Praise for Lora Leigh's Novels of the Breeds

"When it comes to writing this genre, Lora Leigh is the queen!" —Romance Junkies

"[A] highly erotic saga." —Fresh Fiction

"Lora Leigh doesn't disappoint when it comes to sexiness, intrigue and an added little bit of humor. Each time I have finished one of her books I find myself yearning for the next installment and wondering which character will be brought to life for us." —Bitten by Love Reviews

"Lora Leigh delivers on all counts." —Romance Reviews Today

"Heart-wrenching." —Fallen Angel Reviews

"Leigh's action-packed Breeds series makes a refreshing change." —Monsters and Critics

"The love scenes are incendiary." —All About Romance

"The perfect mix of science fiction infused into the paranormal aspect along with a huge dose of sexy characters and romance. . . . I'm a die-hard fan of this series!" —Smexy Books

"Chemistry and wild sex, of just the type to satisfy folks who are already fans of the no-holds-barred sex style from Leigh's Breed novels. Which is to say it happens often and explosively." —Errant Dreams

CROSS BREED

LORA LEIGH

JOVE
New York

A JOVE BOOK
Published by Berkley
An imprint of Penguin Random House LLC
1745 Broadway, New York, NY 10019

ISBN: 9780515154016

Berkley hardcover edition / September 2018
Jove mass-market edition / March 2019

Printed in the United States of America
1   3   5   7   9   10   8   6   4   2

Cover photo by Claudio Dogar-Marinesco
Cover design by Rita Frangie

Thank you, Christina.

Your anticipation, your joy in the story,
chapter by chapter,
made Cassie and her mate want to shine
and go out of their way to please.

I, Cassie and Dog, thank you.

And to my son, Bret—
you've followed this path with me
since Cassie first arrived,
watched my dreams come true and stood by me
through each story written and each story published.
You're the child romance raised
and one of the strongest anchors in my life.

· T H E W O R L D ·
⊙ F T H E B R E E D S

They were created; they weren't born.

They were trained; they weren't raised.

Tortured, experimented upon.

Now that they're free, they're hunted.

Eighteen years ago, a small Pride of Feline Breeds—humans genetically mutated and altered before conception with the DNA of the big-cat predators of the Earth—revealed their existence and shocked the world with the undeniable proof of man's evil.

"Science," screamed their creators, who fought to excuse the demented, depraved experiments.

One hundred and fifty years of death, blood and inhuman practices, of experiments that killed, maimed and forever scarred the incredible beings that science believed they had breathed life into.

The Breeds were taught they had no soul.

Their creators were to be their gods. Those men and women, hearts blackened by greed and evil, held the power of life or death.

More death, sadly, was discovered than life.

The revelation of those first six feline Breeds led to the discovery of the labs and confinement cells that held still endless more—who were sometimes enraged, all burning with hatred for their captors and desperate for freedom.

And the tales they told of their confinement horrified the world.

Daughters kidnapped across generations, used as Breeders, then terminated without thought to the lives destroyed.

Families wailed in the streets and on screens across nation after nation. They sobbed at the horror their children, sisters and grandchildren suffered. They screamed for justice for the children, no matter their genetics or mutations, and raised their fists in demand for atonement.

Yet more revelations of those who had escaped, had been slipped out as babes and other experiments performed in vitro came to light.

Whole families were devastated to learn they were to live in fear that their adopted children or the children conceived in vitro could one day be tested and torn from their arms to be placed in labs where experiments practiced on them were even more demonic than those done to animals in the past.

A cry of horror echoed around the world. A demand for atonement swept through the countries whose politicians and military involved themselves in these atrocities.

Chaos reigned in the capitals across the world. Marches by the hundreds of thousands swept across nations, and for months, the screams echoed to heaven itself. Voices were raised to right this horrible wrong.

The companies revealed to have provided funds for the depraved, horrific experiments saw their stocks crash, and entire corporations were destroyed. Some burned to the ground in the madness of the fury the world felt that their governments, their militaries, had contributed to something so evil.

Government leaders in nation after nation toppled amid the fury until it threatened to decimate whole administrations unless those governing found a way to preserve the lives that had suffered so terribly.

Here, the Breeds found a voice.

They were creatures genetically enhanced to sway public opinion, to pinpoint weaknesses and strengths and use them to their own advantage. The genetics of fallen heroes and villains came to the fore as the Breeds stood before the masses and calmed their fury, suggesting their leaders ensure Breed freedom.

Their genetics were drawn from the greatest minds in generations—long-lost warriors, military leaders, skilled orators, legal geniuses and scientific monsters—and mixed with those of the most cunning and predatory hunters alive.

They understood deception and how to use it. They knew compassion but also the need for force. They became the weapons their creators envisioned, but they were now using those talents against their tormentors.

What science had created and military minds had thought to control, they now found themselves helpless against; they were forced to sit down with creations who held such a fine understanding of legalities, deception and self-preservation that they were able to use the very laws of democracy against the democracies shaking beneath the threat of destruction.

But freedom is still a chimera, a dream the Breeds are reaching for. Because even the laws drafted to protect them can't silence the voices that rose against them.

"God didn't create them," the minority screamed, their voices drowned by those demanding justice.

Allowing the Breeds to move freely would dilute God's genetic design, the purity of human blood, they argued.

They were ignored.

They were the minority.

They became the shadow that haunts the Breeds.

And nearly two decades later, the battle isn't over yet.

It's only begun.

She was only eighteen and she knew she would die soon. Here, on this beautiful island Seth Lawrence owned, surrounded by the protective strength of a Breed force unlike any other, Cassie knew she wouldn't leave alive.

She had seen her own death.

It wouldn't be tonight, though. Not yet. But it was coming. She would have to die so others would live.

Stepping past the wide double doors that opened into the huge atrium, she looked up at the glass-domed roof allowing the night to slide into the enclosed garden and had to fight back the bitterness. The anger.

Turning, she met the eyes of the Breed Enforcers standing behind her, their gazes resolute but compassionate, and snapped the doors closed as they watched her silently.

"Ask to enjoy the gardens at night and this is what I get?" she muttered, swinging around to let her gaze go over the massive enclosure of brick and glass surrounding it.

The grass beneath her feet was surprisingly real. A wide stone walk led into the shadowed greenery, the lush, heavy growth and sultry scent of moisture and fragrant blooms pulling her into the depths of it.

The atrium, Seth had called it. It was a damned greenhouse and nothing more. A well-protected, stone-and-bullet-resistant-glass-enclosed room with only one entrance, the wide doors she'd stepped inside.

This was just perfect. It was infuriating, and she could feel the wild need for freedom clawing at her senses.

Moving farther into the lush greenery, she could find little pleasure there. Despite her bare feet and the feel of grass beneath them, she found no satisfaction here. Just as she found no satisfaction in the deep, wide pond trickling in the center of the trees surrounding it.

The trees were heavily leafed and beaded with what appeared to be dew. The moisture actually came from the water that misted from pipes running along the steel frame supporting the glass above.

The scent of the night wasn't here. The chirp of insects, the scuttle of creatures created to stalk such shadowed beauty, wasn't here. It was sterile. Created by man rather than by nature.

Just as she had been.

She hated it.

At least on her balcony she could smell the night, the creatures that inhabited it and the sea surrounding Lawrence Island.

On her balcony there was a chance of sensing him . . . the man, and she knew it was a man, who watched her through a gun's sights.

Here, there was a chance that he would search the night for her.

That he'd go ahead and take the shot rather than waiting.

Swallowing tightly, Cassie lowered herself to sit on the rough, flat boulder bordering the pond, then shed the matching robe covering the thin, sleeveless white gown she wore. Drawing her feet up to rest on top of the stone, she looped her arms beneath her knees and rested her chin on them as she stared into the trickling water.

What was wrong with her? She knew how dangerous it was to allow herself to stand on the balcony, in clear view, a target to any enemy with the intent to kill her. What force had drawn her there, pushed her to stand there in full view?

Though few wanted to kill her.

The price on her head was for her abduction, her virginity intact when she was turned over to the scientists secretly working with what remained of the Genetics Council.

She was Cassandra Sinclair.

She was unique, not just in her genetics but in her birth. Breed sperm had been used to inseminate her mother's egg without any alterations to the ovum. The same as a hybrid, a Breed born of a Breed-human mating.

But she was even rarer than that. She wasn't created from a single animal species' genetics, but two. She was created from both Wolf and Coyote genetics. The good and the bad. The proud, enduring Wolf DNA altered and forever dirtied by the taint of the Coyote DNA.

Such a beautiful animal, the voice whispered through her memories.

She'd been five, standing in nothing but the white panties she wore, shuddering, sickened by the touch of the bastard's fingers on the mark at her shoulder. The shadow of a paw print. A genetic marker. But as she grew older, another shadow began marring her flesh, one even her parents were unaware of, one resembling that of jagged slices made by claws. The mark of the Coyote stained the flesh just over her womb.

"She was created to whelp monsters," her father sneered as Cassie shook with tears and disbelief.

A part of her had known he wasn't her real father. Unlike her mother's, her father's scent didn't resemble hers. Her momma's scent resembled hers. And her mother loved her.

"She'll whelp my little monsters," Terrence Grange,

drug lord and murderer said, chuckling, then lifted his arm, and a second later the weapon he carried exploded and her father was dead.

She knew he was dead. He fell to the floor, blood spilling from his chest as he stared at Cassie with hatred.

Thirteen years. It had been thirteen years since that night, and still, Cassie remembered every second of it as though it had happened only moments before.

She would whelp monsters.

Many said *she* was the monster, though.

The point was moot, because she'd be dead. She'd seen the blood explode from her head, watched herself falling, and in that vision her eyes had slowly closed as her father's howl of rage spilled into the night.

She'd never been kissed, never been on a date. She was carefully protected, and those who protected her feared Dash Sinclair—her true father in the most important ways—far too much to risk lusting after her. She socialized within the Breed community, rarely among non-Breeds. And if by chance on those rare occasions a human male showed her any attention, then it wasn't allowed for long.

Whoever had watched her while she was on the balcony earlier that day lusted for her in ways she'd never felt with the young men her own age. There had been a sense of maturity, of experience, in the hungry gaze focused on her. She'd felt it, like a wave of heat reaching out for her. Curious and hungry. He knew who she was, and he didn't care.

If he abducted her, she wouldn't be a virgin for long.

As that thought drifted across her mind, she felt him.

She didn't smell him; there was no scent to warn her. She felt him.

Her heart raced, her breathing became faster and she could feel the whisper of the air drifting through the area, against her. It eased past her gown, stroked her flesh, sensitized it.

What an odd sensation. She'd never felt that before, until him.

"If you're caught, they'll kill you." She didn't shift, didn't try to call out to the guards standing outside the doors.

She wasn't frightened of him, though she sensed she should be.

She should be terrified.

"Think they will?" The amused drawl was teasing, playful, his accent just a bit alien. "They didn't know I was here when they checked the area before letting you in. And they were quite thorough."

He remained behind her, hidden within the heavy foliage that had brushed against her back as he sat down. And she let him stay hidden, because she didn't want to know . . . She liked the feel of his warmth against her back as she felt him lower himself behind her, the warmth of his breath against her neck.

"You know they will." Her voice trembled. "Are you here to kill me?"

How wrong it seemed that what she was feeling now would be for the Breed who would kill her. And he was a Breed. She could sense it, feel it, though she wasn't certain which designation of Breed.

"Do you want to die?" Amusement laced his voice, amusement and something more, something dark and shadowed.

Something hungry.

Her eyes closed as she felt a caress against her hair, fingers twining in it, testing the curls, as a hum of appreciation stroked against her senses.

"I'll die either way." She stared into the pond, wondering at her own cowardice. "I won't leave here alive, you know?"

Silence met her question, but she knew he heard her, knew he hadn't left. She could feel him in the air she breathed, in the slow caresses in her hair.

"What makes you so certain of that?" Curiosity filled his voice. A voice that was dark, sensual.

"I know things . . ." Sometimes, she knew terrible things. Things she didn't want to know, didn't want to see or sense. "I see things sometimes . . ."

"I won't let you die, little halfling," he whispered just behind her, causing her to tremble at the warmth of his breath at her ear. "I'll watch over you."

He wasn't taking her seriously, but it didn't matter. She wasn't going to protest the fact. Why argue when this would likely be the only time she knew a measure of what it felt like to be desired, to be touched by a man.

"You were watching me when I was on the balcony," she whispered, her head tilting to the side as she felt a calloused finger stroke down her neck.

"I was," he admitted. "I should have been keeping watch on the property. Instead, all I was watching was you."

Still, that amusement lingered in his voice.

"Why?" She needed to know. She needed something to hold on to, to make the next few days bearable.

"Because, my little halfling, you're mine . . ."

She stiffened in outrage, in anger, but before she could turn and inform him just how insane he was, he was gone.

Wide-eyed, her heart racing, she stared at the swaying leaves of the huge ferns behind her and heard a whisper of a chuckle somewhere in the darkness.

"Cassie." The atrium doors were thrown open as her father's voice echoed through the artificial glade, dark with menace, with warning.

His enforcers rushed through the atrium, at least half a dozen, converging on her as she drew her robe on and tied the satin ribbons holding it closed.

"What's going on?" She jumped to her feet, staring around at the Wolf Breeds suddenly searching the spacious atrium, checking the areas of heavy growth with dangerous purpose.

"Cassie, sweetheart, it's time to go now." Dash Sinclair pushed through the foliage that hid her from the door, his amber gaze piercing as it went over her. "Are you all right?"

Was she all right? His guards had checked the area before she entered it; no one knew the visitor had been there.

"Why wouldn't I be?" Looking around the atrium, seeing the Breeds who still searched it, she turned back to him, realizing with heavy sadness that her time there was finished. "It's not like I'm actually outside, right?"

He stared behind her, his eyes narrowed, nostrils flaring as though testing the air for any unfamiliar scents.

"Why are they searching the room?" she questioned him then. "They searched it before I came in."

If they found her visitor, what would they do to him? Her father would be furious. Whoever he was, he carried no scent, which meant he was trying to hide from Breeds. No doubt he was the enemy.

"There's been trouble in the main house," he told her, a growl in his voice. "Come on, let's get you back upstairs." He held his hand out to her, his expression implacable when his gaze returned to hers. "It's getting late."

She was being dragged back to her room as though she were a toddler. Evidently the trouble had already been taken care of and her father had somehow realized she wasn't in her room when he went to check on her.

"And of course I'm still a child who has no idea how to defend myself, nor do I have guards on my ass twenty-four-seven." She ignored his outstretched hand and pushed past him instead. "For God's sake, Dad, I'm not ten."

She didn't wait around for his reply or the confusion she knew she would glimpse in his eyes. He couldn't understand, couldn't know the hell her dreams were becoming or the anger that clashed through her every waking second.

She was going to die here soon. So very soon.

If her father had just let her have this time, in this place, maybe she could have stolen something for herself. Maybe she could have figured out why the man whose gunsights she'd felt on the balcony outside her room didn't terrify her.

Why he drew her.

Why she ached for his warmth for just a moment, just for tonight. Because tomorrow night would be too late. She'd seen the vision of the bullet, the blood. She'd watched herself fall within that waking dream.

She'd be dead.

♦　♦　♦

He watched her leave, a shadow within a shadow, and waited for the Breed Enforcers who followed her father to clear the room. It took them a while.

Of course, they knew he was there. What they couldn't smell, they could sense, and they sensed him. Rather than moving or becoming nervous because of their continued search, he merely waited, patient, unconcerned. At first, half of them left; the others were still and silent, waiting for movement. They waited for a quarter of an hour; then they all left, but one.

He would have grinned if he didn't know that slight movement would give him away. The Breed they left was damned good. Patient. Deadly. Experienced in the hunt.

This one waited nearly an hour.

"You're good," the voice whispered through the darkness. "Whoever you are, you're damned good."

Yeah, he was damned good.

He remained calm, patient. He wasn't worried in the least. He knew how to do this, and he was good at it.

"I'll be waiting," the Scots Wolf assured him, his brogue more apparent now. "If you want to live, you'll stay the hell away from her."

The Breed didn't attempt to hide his movements or his ire as he stomped to the doors and disappeared through them.

Still, he didn't move. He remained on the ledge far

above the atrium and simply stared down at the pool where Cassie had sat.

He'd nearly been caught, and that fact wasn't lost on him. He hadn't been listening for company; he'd been too busy listening to the quickening of her breath, smelling the spice of her innocent arousal, the sweetness of her. It had been a hell of a risk to take.

She was a woman worth risking his life for.

What Breed wouldn't risk everything for his mate?

· C H A P T E R I ·

This was a very bad idea. She knew it was a bad idea, but she was still here, and she was still doing it. She stopped at the door of the suite she had been directed to, slid the security card into place, then pushed open the door and stepped inside.

The smell of cigar smoke reached her senses the moment Cassie entered the room at the Navajo Suites where she'd been told to meet the Breed she now owed one hell of a debt to. The scent of the tobacco, rather than acrid and distasteful, was a bit mellow, soothing. Rather like those she'd known other Breeds to indulge in.

That was at least something familiar, something not so disconcerting as the decision she'd made to come here.

God, she didn't even know his name. All she knew was the number she'd been left six years ago and the message that accompanied it. *You were beautiful in the moonlight, little halfling. If you need me, call. But there will always be a price to pay,* the note had read.

And she had made the call often over the years, though she was never certain why she could trust him so easily.

The price had begun small, but with each call made it had grown steadily. Still, she had enjoyed the game.

Until now.

But hadn't she known it would eventually come to this?

What woman agreed to sleep with a man whose name she didn't even know? Whose face she'd never seen?

A crazy woman, that was who. Or a very desperate one.

She closed the door behind her softly, set the lock and stared at the opened balcony doors where the shadow of a large, powerful Breed stood. The tip of a slim cigar brightened as he inhaled, then dimmed, clenched between strong white teeth as they flashed in a brief smile.

A Coyote's smile.

"Didn't expect you to keep your word," he said, his voice quiet, deep, as he lifted one hand to remove the cylinder of pressed tobacco.

A second later it was tossed over the balcony railing, its fiery point of light disappearing as it fell to earth.

"You did as I asked." She shrugged. "My sister's safe."

God, if only she had known sooner that her twin, Kenzi, had been taken. She was supposed to be safe. And she'd learned too late, sensed the danger her sister was in after she was taken rather than before.

The gift she had been cursed with as a child had all but deserted her now, in her twenties. When she most needed it. When it could actually help her rather than tear her apart. And this time it had almost come too late to ensure their safety.

She was safe now, though. Cassie had heard the report that Kenzi was in Breed hands. The moment it had been announced Kenzi had been found, Cassie had slipped from the Bureau of Breed Affairs apartments to meet her savior as he'd directed her.

"Didn't mean you'd show up," he pointed out laconically. "It's not as though I could sue for breach of agreement."

He was right, so why had she shown up?

She could have ignored their bargain once Kenzi was safe. But he'd never, in all these years, broken his word to her. No matter how dangerous her requests, no matter how difficult, he'd always come through for her.

As he said, he couldn't sue her. There would have been nothing he could have done if she had chosen to ignore the deal she had made with him. It was just that somehow, it had seemed rather wrong to do so.

"I don't break my word," she finally answered him. "You should know that by now."

A mocking chuckle filled the room.

"Know what I think?" he said then, turning to face her as he slid the balcony door closed. The blinds closed automatically behind him.

"Does it matter?" She was certain she didn't want to know what he thought.

"Oh, I think it matters," he answered, his voice low. "I think it matters very much."

"Are we here to talk or finish the bargain?" No, she didn't want to know what he thought; she wanted to get this the hell over with and get back to the Bureau offices, where she was safe.

Where this Breed couldn't find her.

Stepping to the small table beside the couch, he flipped on a low light, though neither of them really needed it. She would have preferred he left the light off.

If he had, then she couldn't have seen his features in such stark display and breathtaking savagery.

He shouldn't be so handsome, was her first thought. Her second? He was dangerous. One of the most dangerous Breeds she'd ever glimpsed.

She could see it in the hard, savage lines of his face, the piercing gray eyes, the tall, corded strength of his body.

He was one of the most powerful Breeds she'd ever sensed in her life. Not just physically, but in that inner core of strength. And this man's core of strength had no end.

It went deeper than her father's, deeper than Jonas's, and that was saying something. It possibly went even deeper than her own, and that was terrifying.

Shaggy dark blond hair fell around a broad forehead, darker lashes surrounded steel gray eyes, and a strong, powerful chin assured her that he wouldn't be just determined, but arrogant as hell with it.

His lips quirked into a mocking grin. Just a hint of a smile, one that assured her that she wasn't the only one with finely adapted senses. Her Breed instincts bristled, heated, parts of her demanding she challenge him while other parts wanted only to submit.

"Curious, aren't you?" The slight growl to his voice had an unbidden chill racing down her spine. "The Breed princess wants to see what it's like to get down and dirty for a change?"

Her eyes narrowed. Breed princess?

"Haven't heard that little nickname yet?" He chuckled.

Oh, she'd heard it often, actually.

Moving to the bar across the room, he poured two glasses half full of liquor. Picking the glasses up, he walked unhurriedly to where she stood and extended one to her.

"The perfect little Breed," he said as she accepted the drink. "Able to argue Breed Law with a charm that can convince the Council to separate mates and human lawyers to allow a human child to be taken from its father. The Breed with a siren's voice."

"That's ridiculous," she snapped. "Not everyone knows the laws that rule our people, or understands them . . ."

"As I said, very intelligent." He toasted her with his drink before tossing it back. "With a siren's voice."

Sipping the liquor, she watched him carefully.

Siren's voice her ass.

She knew Breed Law and she knew how to argue it. It was that simple.

"What does Breed Law have to do with this . . . ?"

"Do you know when the media mentions you, they simply call you a Wolf Breed? All those little mutant Coyote genetics you possess seem to be forgotten."

Her heart was racing; how unusual. Her breathing was elevated, and she swore she felt flushed. She didn't want to talk about her genetics or anything else. She wanted this done. Finished.

"We're not here to discuss me or the media . . ."

"You made a deal with a Coyote, little halfling," he drawled, his expression somber despite the mockery in his gaze. "You've been aware of that. Right?"

If she hadn't been before, she sure as hell became aware of it the moment she stepped through the door.

"I'm aware." She was a Breed after all; she could smell the Coyote on him . . . though it was faint. "I've known all along what you were."

The scent was subtle, as though something covered it.

"Are you wearing a scent blocker?" Tilting her head to the side, she watched him carefully, drawing the scent in deeper.

"It may be wearing off." He moved back to the bar, poured another drink and tossed it back. "And you're right; we came here to finish a bargain."

He finished the drink, and before she could do more than flinch, he slapped the glass to the bar, took two steps and managed to snag her waist with one strong arm and jerk her to him.

"Now, let's see, what was the deal?" That was a definite growl, a spark of anger in his gaze. "No kissing." His thumb brushed against her lips. "I can't eat what is no doubt a sweet little pussy. And I can't come inside you. Are those the rules?"

Why the hell was her heart racing out of control and why did she suddenly want his kiss as she had never wanted anything in her life? Wanted his kiss everywhere.

She was crazy. This was beyond desperate.

"Those are the rules."

Something hot, hungry, flared in his expression. It tightened, his cheekbones becoming more pronounced as his lashes lowered over his eyes.

"Other than that, it's whatever I want?" he asked, his tone curious, but there was nothing curious in his gaze or his expression. "Tonight, you're mine."

She licked her suddenly dry lips; nerves and fear of the unknown had to be the reasons why she was just a little bit light-headed and fighting for breath.

"Just for tonight," she agreed. "I leave before dawn."

Something akin to regret flashed in his face.

"Four hours," he murmured. "Then we better get started. You have a lot to learn in those hours."

A lot to learn . . .

She was not going to tremble or shake with nerves, she told herself. Show no weakness. Never let anyone see you weak. No one. Especially a Coyote.

When he caught her hand, she was proud to say it wasn't damp and her fingers didn't tremble. She kept her head high, her expression serene. She'd learned over the years how to do that. How to hold back the fear, uncertainty and nerves under trying conditions.

Not that she'd ever been in this particular situation before, and as he led her past the living suite and into the bedroom, she nearly lost her nerve.

The bed was turned down invitingly, pillows lying flat, waiting for a body to lie within it, and there were candles. Three lit candles.

The door closed behind them, almost silently; still, it was all she could do to control her flinch.

He dropped her hand immediately. "Go home, princess." Disgust edged his voice as he flashed her a look of scorn. "Consider tonight's work a freebie."

Anger. She could feel it inside him. It wasn't rolling off

him in waves; it came out as mocking unconcern, but it was there all the same.

She'd made the deal. Her sister was safe, and she'd come this far. If she backed out now, she'd never regain her courage. And he might never be there to help her again.

She reached behind her and released the small catch on her skirt, then slid the zipper down. The sound was a quiet hiss in the otherwise still room. Staring at him, she let the material drop, leaving her clad only in the camisole, vest and high-cut black lace panties.

With a shrug of her shoulders she released the vest.

"I'm a virgin," she whispered, refusing to drop her gaze or show any shame. "If you're looking for experience, or for me to know how to please you, then that isn't going to happen."

She pulled the camisole over her head slowly, slid it free of the long length of her hair and dropped it to the floor, then stepped from the four-inch heels she wore.

And he didn't speak. Not a single word. He watched her, still and silent, but the scent of male lust suddenly filling the room was unmistakable.

Then, with the same unhurried movements, he sat down and pulled his boots free of his feet. Rising once again, he pulled the shirt from his pants and began unbuttoning it.

She didn't know his name, and for a moment, she wished she did.

Then he was shrugging the shirt free, revealing the depth of strength in his body in the play of muscles beneath dark bronze flesh. Strong biceps, wide shoulders and chest, tight, hard abs.

Slowly, he released the wide leather belt that cinched his hips and worked free the button and zipper of the dun-colored pants he wore.

Fear.

Uncertainty.

What was she thinking?

She'd never done this before so she couldn't even guess. She didn't know how to do this.

She was standing naked but for the panties that hid the genetic mark of the Coyote just below her womb, in front of this Breed. A Coyote . . .

Swallowing tightly she hooked her fingers in the band of black lace and lowered them, forcing herself to slide them over her thighs before letting them fall to the floor. His gaze touched the hardened points of her nipples, then lowered to that mark. The faint lines, in the form of jagged scars, shadowed her flesh and had the scent of male lust spiking in the womb.

Rather than removing his pants as his need increased, he stepped to her, calloused fingers touching her cheek before cupping it gently.

He was warm. So warm.

"No kisses," he whispered. "But you didn't rule out this."

As he spoke, he swung her up in his arms, sweeping her from the floor and striding to the bed, where he laid her in the middle of the mattress. Lying down beside her, his head lowered, but he kept his word. He didn't kiss her lips.

What he did was even more maddening, more erotic. His lips touched the corner of hers; just the tip of his tongue edged at it before his lips moved to her neck, his tongue taking little tastes of her flesh as her breathing accelerated.

Because it felt good. So damned good.

One hand twined in her hair, gripping the curls and pulling just enough that the slight sensation was a merging of erotic and the edge of pain. And she liked it. Dark need and that restless, shadowed force inside her merged, clawing at her, demanding she take what was hers.

"There, little halfling," he whispered as his lips moved to her neck, smoothing over her flesh as his tongue, ah mercy, his teeth, awakened nerve endings she didn't know she had.

Before she knew it, her hands were on his shoulders as he rose over her, then in his hair, sliding through the cool strands, clenching in them as she arched to him. And she tried to make sense of the sensations racing through her.

The rush of heat that engulfed her body, the pinching tightness of her nipples, the warmth growing between her thighs. The ache centering in her clit as she felt her juices flowing from her sex and the demand building in her that she let go, give in, that she free the hunger raging through her.

"Feel good?" he whispered as his lips kissed slowly lower, moving for the heaving flesh of her breasts.

"Feels good." She didn't even sound like herself.

Why did he care if it felt good?

"You taste like heaven." The rasp of his voice was deeper, more animalistic. "Son of a bitch, love, you taste good."

Sensation was overtaking her, pleasure like she hadn't expected, couldn't have anticipated.

"Oh God. Yes . . ." She couldn't hold back her moan as his lips covered a sensitized nipple, drawing it into his mouth, sucking with firm, hungry draws of his lips, licking it, rasping nerve endings with such pleasure.

She arched into the sensations, her eyes closing, though she wanted to hold them open. The heat was building, sensation upon sensation as he moved from one engorged peak to the other. She wanted to be closer . . .

She wanted his kiss.

Her head twisted against the pillow as he slid one hand down her side to her thighs, then settled between them, covering the slick folds he found there with his broad palm.

It wasn't supposed to feel good. Not this good. She could feel the perspiration gathering on her skin, hear her own moans as she felt him working his pants free of his thighs.

His lips were still at her breast, sucking, his tongue abrading her nipple. His hand moved from her sex, pushed her thighs apart, and then he was kneeling between them. With one hand he clasped her hip, his lips moving from her breast to her neck.

She felt the crest of his shaft, broad, throbbing as it pressed against the entrance between her thighs. So hot, pressing inside her, opening her, stretching her . . .

Each hard, pulsing throb was followed by heated pleasure, like a rush of liquid fire filling her, easing her, amplifying the sensations.

She arched to him, knowing she shouldn't, knowing there was something she should remember; something wasn't right. Then he was pushing inside her, pleasure and pain merging, white-hot in its intensity, tearing through her as the short strokes inside her vagina tore through her virginity, lengthened, became quicker, harder, burying him inside her fully.

She could feel the hard throb of his cock, followed by a sense of heat and incredible pleasure.

She couldn't halt the cries falling from her lips, couldn't stop the whirlwind of sensations obliterating everything but the pleasure. With a sense of disbelief, she realized she'd completely lost control; then even that thought was torn aside as he began moving inside her.

Each thrust was followed by the sweet, burning trail of heat, the clenching of her vagina and a rush of liquid pleasure falling from her. Her hips lifted as she fought for more, deeper, harder.

She could hear him whispering against her shoulder, his lips and tongue caressing, teeth scraping as the thrusts became faster, rhythmic, pushing her into a storm she could feeling racing out of control inside her own body.

Her nails dug into his shoulders as each stroke of his cock pushed her deeper, as the pleasure, so extreme, so brutal it bordered on pain, began tightening inside her.

Pushing her, clenching in her sex, her clit, bands of pleasure and pain until she felt her orgasm imploding, destroying . . .

His teeth sank in her shoulder. Wicked, sharp and curved as she felt him thickening impossibly inside her, stretching her inner muscles further, pushing her orgasm higher even as a sense of horror tore through her.

He was locked inside her. Releasing, ejaculating inside her because he couldn't pull free of her clamping muscles as the mating knot pulsed inside her.

She was crying out her pleasure even as she felt her tears falling. Reveling in the sensation of his teeth buried at her shoulder, his tongue laving the wound, his cock spilling his release.

Physically, nothing could ever be so good. It was the most intense, most incredible pleasure, and it was destroying her.

From the inside out, it was destroying her.

His teeth released her, his head lifted slowly. "Well, fuck, guess the rules don't apply now . . ." And his lips were on hers, hard, hungry . . . addictive.

No, the rules didn't apply, but the destruction sure as hell would.

◆ ◆ ◆

This wasn't happening.

A rarely felt, overwhelming panic began to invade Cassie's senses once she'd regained them again, threatening to rip away the logic and careful thought she normally approached all problems with. It was rising by the second, tearing through her and beginning to exacerbate the fear that the knowledge of a mating had brought.

This had just slipped past anything even remotely resembling fear. She realized in that moment that she could have handled a mate after all. A Wolf Breed mate, a Feline Breed, hell, a Reptile Breed or a human mate.

She could have handled a mate.

She couldn't handle this.

"Breathe, Cassie," he whispered, those strong arms she'd once longed to feel around her, enclosing her like iron. Like a prison. A cell from which there was no escape. "It's okay, baby, just breathe."

Baby.

Just breathe.

She heard the words; she didn't respond, didn't react. She stared at the wall across from her, focused on it, tried to push back the fear and . . .

Rage.

It clawed at her, mixed with the panic, with the over-whelming sense of helpless confusion. It burned inside her chest like a viciously hot poker, stabbing at her over and over again.

"You lied to me." The words escaped despite the tightness of her throat and the feeling that she was strangling on her emotions. "You lied to me. You assured me we couldn't be mates."

Mates weren't supposed to ever lie to each other. She had never lied to him. She had always been completely honest with him. Always.

She hadn't even considered that he could be her mate. He was her partner in adventure since those few moments they'd spent in an island atrium, albeit mostly through messages. One didn't lie to one's partner.

Those strong arms slid away from her, but that feeling of imprisonment didn't recede. It couldn't recede. There was no escaping.

She hurt now in every molecule of her body. The pain resonating with blistering intensity.

His scent followed her.

Sitting on the side of the bed, she propped her elbows on her knees and covered her face with her hands. She wanted to rock into herself, scream and rage and claw at his face with her nails. She wanted to give in to the demented pain rising inside her and show him the lethal, killing instinct that had been bred into her. The one she held inside, always hidden, restrained.

"Well, little halfling, you must admit you suspected it; otherwise, you'd have never made up those ridiculous rules," he said with a grunt, as though that excused him.

Mocking amusement was a trademark she'd always sensed, yet until now, he'd never turned it on her.

What was she going to do?

She couldn't deal with this!

She had to run, to leave . . .

Yet even now the despised reaction of her body to the Mating Heat was already building again, sensitizing her, forcing her to fight herself, to fight the steady increase of the hormones now racing through her.

She wanted him again. Wanted his flesh throbbing between her lips, wanted his tongue burrowing inside her sex, spreading more of that sickening hormone.

Her hand clamped over her mouth as she felt her womb tightening, demanding his release, demanding he flood her body with his semen again.

She pushed to her feet, only distantly aware of him moving from the bed, but all too aware of the fact that he was aroused, erect and ready to give her body exactly what it was beginning to burn for.

For a moment, all she could do was ache for her mother, her father. Ache to beg them to fix this as they had so many other things in her life. To smooth it over, to make it better, to help her find a way out.

And there was no way out. She knew there was no way out.

"Should I take you again, mate?" There was an edge to his voice that sliced at her, that dug into her chest and made the pain brighter, more intense. "Shall I just bend you over

the bed and push inside you? Ride you hard and fast until I
knot you and give your body what it needs? Just stay behind
you so you don't have to see the Breed you mated?"

Cassie jerked, barely holding back a cry rising unbidden
to her lips as her sex spilled its liquid heat and her stomach
rippled with the clenching of her womb, with the need, the
hunger.

Yes, that was what she wanted, she screamed silently,
agony tearing through her. Take her like the animal she
now knew lurked inside her.

A low, male chuckle followed her as she shook her head
and headed for the shower. She had to think. She had to
figure out what to do.

"Cassandra . . ."

"Cassie . . ." She corrected him almost automatically,
feeling so dazed, so off-balance and filled with violence
that keeping the explosion of pure murderous fury contained was the hardest thing she'd ever done.

"What?" Clipped and short, his voice raked over her
senses, stroking her like a physical caress as she felt her
sheath clench, felt more of the hot, silky wetness spill
from her.

"Cassie," she had to force herself to answer. "My name
is Cassie."

She was Cassie Colder. She wasn't Cassandra Sinclair,
no matter how desperately she wanted to be, how hard her
mother and father—her stepfather—had worked to give her
that illusion. She wasn't a Wolf Breed. She wasn't Dash
Sinclair's incredible, amazing, intelligent daughter. She
was Daniel "Dane" Colder's science experiment. The dirty
little animal he'd helped create.

"I need a shower," she whispered. She needed to think.
To turn back time.

"A shower won't wash my scent from you." It sounded
like a promise. A warning.

"Guess we'll find out . . ." Straightening, she'd almost taken that first step when she felt herself jerked around, her mate towering over her, glaring down at her, his gray eyes like thunderclouds as a warning growl left his throat.

That sound was the trigger.

It ripped through her, exploded through her mind and tore aside that veil of civility she was always so certain she possessed.

"Don't push me, Cassie," he snarled in her face, his head lowering, almost nose to nose with her.

Lifting to her tiptoes, she bit him. Her teeth snapped at the thin line of his lips, and she tasted blood, tasted that hormone and lost control of the low, warning growl that left her own throat as she jerked back.

One hand latched onto the hair at the back of his head, the other gripped the thick, throbbing stalk of flesh that extended like iron from between his thighs. Grabbing at his hair, she pulled his head down to get her fix. To pull in the hormone spilling from the glands beneath his tongue and allow the creature inside her to fully awaken.

The kiss was like a sensual explosion. It imploded inside her senses, laid waste to logic, to common sense, to the dreams, the hopes, the certainty she could overcome what she'd been created to be.

His tongue pumped between her lips as she licked at it desperately, allowed it to duel with hers, to spill the mating poison, to rush through her senses and jerk her on that wild, furious ride once again.

Long minutes later, dazed, drugged with the sensual heat, she pulled her head back. Retaining her grip on his hair, she met the challenge in those wild gray eyes and the less-than-perfect features. As she stared up at him, one broad, calloused palm cupped her breast; his fingers gripped her nipple, tightened, and her head slammed back against the wall.

The sensations were terrible; they were exquisite. Agony and ecstasy slamming into the hard tip before ripping a line of sizzling electric heat straight to her pussy.

"Again." Her voice was strangled. "Do it again."

Easing the pressure, he did it again, this time harder, dragging a demented cry from her lips as his other hand slid between her damp thighs.

Damp because the slick moisture was weeping from her, spilling from the swollen lips between her thighs to the fingers now tucking between the folds to catch the silken heat.

"Come here, mate." Releasing her nipple and the desperately aching flesh between her thighs, he lifted her to him, turned and sat her on the top of the tall table.

Still gripping his hair, she jerked his head to her breasts, her breathing hard, heavy, her chest tight with the screams she was holding in, the denials she so desperately wanted to give voice to.

"Suck my nipple," she demanded, pushing one enflamed tip to his lips. "Hard. Like you gripped it. Do it."

She watched him. Their gazes locked as he snarled, then gripped the tip between his teeth and applied the painful, ecstatic pressure she needed.

White, strong teeth, curved canines at the side, a brutal snarl of lust on his lips.

His hands gripped her legs beneath her knees, yanked them up and forced her feet to the top of the table. With his teeth gripping her nipple, his tongue lashing it, his hand moved between her spread thighs. A second later a long, agonized sound of keening pleasure escaped her lips.

Two fingers pushed inside her, hard, deep. There were no preliminaries, no warning, just the sudden fullness and a firestorm of sensation tearing through her.

Her hips jerked, then bore down on the fingers as he sucked her nipple into his mouth, devouring first one, then the other. Lips, teeth, tongue, suckling pressure and mind-consuming ecstasy. She didn't have to think here. She didn't have to consider what she was, what he'd turned her into.

"That's it," he snarled, lifting his lips as she fought to drive herself on his fingers. "Ride my fingers, mate. Look." He lifted enough to stare down their bodies, to watch her hips, to see the penetration of her body as she ground herself onto his palm. "Greedy baby. How much do you want? How much before you beg me to stop?"

Beg him to stop? She could take anything, everything he wanted to dish out.

"Go to hell," she cried out, but she couldn't help but watch as her hips pulled back, revealing the heavy layer of thick juices that clung to his fingers, before she slammed onto his fingers again, burying them inside her.

She froze for only a second. Before she could halt the downward thrust he added a third finger and pushed inside her, even as she slammed her hips onto the penetration. She could feel her muscles clenching around the invasion, rippling with involuntary spasms.

"Enough?" She hated the challenge in his voice. Hated it. "Or more?"

His fingers curled, found a spot so sensitive, so explosively responsive, that she couldn't hold back the climax that shot through her system. And it wasn't enough. It just wasn't enough. It only made her body hotter, made her senses more maddened.

"You bastard!" she cried out, her hands gripping his forearms, nails biting into his flesh.

Seconds later the thicker, hotter flesh of his shaft pressed against her, a hard spurt of hormonal pre-cum shooting inside her. His shaft parted flesh still highly sensitive, still clenching in pleasure, and slowly—oh God, so slowly— began parting her inner flesh, penetrating her, filling her until she was certain she could take no more even as the hormonal ejaculations continued.

Dragging her gaze from the penetration, she glared up at him. The hint of softening in his expression disappeared; the arrogance and challenge returned.

"Do it," she snarled. "Fuck me and get it over with it. Go ahead, you bastard Coyote. Do your worst."

His worst. He destroyed her. Powerful, deep thrusts filled her, pushed inside her, stretched her with such exquisite pleasure she couldn't help but hold on to him.

Stars exploded behind her tightly closed eyes and she sobbed in a mix of ecstasy and fear. Because she knew nothing, nothing, could ever be the same again.

• C H A P T E R   2 •

The sun was high and painting the desert with the coming heat of a rapidly approaching noon, not that the penetrating rays could find its way into the comm center of the Western Bureau of Breed Affairs. From there, digital displays of the desert and surrounding towns were lit up, pinpoints of light indicating the Breed forces working in search patterns as they scoured the land for one tiny, far too delicate Breed female. "Find her! Now!" Jonas Wyatt, director of the Bureau of Breed Affairs, snarled the order in a voice filled with demand. A demand backed by the genetics of one of the most predatory animals in the world. The lion.

The snarl of rage that slipped from him had Bureau agents, both human and Breed, jumping and running from the communications room as techs and satellite ops went to work.

The air of fear that hung over the room was smothering, stifling.

Cassandra Sinclair, the face of the Breeds, the much-loved, deeply revered and most hunted of the Breed species, was missing. Her capture could cause a true war between Breeds and humans to erupt.

The human-Wolf-Coyote blend of her genetics made her unique, a true halfling as some called her, but the fact that those genetics were created outside of the Genetics Council labs, and the child born naturally, her mother's ovum unaltered, made her truly one of a kind.

The only Breed that contained the genetics of not just one, but two of the predatory animals used to create the Breeds—Wolf Breed sperm altered with Coyote genetics and used to fertilize an unaltered human ovum—was unheard of. And as Cassie matured, it was obvious those genetics were somehow mutating, strengthening in ways Jonas couldn't quite put his finger on. In ways he'd never figure out if she wasn't found.

Beauty, innocence, compassion and a kind heart made her a favorite of both Breeds and humans lucky enough to meet her.

There was an air about her, one reporter had stated after an interview with her, that drew one to her, that filled one with warmth.

And now she was gone.

Jonas slammed out of the operations room, the animalistic snarl that erupted from his lips terrifying in its pure rage.

He'd helped raise that child. Looked after her. Protected her. And now someone had dared take her.

It had to be the Council. Those fucking scientists and war dogs that banded together to create then torture the Breeds would never stop, if he didn't find a way to destroy them. And God help them if they had Cassie. There wasn't a Breed outside those ranks that wouldn't erupt in pure animalistic rage if they had her.

Fists clenching, he hurried through the halls of the Western Bureau of Breed Affairs, and rather than taking the elevator, he took the stairs up. Two and three at a time he rushed to his offices, intent on calling in every team, every Breed, every mercenary the Bureau employed, to find her.

They had hours. Only hours to find out what had happened. Callan Lyons, the Prime of the Lion Breeds, was already preparing the Lion Breed community of Sanctuary for war, just as the Wolf Breed and Coyote strongholds of Haven and Citadel, respectively, were preparing while their alphas joined the search.

And it would be war.

Whoever had taken Cassie would pay, because no doubt, before they could reach her, she'd be dead; that, or so damaged that the very acts that damaged her would send rage cascading through the Breeds.

They were human, but they were animal as well. The world had no idea what was about to be unleashed on it, and for once, Jonas wouldn't try to stop it.

Hell no, he'd help it along.

"Director Wyatt, your mate and child are waiting for you in your quarters. We're prepped and ready to fly as soon as you're ready." The Breed security detail awaiting him as he stepped into the hall closed around him.

Six powerful, savage Breed warriors trained for two decades for nothing but death. Twelve more were with his mate and their child.

"Ten minutes," he snapped to the commander. "Have Rachel and Amber brought to my office. We'll leave from there."

He had to get his pregnant mate and their child to Sanctuary before blood was shed. It was the only safe place. And if war did erupt, they, along with the other mates and children among the three Breed communities, would be flown to Africa and hidden deep in Congo with the Breed known as the First Leo. It was the final refuge when the world turned against them.

"Delay that order." The brooding Scottish burr of that voice had Jonas and his detail turning quickly to face the

Breed moving easily up the hall despite the weapons trained on him.

"What the hell are you doing here, Styx?" Jonas growled, watching the redheaded giant as he brushed past the other Breeds. "Get your ass back to your mate."

"You'll want to wait a few minutes more," the Wolf informed him. "At least until you and I chat a minute."

He was one of the few Breeds Jonas didn't have to look down at to meet his gaze. They stood eye to eye, nearly toe to toe, and something in the other Breed's eyes warned him this was no ordinary meeting.

"Delay the order." Jonas glanced to the Coyote, the commander of the team, long enough to receive his nod in reply.

"This better be good," Jonas informed Styx as he slapped his palm to the security scanner beside the door. "Endangering my family isn't something I'll take lightly."

He stepped into the office, waited for Styx to join him, then slammed the door.

And froze.

The fragile figure that rose from the leather office chair in front of his desk was a shock. Slender, barely five-four until she put on those high-assed heels she preferred. Long, silky curls rioted around her delicate face and fell down her back to her hips. Black, pencil-slim skirt, matching camisole and sleeveless vest paired with black heels.

He nearly lost his breath in sheer, overwhelming relief.

"God. Cassie." The words were a prayer of thanksgiving as he rushed for her.

Only to stop a mere foot away, the arms he'd lifted to embrace her falling to his sides as the scent that surrounded her hit his senses. As did the trace of tears on her face. He stared at her, confused. He should have scented her presence long before he reached the office, especially considering the sheer strength of the mating scent she carried. Yet, it was as if she'd managed to pull it back, to contain it within a few feet of her. Something no Breed had the power to do, especially where the strength of his senses was concerned.

"Cassie . . . ?" He could barely breathe as her chin lifted and those eerie blue eyes of hers flashed with pain and fury. "Who?"

She inhaled deeply. "Is my sister safe?"

In his life, he could count on one hand the times he was actually shocked. This one overshadowed all others.

"Kenzi's safe." He nodded, more off-balance than he wanted to acknowledge. "She's with Rhyzan." His deputy director of Breed Affairs had the other woman in secure quarters until she could be airlifted to Sanctuary with the rest of the females and mates.

Cassie nodded, then stepped away from him, folding her arms across her breasts defensively. As though she could hide or ignore the scent that surrounded her.

A mating scent.

"You've been missing for over four hours . . ."

"I knew exactly where I was." She sounded as lost as she looked as she put more distance between them. "I was making an exchange, you might say." Bitterness filled her voice.

He stepped toward her, only to stop as her hand lifted in a gesture that told him to remain where he was.

He stopped, but only because that delicate hand held him still as he stared at it. It was trembling. He'd never seen Cassie's hands shake. Not from nerves, weakness or any other reason.

"Are my parents here yet?" The trace of tears in her voice enraged him.

"They're helping coordinate the search for you . . ."

"Call the search off." Her head lifted, and for a second, her lips trembled and tears sheened her eyes. "Tell my parents I'm safe . . ."

"Oh yeah, Cassie, *that's* going to work." Finding his equilibrium once again wasn't easy. "Your father will take my door down in about thirty minutes after that order goes out. Him, Callan, Wolfe, Del Rey and every other fucking alpha leader out there are beating the desert searching for you."

The Wolf Breed Lupine Leader, Wolfe Gunnar, as well as the Coyote Coy, Del-Rey Delgado, were pouring all their considerable strength into joining forces with the Prime Lion Breed Leader, Callan Lyons, to find her.

Jonas couldn't touch her, but he wanted nothing more than to pull her into his arms, assure himself she was there, and try to ease the pain he could feel pouring from her.

"Were you raped, goddammit?" he finally snarled. "Did your fucking mate rape you?"

Her breathing hitched, her fingers moving to cover her lips as she fought for control and shook her head quickly.

"No." The word was strangled and torn, but he didn't sense a lie.

He could smell her pain, her confusion and Mating Heat. But he was damned if he could believe the male scent that infused the mating.

"I didn't know about Kenzi in time, not until her abduction." Her voice trembled. "Not until it was too late." She shook her head and turned her back to him, hunching her shoulders as though to avoid a blow. "There was no time to contact you. But I knew he would be in place; after all, isn't he always the one the Council calls first?" She was fighting the sobs he could feel building in her. "I contacted him to make certain she was safe if he was in the area." She turned back to him slowly and another tear fell before she reined them in again. "I agreed to the price. I simply didn't expect the outcome."

She'd bargained her body for her sister's safety. She'd bargained with her mate.

"Where is he?" Because Jonas knew he'd kill him.

God, he couldn't even kill the bastard son of a bitch. He couldn't kill him, because no matter the stakes, no matter the rage that would pour through the Breed community if they learned the truth of who had mated her, he was still her mate.

No one could touch him.

"Can you believe it was a Coyote?" Disbelief filled her voice, her expression, as guilt flayed Jonas.

"Cassie . . ." He believed it. Hated it, but he believed it.

"You knew." She breathed out the words, the sound ragged, filled with pain and with betrayal.

"I suspected your mate was a Coyote." He shook his head wearily. "I had no idea who he was, though, Cassie. If I had, I would have found a way . . ."

Bitter mockery filled her face. "You would have found a way to what? To fix it? To manipulate it?"

"To kill him first," he snarled. "Mate or not, I wouldn't have allowed this to happen to you."

It wasn't the first time he wanted to kill a mate, and he knew it would likely not be the last. Mating Heat was hell for a woman in some circumstances, more so for some than for others.

She blinked back her tears and he swore he could sense her releasing that incredible store of strength he'd always known she possessed.

That steel spine locked into place, her stubborn little chin lifted, and he watched the woman she'd grown into straighten her shoulders and face him with far more control than he had at the moment.

"Styx flew from Sanctuary yesterday. He can help me for a day or so." She completely ignored his statement. "You'll be rather busy with other things, and I need a friend . . ."

"Ya need yer mate," Styx growled, but there was no heat in his words.

A bitter smile twisted her pale lips as her gaze moved back to Jonas. "And here he's known for being agreeable and easy to get along with. I'll have to check with Storme and see if she cut off his chocolate supply again."

Styx merely grunted at the comment.

"If you want to avoid the Breed that's mated you, then send Styx home," Jonas advised her. "Your mate won't allow this and you know it. Your name was linked with Styx romantically before he mated Storme. Just because his mate trusts him doesn't meant yours will."

Pure fury flashed in her eyes, brightening them, making them more eerie than before.

"Bastard Coyote," she enunciated with a dagger-sharp tone. "He'll be lucky if I don't castrate him myself."

"Cassie . . ."

"He knew we were mates," she suddenly cried, the anger erupting with such fury that Jonas felt the need to step back. "He knew, and he let me make that damn bargain anyway. All these years he'd done nothing but manipulate me when he should have told me."

Her fury was overpowering, lashing through the room, the scent of it, the sheer power of it like an invisible wave of heat.

What she said simply wasn't possible. Even Jonas hadn't known, and he'd run her DNA through every sample they had, looking for a match. He'd even run it through that Coyote DNA database and it had come up negative.

"He knew." She was so tense, so determined to control that fury, that her body was strung as tight as a bow. "He knew before he touched me. Before he . . ."

Before he mated her.

"Cassie. Sweetheart . . . ," Jonas whispered, aching at the need to hold her as he always had when she'd come to him, when she was hurting.

But the scent of that mating was one of the strongest he'd smelled since he'd learned what the scent meant. That meant any touch, male or female, would be painful, too painful for him to attempt.

She rubbed her bare arms, breathing hard as she licked her lips and glanced toward Styx.

"Call off the search. Tell Mom and Dad to concentrate on Kenzi . . ."

Jonas laughed at that, amazed she'd even suggest it.

"You know better than that, Cassie. Won't happen. They've only just learned of her existence but you're still their child." He propped his hands on his hips, and as much as he hated to, he pushed back his affection for her, his regret for her position, and injected just the right amount of censure in his tone. "Get your head together, goddammit. I trained you better than this and I'll be damned if I'll let you turn into one of those simpering little woe-is-me females."

Not that she didn't have good reason to let her inner woe-is-me damsel free; he just refused to allow her to sink to that level.

"Unlike others, you're not my boss—"

"Test me." Just enough growl, just enough deep-throated warning to shut her up, and it worked. Thank God. "You obviously created this situation, from what you just said. He couldn't have manipulated you if you weren't associating with him somehow, and before I see a fucking bloodbath on my hands between Wolf and Coyote, I'll lock your ass up myself. Now, get your goddamned big-girl panties on and try to act like the intelligent, capable young woman I've trained you to be instead of a fucking spoiled-ass brat. And think about this." He paused just long enough to be sure he had her attention. "If your father even suspects, even has a moment's suspicion, that this isn't a voluntary mating, then Breeds will be warring with Breeds instead of humans. Is that what you want?"

Those pale lips trembled again, and he had to still them. Still them or kill that damned Coyote himself.

"Is it what you want?" he yelled, taking two fast steps and lowering his head until they were almost nose to nose, until the scent of her Heat slapped at his senses with the demand that he retreat.

"No!" she yelled right back at him. "That's why I came

to you, you overbearing, conceited Lion. It sure as hell wasn't for your understanding."

Straightening, he nodded, stepped back and let his expression soften marginally.

"But I do understand," he said, his tone gentling. "More than you know. But *you* knew the moment that hormone hit your system what you had to do. Now, by God, do it."

She didn't speak, but she didn't have to. He'd known her long enough, knew her well enough and sensed things deep enough to know she knew exactly what she had to do.

The question was, could she actually do it?

Her hesitant nod was the only answer he needed.

"Styx?" He spoke to the Breed watching them.

"Aye?" That was definitely a hint of amusement in the Wolf's tone.

"Take Loki and three others from my team." He kept his gaze on Cassie as a hint of fear flashed in her eyes, then just as quickly hid once again. "Find Dog."

• C H A P T E R 3 •

He wasn't one to hesitate when he knew something had to be done. The moment he'd intercepted the transmission that the Council had a sibling to Cassandra Sinclair, he'd known he'd have to go after her. It was simply a stroke of luck that put him in the right place at the right time.

But having Cassie's message come when it had had been surprising, and just as in the past, he'd added it to their little game. Then on a last-minute whim he had raised the stakes. Just to see if she would go along.

The fact that she had agreed to meet, to give him her body for a single night, had presented a challenge he couldn't resist. It was almost a dare, and he'd warned her once not to dare him.

His mate.

He'd known for years she was his mate, just as he'd known she'd fight him. The knowledge of that fight had held him back. He'd concentrated on other matters, on Breed freedom and his deceptions against the Genetics Council. Until last night.

He'd lost his mind, and now there was no saving it.

Son of a bitch.

Pushing his fingers through his hair, he lifted the bottle of whisky to his lips and drank deeply. Not that he could get drunk with the damned rotgut shit he'd bought at the hotel. The burn wasn't even enough to take his mind from the hell he'd created for himself.

He'd thought for certain if he obeyed her insane little conditions he could still have her without the consequences that came with mating one's mate. By not sharing the hormone that had filled the glands beneath his tongue, surely she'd escape relatively unscathed and he could still touch her, take her.

Oh, how very wrong he'd been.

He'd avoided this for six years. Since those stolen moments in Seth Lawrence's atrium when he'd realized what she was to him, he'd tried to avoid this.

Or had he? He hadn't exactly been thinking clearly for weeks now, ever since he caught the faintest scent of another Breed clinging to her. So faint at first, he hadn't been certain it was there. He'd had to get closer, brush against her, and his head had nearly exploded with rage.

"Jonas is getting testy." Mongrel stepped into the room, careful to stay way back as he made the announcement. "Loki said the director's at that do-or-die stage."

Dog merely grunted. Jonas stayed at a do-or-die stage. It was part of his genetics.

"He says the Wolf Styx is in the director's office with her. No one knows what the hell is going on, though," Mongrel added.

Dog's lip lifted in a silent snarl as he fought back his fury.

Styx Mackenzie. That fucking Wolf Breed had nearly met a bullet more than once because of his closeness to Cassie. Had he not mated when he did, then he'd probably be dead.

Dog lifted the bottle and drank deeply once again.

He was going to have to get better booze if he wanted to get drunk. Hell, he could use a good drunk right now.

"Report is Vanderale's heli-jet left Johannesburg less than an hour ago. Dane's flying in. Things are getting ready to go to hell, Dog." There was an edge of worry in his friend's voice.

Things had already gone to hell.

Dane Vanderale, a hybrid breed, son to the first Leo, and a manipulating son of a bitch unlike any Dog had ever known, was sure to stick his damned nose into the situation.

Pushing his fingers restlessly through his hair, Dog placed the bottle carefully on the table and turned to face the other Breed.

"Initiate immediate evac," he ordered him decisively, knowing what had to be done. "Get our people out, have them rendezvous at the house. I'll need everyone in place."

Years of planning, manipulating and careful calculations were coming to an end. The end he'd been working toward was in sight, and it was now endangered by a mating he'd hoped to delay.

"It's already been done. I sent out the call myself. Everyone's moving," Mongrel assured him. "The mating scent's damned strong. Won't matter where you go, you won't be able to hide it."

Sometimes it could be covered, even hidden for short lengths of time, with the right hormonal treatments. But for some, there was no way to hide it. He'd waited too long— the hormone had only strengthened in his system over the years—and now it was raging through him.

Shit. Dane had warned him. Now he was going to have to listen to the bastard's I-told-you-so's. That was never pleasant. Hell. He should have just kept her.

Now he was going to have to find a way to slip into Jonas's office, then slip into his mate's bed. Because even if the Heat wasn't burning her alive yet, by God, it damned sure was burning through him like wildfire.

"This is going to turn into a hell of a problem," Mongrel warned him as he slid a slim cigar from his shirt pocket, lit it and turned for the door. "If you're not careful, things are going to get really bad."

Dammit, hadn't that already happened? At least, according to his enraged mate.

"Naw, it's just going to get more interesting." He grinned, a tight, hard curve of mocking amusement. "That's all, brother. It's just going to get more interesting."

Mongrel's dubious look was almost amusing. "You scare me, Dog. I'll be damned if you don't scare me."

But that was okay; as long as he wasn't scaring himself he was doing good. So, was he scared yet?

◆   ◆   ◆

Jonas was waiting for him. Pushing open what appeared to be a section of the wall an hour later, Dog entered the other Breed's office as Mongrel stepped in behind him.

Mongrel. That name had the power to irk him at times, just as the name of their partner, Mutt, did. His own, he'd learned to live with. What could they expect when they were known for following the Genetic Council rather than fighting for Breed freedom?

But for the first time in his entire adult life, Dog admitted to a thread of regret that he hadn't given Cassie reason to suspect that he wasn't Council controlled.

"You could have warned me, Dog." The brooding frustration on Jonas's face wasn't exactly a welcome when he entered the room. It looked more like pure disgust.

He arched a brow in inquiry. "I assumed you'd be expecting me."

Yeah, that was a deliberate misdirection if there ever was one. The look on Jonas's face assured him it wasn't going to work, though. Not that Dog had expected it to.

"Where's my mate?" He stared around the room.

He could smell her scent, sweet, spicy. An intriguing

mix that made him harder than he was before he entered the room.

The look Jonas shot him was rife with frustration, and perhaps even anger. With this man, it wasn't always easy to be certain which was which, but Dog had never let the look bother him either.

"She's with her mother and several of our specialists. You know the deal. A hormonal treatment has to be worked up for her." Jonas moved behind his desk and took his seat, staring back at Dog with liquid-mercury eyes that were almost as eerie as Cassie's blue ones.

Okay, hormonal treatments. He wasn't going to object to that. They weren't a cure, or even a treatment that would allow her to deny him. It would just make it easier for her to bear the effects of the Mating Heat. Wouldn't be so bad if they could come up with a similar drug for the males.

That was, if it worked for her. Rumor was that Coyotes didn't respond so well to hormonal treatments.

"Sinclair's here, then?" Yeah, he'd expected that too, and that meeting he might not be looking forward to.

Dash Sinclair was an incredibly powerful alpha. If he let it be known he wanted Dog dealt with, then survival might be iffy.

Jonas leaned back, his arms settled comfortably on the arms of the desk chair, and just stared back at Dog silently for long seconds.

This could become a problem. If he let it.

"If Sinclair attempts to take her, I'll find her," he told Jonas, ensuring that Jonas knew he was serious. "I'll find her, and she'll disappear. Not what I want to do. Not a choice I'd like to make. But I will."

Cassie would probably kill him herself. Son of a bitch, he should have kept the game to messages alone . . .

Like hell. Nothing, not one damned thing in his life, had been so good as being buried in his mate.

"This is a fucking mess," Jonas muttered, leaning forward

then and placing his arms on his desk. "Why didn't you tell me you were her mate?"

"None of your business." He wasn't going to be questioned by this Breed either. "Now, take me to my mate's rooms or have her prepared to leave with me. One or the other . . ."

"I'll ask you the same question I asked your mate." Jonas overrode the demand. "Do you want to see a war between Breeds? Or risk Cassie losing her mate to his own foolishness?" The director's voice deepened, the innate command in the animalistic rumble a challenge to the animal Dog was created from. "I'm not willing to risk either, Dog, but that's what will happen if Sinclair believes even for an instant that Cassie is not a willing mate."

Dog advanced on the desk, leaned forward until his palms were flat on the wood and stared Jonas fully in the eye.

"Prepare my mate to leave or show me to her rooms. Your choice. I'm in no mood to play footsie with her father, or with you. My mate. My choice." The director should know better than to challenge an alpha Breed male where a mate was concerned.

He damned sure should know better than to challenge Dog in such a situation. He hadn't survived amid the stench of the Council and its evil without learning how to navigate any challenge to his decisions or his actions.

Jonas simply stared back at him silently for long moments.

"Jonas . . . ," he began warningly.

"Cassie's willing to meet this situation halfway." The director shocked him with that information. "She'll publicly accept you as her mate. She'll keep the true details to herself regarding how you bargained with her for a night of sex to save her sister's life, and she'll deal with you privately." Was that a measure of satisfaction he heard in Jonas's voice? "In exchange, you will not antagonize her parents or her friends during this time. You will play the considerate, loving mate at all times whenever others are around." Jonas leaned forward then. "And by God, you will be a considerate mate when in private or you'll deal with me."

Those liquid-mercury eyes flashed, the color bleeding into the whites as claws slowly emerged from the tips of Jonas's fingers. A phenomenon Dog had seen only rarely. Jonas's control was usually far better than this.

"You make me wish I had plans to do otherwise, Director." He smirked. "For the simple joy I'd find in accepting that little dare you just threw out." He stood back, wanting to chuckle.

Hell, he was a fucking Coyote. What made Jonas think he could intimidate him so easily?

"You've been a hell of an ally over the years." Jonas sighed. "But too many people believe you're Council first . . ."

"My mate comes first." The Council had never come first. The appearance of it had been necessary but was no longer an option. "Above everything else, never doubt that, Jonas: My mate comes first."

"And the operation you've been conducting?" Jonas asked as Dog went to turn from him. "What about your people, Dog? The information you've been working to attain?"

"The evac order went out," Dog informed him. "As of the moment I claimed my mate there was no other choice but to move the timetable up. It'll take a few days to get the teams in place, though. Until then, as far as you, Sinclair or anyone else knows, I'm Council. Am I understood?"

The fact that Jonas didn't think much of the information was evident.

"You couldn't do anything easy, could you?" Jonas grunted. "I should have expected this. Son of a bitch if I shouldn't have."

To that, Dog shrugged while tossing him a hard smile. "Hindsight, my friend," he stated mockingly. "Hindsight. Now, my mate, if you don't mind."

Not that he gave a damn that Jonas minded. Hell, at this point he didn't care if his mate minded.

All he cared about was finding her and relieving the hunger ripping through his body. A hunger he knew his mate would share.

◆   ◆   ◆

She was going to puke.

Cassie could feel the nausea rising. Again. She'd thrown up twice already during the examination she was forced to endure by both the Wolf Breed specialist, Dr. Nikki Armani, and the Coyote specialist, Dr. Katya Sobolova.

It seemed as though the examination was never ending. Vaginal samples, blood taken, saliva and perspiration. The specialists were so thorough and intent they had her ready to scream more than once. But though the doctor's touch was uncomfortable, it wasn't horrendous. It was just sickening.

For more than four hours she endured it before lifting her hand as they came at her again.

"Enough." She really didn't want to throw up again.

Drs. Armani and Sobolova shared a concerned look before turning back to her.

"Don't argue with me," she snapped. "I've had it. I'm showering, dressing and returning to my room."

"The more samples we can get before your mate arrives, the better," Sobolova stated. "He's not known for his co-operation, Cassie. And such males can be territorial . . ."

"Then he can be territorial by himself." She lifted her shoulder in unconcern as she slid from the table, aware of her mother's silence as she stood next to the examination bed. "Now leave me alone."

"Elizabeth." Armani turned to her mother almost beseechingly. "Talk to her."

Gathering her clothes, Cassie wondered if this would be the one time her mother sided against her.

"Cassie's made her decision," her mother stated, though her expression was concerned. "You have all you're going to get at the moment. Besides, according to her father"—she tapped the communications device at her ear—"her mate's arrived. As soon as Cassie's taken to her suite he'll be here for his own examination."

Cassie tensed. His examination? They'd touch him? See him naked and aroused? Something feral rose inside her.

Before she could halt the sound, a low growl left her throat as her gaze sliced to Armani and Sobolova.

"Cassie." Elizabeth Sinclair stepped between her and the doctors. "The males don't receive a physical examination. They won't allow a female's touch this early in the mating, I promise you that."

Of course they didn't. She knew that.

God, what was wrong with her? It wasn't as though she wanted him herself, did she?

"I'm not feeling well, Mom," she said faintly, pushing past her mother and heading for the showers. "I'm sorry." She hated this. The arousal tearing her apart, making her hypersensitive. She hated what this mating shit was doing to her. All the dark, furious emotions she'd kept buried so deep inside her were pushing at the shield she'd always kept in place, trapping them.

Those emotions terrified her. She'd kept them locked inside her for so long that she feared what would happen if they suddenly surged free. And what she was experiencing now was tempting them in ways she couldn't bear.

As she stepped from the shower fifteen minutes later and hurriedly dried and dressed, a knock at the door assured her that her mother had waited long enough to talk to her.

The woman who had risked her own life, countless times, to save her. The mother who had fought for her, nearly died for her. And believed in the goodness Cassie showed the world. She never, never wanted her mother to know what she hid inside. She didn't ever want to see the distaste and disappointment she was certain her mother would feel if she even suspected the animal Cassie kept contained.

"Cassie?" The door opened as she finished dressing.

The black silk slacks and matching T-back camisole gave her a small feeling of confidence. Sliding her feet into the four-inch heels, she met her mother's gaze as Elizabeth pushed open the door.

"Well, that wasn't fun." She gave a small, uncomfortable laugh as her mother stepped inside and closed the door behind her. "No wonder everyone avoids it as much as possible."

Her mother watched her intently. "It's usually quite painful actually. The first year your father and I were mated, it would feel as though knives were piercing my skin at times."

She could hear the question in her mother's statement. Why wasn't the effect so extreme with her daughter as well?

"Ask Drs. Frankenstein," she said with a snort as she removed the ebony hair sticks she used to pin her hair out of the way of the water.

Her mother simply stood still and silent, watching her.

God, her mom didn't look any older than she had when Cassie was nine. In fifteen years, she didn't appear to have aged a year. Her skin was still unblemished, her blue eyes sharp and missing little. Dark brown hair fell just below her shoulders, and she was still trim, with a slight athletic build.

Her mother trained often with her father, believing that should danger come, she should fight at her mate's side, not wait for him to protect her. And many times she'd had to do just that. Fight at his side to help protect her family.

"Cassie." There was a bit of chastisement in her mother's voice. "Talk to me."

Cassie shook her head, frustration and even fear building inside her. "What do you want me to say?" she demanded, more agitated now than she had been during the examination. "You said my mate was here. I need to see him."

She flushed. It was a lie, but it wasn't. Her body was dying for him. The very knowledge that he was in the building was enough to increase the arousal.

"I want you to assure me this is voluntary," her mother said softly. "Your father and I need to know this is what you want."

What she wanted?

Was her mother crazy? Had she and her father somehow gone senile and she hadn't seen it, suspected it? And here she thought they knew her so well.

"As voluntary as any other mating?" she asked in disbelief. "I slept with him willingly. I didn't suspect he was my mate before he touched me. What more can I say?"

That he knew?

That the lying bastard had known they were mates and rather than warning her had let her step into her own destruction?

Her mother was watching her too closely, too compassionately.

"Do you know who he is?" she asked long moments later. "Cassie, do you know who your mate is?"

She wasn't going to cry. She wouldn't let her lips tremble, her tears fall. She wouldn't give in to the betrayal she felt, no matter how much she wanted to.

"I know who others believe him to be," she finally stated, using the line Jonas had given her. "Just as I know he's not what others believe. He's my mate."

She had to stare into her mother's eyes and say those words. She had to lie to her mother. It wasn't the first time she'd done so, but it was the biggest lie she'd ever told her and Cassie hated it.

Thank God it wasn't her father questioning her. He could smell a lie. She didn't know if she had enough self-control to lie to him and keep that scent from emanating from her. Even at the best of times that ability was iffy.

"Very well." Her mother nodded. "I'll let your father know. But you know he'll want to see you soon, don't you? Both you and your mate."

Her chin lifted. "He has a name."

She stared back at her mother defiantly, and she couldn't even say why, because she hated the deceptive bastard.

Compassion softened her mother's face. "He'll want to talk to you and Dog soon, then," she said gently, nearly breaking Cassie's determined façade. "You know, Cassie, your father and I would do whatever it took to ensure your happiness. You have only to ask."

And what could they do?

Kill her mate? Breeds had only one mate. Endure this arousal, unquenched, for the rest of her life? The way it was building now, she couldn't imagine such a thing. She'd never survive it.

As much as she hated the Coyote, she was stuck with him for the time being. Possibly for life.

No falling in love. No happily ever after. No mate that she at least knew one good thing about. No, her mate was a Coyote. A Council Coyote at that.

"I went into this willingly," she finally whispered, hoping, praying, her mother believed her. "Please, don't let Daddy think otherwise, Mom. He's not what others think he is."

He had helped her every time she needed that help. He had saved Kenzi, and in doing so, saved Cassie's sanity.

"Have you seen Kenzi yet?" she asked her mother, hoping to change the subject as they left the shower room.

"She's refusing to see us." The strain in her mother's voice could be heard now. "I left your father to talk to Rhyzan. There seems to be a problem between him and Kenzi."

Rhyzan Brannigan was the Coyote Jonas had picked as his deputy director of the Federal Bureau of Breed Affairs. An exceptionally striking, cold Breed.

"He could be a problem," Cassie admitted. "Rhyzan doesn't care much for me for some reason. It could affect how he's treated Kenzi."

She had no idea why Rhyzan was antagonistic toward her, but from the moment they'd met, she'd felt it, despite his later attempts to seduce her.

"You never told me that." Once again, a statement with a question behind it. Her mother was incredibly good at that.

Once again, she shrugged negligently. "I'm a big girl, Mom. I've learned to do my job without allowing other's distaste for my presence bother me."

She was a Cross Breed. She'd heard the distinction far too often. She was neither Coyote nor Wolf to other Breeds. For the most part. Strangely enough, it was the felines who were more accepting of her. But they'd known her since childhood.

The majority of the Wolves and Coyotes she knew regarded her with suspicion; some, like Rhyzan, just hid it better.

"I'll discuss this with your dad, then. Jonas will need to revise his decision to keep Rhyzan in charge of Kenzi's debriefing. I won't have her bullied. Not after all she's been through." The sorrow in her mother's voice was deep, the scent of it strong.

Kenzi was her child. Cassie's full sister despite the fact that Kenzi had been created without the Wolf DNA.

"I'll see her soon as well," Cassie promised, though she sensed the fact that Kenzi wouldn't welcome her.

She could feel it inside, deep, where that gift she had once possessed had retreated to.

"I'm here for you as well, Cassie," her mother promised as they entered the elevator and Cassie pressed the button that would take her to the residence level of the Bureau's offices.

"I know, Mom." She stared straight ahead, refusing to give in to the need to spill the hurt, the pain, into her mother's loving arms.

If she spilled that much, the rest would come rolling free. She wouldn't be able to hide everything she'd kept from her parents for so very long.

Everything she'd kept hidden even from herself.

· C H A P T E R   4 ·

He was waiting for her when she stepped into her suite on the upper floor of the Western Bureau of Breed Affairs. The dun-colored buttoned shirt and matching pants were paired with work-scarred boots and a wide leather belt. The sand-colored fall of hair around his face was both rakish and almost boyish. But there was nothing boyish about the look in his gunmetal gray eyes.

He wasn't armed—at least she couldn't see or scent any weapons on him. They had a distinctive smell, one that reminded her of death.

Sprawled back in her recliner, remote in hand as he scanned the channels on the HD screen. On the table beside him sat several empty beer bottles and one half full and a half-eaten ham, roast beef and cheese sandwich.

He flipped off the screen and in a move that bespoke pure male confidence tilted his head and grinned back at her mockingly.

"Well, mate, did they get all their samples from you? At least until after we have sex again?" A dark blond brow arched with curious sarcasm.

She hated him. She was sure of it.

Bastard.

She made certain her smile was cold. "Examinations are all finished and hopefully a hormonal treatment that will counteract the mating will be here soon."

Of course, nothing could counteract the mating; it could only help ease it, nothing more. But even an easing would do, because she was damned if she could clear her head enough to think past the Mating Heat.

He flipped the recliner back to a sitting position, his booted feet meeting the carpet as she watched him warily. And he laughed at her.

"Nothing counteracts the mating, mate," he assured her, the laughter still lingering in his voice.

His expression was frankly insulting.

Now she knew why Ashley, the Coyote female she worked with, swore she was shooting her mate at first sight.

Before he had a chance to exchange any bodily fluids with her.

"I can only hope this will be the exception." She had a feeling it was anything but.

Arousal was burning through her, creating a fine film of perspiration along her forehead, and her hands were getting ready to shake.

She just wanted to touch him.

Taste him.

"So . . . ," he drawled, rising slowly to his feet. "They tell you who I am?"

Cocky bastard. Did he think she couldn't figure that one out on her own?

"Are you a Breed?" she snapped.

His brow arched. Was that surprise she saw in his face?

"Why, mate, I do believe I am." He was laughing at her again.

Propping her hand on her hip, she restrained the need to snarl back at him in fury. "Do I smell as though I give a fuck what your name is right now? Yes, I know what your goddamned name is, and I'll be damned if I'll scream out 'Dog' while I'm coming. So please be kind enough to choose another."

Choose another name?

She was worried about the name she called out when she orgasmed, when the scent of her Heat was like a drug hitting his system?

He didn't even have time to tell her what he thought about that demanding little statement before she turned with a little twitch of her nose and a toss of her head and stalked through her bedroom door.

Had anyone ever delivered such a stinging rebuke only to sweep away before he could deliver a comeback?

He didn't think so. And he didn't like it. He couldn't remember a time anyone had left him speechless. And the knowledge that his fledgling mate had done so didn't sit well with him.

He grinned, raw, primal lust rising hard and fast, releasing the hunger he'd been holding back.

He'd warned her the night he slipped into her hospital room so long ago to never dare him. And though she might have been unconscious when he bent over her, she'd damned sure come awake once he'd whispered the words.

She might not say the words, but every look, every word out of that smart mouth of hers, was a blatant challenge, and it was time to meet that challenge in a way she couldn't refute.

Dog slipped silently into the bathroom minutes later, naked, anticipating a confrontation with his mate, when he was brought to a hard, sudden stop.

The scent of feminine arousal was heavy in the small room. Tempting. If ambrosia had a scent, then it was the smell of his mate's need for him. But mixed with it, and vying for supremacy, was the scent of her pain and her fear.

Never had he scented her fear.

Trepidation on occasion, anger, confusion a few times, but he'd never smelled fear.

Moving silently to the entrance of the shower, he expected to see her tears, a ravaged expression. Instead, she stood beneath an icy spray, her forehead and hands resting against the tile wall, her profile composed and eerily calm.

There wasn't a hint of the turmoil he could sense pouring from her, mixing with her arousal but doing nothing to dim it.

Standing so still and silent, the soaked silk of her hair flowing down her delicate back, she made him more aware of his own strength and larger build in a way he'd never been before. But it was the mix of chaotic emotions that held him, that had his chest clenching, had him pausing before he reached for the shower's controls and pushed the temperature from icy to something far warmer and more inviting.

He waited for the fall of water to warm as he watched his little mate. As she stood like a statue, silent and so very still, he could sense the battle inside her, feel it tearing at her. And only a fool wouldn't be aware of whom she feared so deeply that she was standing there fighting to control herself.

She feared him. Feared him with the same depth that she wanted him.

And there wasn't a damned thing he could do to fix it. He didn't dare give voice to his own secrets, because once they touched the air around him, they'd be secrets no longer, and he couldn't protect her if that happened.

"So, tell me, mate," he said instead. "What name would you prefer I carry?"

Cassie swung around, so shocked that she hadn't heard him, hadn't smelled him enter the room, that she could only blink back at the Breed standing in the shower's open doorway.

"Is there something else you'd prefer to call me?" There was nothing mocking, cruel or censorious in his tone. He spoke as though merely curious as to her answer.

She could only shake her head, uncertain now.

For a second, he lowered his head and stared at the floor as she slowly became aware of the fact that the water flowing around her had become much warmer, steamy, in fact. And within the warmth she could swear the hunger emanating from him was sinking inside her and increasing her own.

When he lifted his head, those steel gray eyes met her own gaze, and though she couldn't sense any particular emotion from him, rather than lashing at her, his lust seemed to surround her, almost comforting instead.

"Why didn't you tell me?" she asked him instead. "All these years we've messaged, why didn't you tell me you were my mate? You knew. I know you did."

He gave a quick, firm nod. "I knew. I've known since I first saw you and caught your scent flowing toward me. And I think I showed remarkable restraint in waiting to claim you."

He chose that moment to move into the roomy shower, taking up space, surrounding her with his scent, with his hunger, as his larger body blocked the shower spray.

But he still hadn't answered her question, and she would have demanded the answer again if the need for him wasn't swamping her.

She fought to breathe, to hold back all the needs and sensations, the hunger beating at her, pushing past control, confusion and fear and reaching out to him.

Oh God, she ached for him. Needed his touch as she'd never needed anything before him.

So much power filled his hard body, more than was normal for most Breed males. Broad shoulders, hard biceps, golden flesh stretched across his chest and down his lean, muscular abs. Strength honed by training and necessity, each inch of his body built for endurance and in prime, peak condition.

Between his thighs, his engorged cock stood out from his body, the mushroom-shaped crest and heavily veined shaft throbbing in arousal. She'd heard Wolf and Coyote Breed males were exceptionally endowed, but until Dog, she hadn't seen proof of it. That hard flesh was thick, powerful and imposing, like the Breed possessing it.

Water sluiced down his body, the steam infusing with the scent of his lust and of the male facing her. Heated, redolent of the desert itself, a whisper of safety, a hint of a storm. Enduring. Alive.

She licked her lips at the remembered taste of him filling her, taking her.

She'd deal with his name later. For now, this need for him was clawing at her, destroying her.

"What do you want, mate?" His fingers slid into the sodden length of her hair as he gripped his shaft with the other hand. "Or shall I help you decide?"

It didn't take much pressure to push her to her knees.

She remembered how he'd pressed his cock to her lips in that hotel room, the taste of him, and suddenly, she was beyond desperate for more. She was dying for him.

Her lips parted as the broad crest pressed against them, her tongue catching the essence of the mating hormone seeping from the glands beneath it as her mouth closed over the wide crest.

Silk over steel. The dark, plum-shaped crest pulsed, the slight taste of the pre-seminal fluid infusing her senses.

A helpless moan welled from her throat as she sucked him in eagerly. Her lips closing over his hard flesh, drawing on it and giving herself up to the Heat flaming through her body.

"That's it, mate. Suck me." Her mouth tightened at the explicit growl, her hand lifting, covering his where he gripped his hard flesh.

Thick, throbbing, his cock head filled her mouth as she worked it over, thrusting in shallow strokes past her lips as he stared down at her, his expression savage with lust.

She couldn't hold back her moans as his hand moved from beneath hers, allowing her to stroke the thick stalk as she milked the sensitive head with her mouth. His fingers tightened in her hair, tugged at it as another flex of the broad crest gave her another heady taste of the hormone-rich pre-seminal ejaculation.

Her body sensitized further at the taste, her mouth becoming greedier.

"Cassie . . . ah hell . . . your sweet mouth . . ." The inherent growl in his voice only made her want more, the sound of his pleasure as she took him goading her further.

She worked her tongue over the thick crest, hungry for more of him. His taste, his need for her, the hunger for him rising ever higher. She ached for him, his ragged groans, the explicit words fueled by his need.

"Fuck! Yes . . ." The sound was a snarl of pleasure as she managed to take him deeper. "That's it, baby . . . so damned good."

The roughening sound of his voice, the brutal need filling it, edged her own need to a critical level.

She took the engorged crest as deep as possible as another pulse of his pre-cum coated the back of her mouth, easing it. She worked her tongue against the sensitive underside, her own moans impossible to hold back.

Each shallow stroke took him nearly to her throat now. Thrusting in and pulling back, each impalement controlled even as she rapidly lost her ability to restrain herself.

The sound of their heavy breathing mingled with the shower and that of her mouth on his cock, greedily taking each thrust as his movements increased. His hands tightened in her hair, his breathing rapidly becoming more ragged.

"Ah hell, Cassie." His groan was a rumbled sound of pleasure.

She sucked at the head of his cock, tightened the draw of her mouth, increasing the movements of her tongue against the sensitive underside of the iron-hard flesh.

"Take it, damn you . . . Take my dick, baby . . . all of it . . ."

The first eruption of silky, hormone-rich semen hit the back of her throat, followed by another.

Sensual greed took over. The taste of his release had her sucking him with abandon, desperate for each taste as she swallowed his release and felt the need raging through her increase.

Hard hands pulled at her hair as he forced her head back and drew her quickly to her feet. In the next instant he pushed her around until her back was to him, placed his hand under her knee and pushed her foot to the shower seat built along the wall. And before she could draw a breath his erection was parting the folds of her desire-slick inner lips.

A pulse of heat as the pre-cum hit the entrance; a second later nerve endings became so sensitive, so desperate for touch, she could barely breathe through it.

His head bent to hers, his lips caressing the shell of her ear. "Your pussy's wet, Cassie. So hot and wet and sweet." As he held her steady, his hips shifted, his cock pushing inside her. "So fucking tight."

Another ejaculation of the pre-seminal fluid shot inside her, sensitizing, searing her with increasing sensation.

She couldn't stop her cry, part pleasure, part pain, as her inner flesh began to give way to the intrusion.

Oh God, he was so thick, stretching her, working inside the snug entrance with firm, determined thrusts.

"Sweet, tight pussy," he growled as the Breed pre-cum shot inside her again. "So fucking hot . . . take me, baby. Take all of me . . ."

Panting cries fell from her lips as she backed into each

thrust, needing more. She was dying for him, desperate for each inward stroke, each lance of agonizing pleasure.

"It's good, Cassie," he crooned, his voice guttural, roughened with his pleasure. He pulsed again, harder this time, the ejaculation of hormonal fluid building her need, the sensitivity of her flesh and her lust. "So tight around my dick . . . sucking me in . . ."

She screamed as the next thrust buried him to the hilt inside her.

She could feel every inch of his cock as it stretched her, throbbed inside her. Her vagina gripped, rippled around the intruder and grew increasingly sensitive with each pulse of pre-cum. Her inner flesh was rippling with need, clenching, tightening, giving way to the heavy erection, stretching around it as each nerve ending blazed into brilliant life.

Her vagina flexed, spasming in intense pleasure at each ejaculation, greedily taking the fluid that somehow allowed a female to take such an excess of flesh inside her. To take what she knew would soon result.

"Please . . . please . . ." She had no idea what she was even begging for at this point.

The sensations were more intense, driving deeper, harder inside her than before. The driving excess of pleasure, pain and desperate hunger was all she knew, all she could process.

"Easy, baby." He groaned as another hard pulse of heat infused her flesh. "Damn, you get tighter every time I fuck you. Greedy little pussy sucking at my cock."

His hips moved, flexed, the thick length shifting inside her with devastating results.

There was no warning. Her orgasm tore through her, blazing through her senses in wave after wave of a pleasure so violent she could barely process the sensations.

"Fuck me . . . damn you . . . fuck me . . ." That was her cry, her demand, and even as it fell from her lips she couldn't make herself care about language.

The world blurred around her as he began moving, nearly drawing free of her, pushing back, hard, hammering thrusts until she completely dissolved.

The peak of the extended orgasm was cataclysmic. The pulse of his release, the thickening of the Breed knot inside her, stretching her further, throbbing hot and—God help her—giving her agonizing pleasure.

Each hard throb of the swollen flesh was a pulse of release. A hot flick of lightning-sharp sensation that went beyond pleasure. Buried deep, the head of his cock nudging at her cervix, his semen unimpeded as it shot to the very depths of her body.

And as he destroyed her, his arms surrounded her, held her secure against his hard chest as she sobbed out in ecstasy. His teeth bit into her shoulder; his tongue probed at the wound. He held her, whispered her name, eased her as the knot held him locked inside her, extending the pleasure until she lay limp against him.

She was only barely aware of him pulling free of her sometime later. Turning off the water, he lifted her hair with one hand and quickly managed to secure a towel around the sodden length. Then, picking her up, he carried her back to the bedroom, and laid her gently in her bed.

She lay, floating in satiation and exhaustion, but still aware of him. Aware of his cleaning their combined releases from between her thighs before drying her gently.

When he moved, she assumed he was finished, that he'd go back to the television, leave her lying alone. Instead, when he returned, he pulled the towel gently from her damp hair and began rubbing the moisture from it with a dry towel.

She drifted on waves of relaxation, distantly amazed when he rolled her to her back, finished drying her hair, then went to work separating the mass into sections and combing the tangles from it. Patiently murmuring his appreciation of the silken texture, the unruly curls, he worked the comb through them. And when he finished with the nearly dried strands he weaved them into a loose braid and secured them.

At no time did he seem frustrated with the task, or in the least impatient. Amazingly enough, she thought as she drifted into sleep, she could have sworn she sensed his enjoyment.

CHAPTER 5

Cassie awoke just before dawn the next morning, alone, all too aware that she shouldn't be. The clock on the bedside table assured her that she hadn't slept for more than a few hours despite the fact that her internal clock assured her it was time to wake up.

She'd spent most of the evening and night completing reports and ensuring that her Bureau files were ready for whomever Jonas chose to take her place among the agents who worked to pull in information concerning the Genetics Council's attempts to sabotage the Breed community. Establishing a base on Navajo lands hadn't come easy. Ensuring it survived would be even more difficult if they weren't diligent in keeping the Council out of it.

As she'd filed the reports before lying down, there had been a heavy regret, though. She'd enjoyed working with Jonas and the agents he'd assigned to her. Stepping away from it hurt. But better to do it willingly, her head held high, than to be forced to relinquish her job.

Breed Law itself wouldn't allow her to hold the position. Her mate wasn't part of the established Breed community.

He was actually considered "rogue," a Breed who refused to declare his loyalty to the Breed community and worked often with the Council.

Smothering a yawn, she sat up in the bed, aware of her nakedness, the sensitivity of her skin, and the tenderness between her thighs and at her breasts. Just as she was aware that her mate wasn't in the suite with her.

So where the hell is he? she wondered, rising from the bed and heading for the bathroom. She hadn't heard him leave. Hell, he hadn't even told her that he would be leaving.

Genetics Council business? she wondered bitterly as she washed her face.

Twenty-four years of achievements, of ensuring everyone could overlook her Coyote genetics, if not forget about them, and what did she go and do? She hadn't just mated a Coyote, she'd mated one known for the fact that he often worked for the very monsters who created and tortured Breeds for so many decades.

And not just any Council Coyote either. Hell no, she'd mated one of the most notorious, lethally dangerous Coyotes known. A hell of a way to convince Breeds and humans alike that her Coyote genetics didn't matter.

She applied her makeup quickly, paying close attention to the shadows under eyes before she brushed her hair back and secured it with a clip. She pulled on black silk slacks and a sleeveless violet blouse. Pushing her feet into black heels, she checked her appearance in the bathroom mirror.

At least she looked no different from how she had the day before, she told herself silently as she strode through her bedroom and into the living area of the suite. Dog's pack still sat next to the door, though he'd at least cleaned up the beer bottles and remains of the sandwich he'd had the night before.

According to Anya, Coya of the Coyote packs in Citadel, she often had to threaten the Coyotes there to get them to pick up after themselves in the community rooms.

Striding to the desk on the other side of the room, she picked up her mobile phone and activated the power.

When the screen came up she stared at the message displayed with a sense of disbelief.

ACCESS DENIED

She could feel her throat tightening, a band of impending anger forming in her forehead as she placed the phone carefully on the desk and picked up the tablet next to it.

ACCESS DENIED

The message displayed when she powered it up had her fingers tightening on the device before she carefully replaced it on the desk and turned toward her laptop and powered it on. The same message again. Picking up the slender black purse at the edge of the desk, she retrieved her personal mobile phone, activated it, and stared down at it with such a sense of overwhelming betrayal that that she had to fight to process it.

ACCESS DENIED

"Well, that didn't take long, did it," she muttered bitterly.

Turning on her heel, she moved back to her bedroom and went to the small jewelry box she kept on the dresser there. There, she extracted her watch and latched the leather band around her wrist.

She was often teased about the piece of jewelry whenever she wore it, but no one would give it a second thought. More to the point, when she passed through the scanners outside the elevator in the lobby, the small chip hidden within it would be undetectable. If worse came to worst she'd be able to send an emergency signal to her father. But other than that, she was now unprotected. She had no idea

where her security detail was, or her parents for that matter.
And she wouldn't be able to roam the Bureau searching for
them. Furthermore, she'd be damned if she'd beg anyone to
contact them.

Collecting her purse, she left both her work phone and
her personal phone lying on the desk next to the tablet and
strode quickly to the door. Opening it, she nearly betrayed
her shock at the two Breed Enforcers outside her door.

She was now considered such a risk that guards were
securing her room?

Wolf Breed Enforcers. Wonderful. And two she didn't
recognize.

She could sense the instant distrust and instinctive aggression they kept in check. It was in their gazes, in the hint
of censure in their expressions. And telling herself it was
natural, even instinctive, didn't help. When it was all said
and done, it was her own fault. She'd allowed herself to be
mated to a Coyote no one, even his own species, trusted.
She could blame no one but herself.

Keeping her head high, she turned to the elevators,
aware she was being followed by one of the enforcers. Stepping into the elevator, she ignored the Breed as he followed.

"Lobby," she spoke to the automated control.

The trip down was made quickly, but not quickly enough
to hide the scent of the Wolf Breed's distaste and resentment.

When the door opened, she wasn't certain which of
them was more relieved: her or the enforcer.

"Miss Sinclair." The Breed manning the scanners was
cool, polite, where he'd always been friendly in the past.

She passed through the scanner and didn't pause as she
moved for the entrance.

Never had she been unable to contact her security detail
before leaving the Bureau, or anywhere else for that matter.
Walking through the doors of the Bureau took more courage than she actually wanted to admit to. To face the fact

that if—when—a Council Breed realized she was alone, she'd have no one to depend on but herself.

As she stepped through the glass door and let it swing closed behind her, she refused to allow herself to give in to the uncertainties she could feel building inside her. The area outside the Bureau wasn't exactly deserted. At this time of the morning, shifts were changing for communications and clerical staff. Meetings would be beginning soon, the business day just gearing up for the Breeds and humans milling about the front of the buildings.

Striding through the workers coming and going, she made her way to the curb and lifted her arm to signal one of the cabs idling in a waiting area well beyond the entrance to the building.

As her arm went up, she was suddenly jostled from behind, thrown to the side into a male's hard body. His hand gripped her arm, the hold like fire against her flesh. Cassie jerked back with a cry, only to have her head collide with something much harder.

"Council whore . . ." Pain racked her side, stealing her breath and taking her to her knees as her vision dimmed and she felt herself toppling to the ground.

They would attack her now? Her own people?

As she felt consciousness slip away, she could have sworn she heard Dog screaming her name, her father's enraged voice joining it.

◆   ◆   ◆

He was crazy to have let his lust and possessiveness for his little halfling get the best of him, Dog thought as he pulled the Dragoon in among the sedans, SUVs and pickups in the parking lot. The instinctive animal senses he'd possessed had gone insane at the thought of another Breed so close to her that the essence of his scent had been left on her. He'd made that damned bargain with her, believed he could have her without sparking the Mating Heat, and now, he'd only complicated both their lives and ensured a lack of trust from not just his mate, but those Breeds that his mate depended upon.

And there wasn't a damned thing he could do to fix it. At least not yet.

The meeting scheduled with Mutt and Mongrel for an update on the extraction of their people from various Genetics Council holdings had taken longer than he expected. There were more than two dozen Breeds, male as well as female, working for suspected and known Genetics Council associates, risking their lives to complete the evacuation. That had been only one of the deceptions he'd been working on; the other was the identification of those funding the labs. The search for the identities of the twelve-member Council had been ongoing for more than two decades, and because he couldn't stay away from his mate, it was over.

Not that they were any closer to those identities than they had been when he'd begun his own search ten years ago. But according to the reports coming in, several of the Breeds working with him had gotten out with downloads of encrypted information from several select locations.

So far, the mission was progressing with no apparent suspicion from the wrong people. There were no teams of Council soldiers or Breeds being gathered together or sent out; everything was business as usual.

He could only pray it continued as smoothly, though he knew once word of his mating with Cassie made it to the higher ranks within the Council, notice would be taken.

But there were no reports of it coming through their normal channels.

Reaching across the console, he grabbed the bag filled with breakfast to share with his mate, pushed the door open and stepped out of the Dragoon, very well aware of the Wolf Breeds slipping along both sides of the vehicle.

Pushing the door closed, he faced Cassie's father, Dash Sinclair, and six of his highly trained Wolf Breeds.

Brown eyes lit with amber and a hint of hazel narrowed on him from between black lashes. Thick black hair was neatly trimmed, almost military short, though he'd been out of the military a good fifteen years. At six-four, Sinclair matched him in height, and no doubt when it came to pure mean gutter fighting, Dog wouldn't find it easy to defeat him without releasing the demented fury of the creature lurking inside him.

Son of a bitch. If he got into a fight with his mate's father, or the Breeds who followed him, then she wasn't going to be happy in the least. She loved her parents, and a fight with this Breed was guaranteed to piss her off. Or worse yet, it would hurt her, cause her to distrust him if her father were harmed.

Hell, if they struck, he was going to have to let them kick his ass. She would never countenance him striking her father, and he hadn't secured her emotions yet, let alone enough loyalty to balance out her anger for him. "Well, fuck, get it over with," he growled, lifting his lip in a disgusted sneer. "But I promise you, I'm going to make her feel so sorry for every bruise and broken bone that it will be years before she forgives you."

Taking a beating was something he'd never done in his life. Even during his very brief time in a Council lab. He'd never allowed it. Knowing he was going to have to allow it now was making his ass itch for sure.

Sinclair crossed his arms over his chest and tilted his head to the side, surprise flickering across his expression.

"You think I'd damage my daughter's mate?" The rumble of displeasure in the alpha's voice was unmistakable.

"I think you'd kill me if she wouldn't suffer for it," he grunted, placing the bag of food on the hood of the Dragoon.

Sinclair's lips quirked in mocking acknowledgment.

"Did you know before you met with my daughter that

you were her mate?" Dash asked then. "And before you answer, let me tell you, I've already spoken to Styx."

Well now, he bet that conversation was damned interesting.

"And what does that Scots bastard have to do with any of this?" Dog snapped, still more jealous of that redheaded fool than he liked to admit.

"Styx caught a hint of your scent in that atrium six years ago, and he didn't forget it. Your scent. You knew Cassie was your mate and you tricked her into meeting you, didn't you?" No one could accuse this Breed of a lack of intelligence.

"'Tricked' is a rather strong word," he admitted with a cocky grin. "I merely suggested a meeting." The snarl that pulled at his lips wasn't entirely voluntary. "I waited six years to claim her; you were damned lucky I didn't do it then."

"Does she know you're also the bastard that nearly killed her on that island?" The guttural tone, rough with the animal rising inside the Breed, was indicative of the anger brewing inside him.

"She knows." Dog had made certain she knew several years ago during one of the infrequent phone calls he'd bargained for.

"Goddammit," Dash muttered, grimacing at the weapon he thought he'd have, though what good he thought it would do, Dog wasn't certain.

As the other Breed cursed, a subtle, faint scent caught his attention. Cassie's scent.

Turning toward the entrance of the Bureau, he searched for her, certain he had to be wrong. She wouldn't be out in the general public when the smell of her Heat was impossible to miss.

Surely to God she knew better . . .

Son of a bitch, she didn't know better.

She moved across the concrete concourse as graceful as

life itself. Head held high, her expression placid as she stepped for the curb and as Dog cursed and moved quickly for her. Behind him, the Wolf Breeds followed as her father caught sight of her as well.

As she paused, a group crossing the street blocked his view of her for precious seconds. But he still heard her cry as it drifted from within the group. When they parted, he snarled in fury, running to get to her, screaming her name as he watched her hit her knees, then slowly topple to the side.

He caught her before her head hit the cement.

"Follow them," he heard Dash yell out to his men.

Swinging Cassie into his arms, he ignored her father, ignored the chase for the group of Breeds racing from the area and rushed for the entrance to the Bureau.

"The labs," Dash snapped as they headed for the security scanners. "Take the stairs."

Pushing past the Breeds and humans as they paused, watching them in shock, Dog rushed through the scanners, only to find his way blocked by six Bureau Enforcers.

"She no longer has clearance, and you damned sure don't," the Wolf Breed Enforcer facing him sneered as he glanced down at Cassie's unconscious form.

Before Dog could snarl back, or her father could push in front of them, the Wolf Breed was thrown aside, along with the two enforcers flanking him.

"By God I do," Styx Mackenzie snarled, canines flashing. "Get the fuck out of the way, morons."

Dog rushed past, heading to the door one of the Coyote females was holding open for him, her expression filled with concern.

"We saw the attack on the monitor," Ashley snapped as he and Dash rushed past her. "Sobolova and Armani have been notified you're bringing her down."

"Get her mother," Dash ordered the Breed. "Now."

"She's on her way; she was notified immediately along

with Jonas," Ashley assured him as Dog rushed down the stairs to the medical area of the Bureau's offices.

Cassie lay limp in his arms, unmoving, her face pale. She barely appeared alive. His heart was in his throat, rage pounding in his head. He was only barely aware of the growls leaving his throat or the savagery that echoed in them.

That attack wasn't meant to capture her; it wouldn't have been Council ordered. It was meant to hurt. A spur-of-the-moment attack by Breeds. More than one. He caught their scents on her clothes, drew them in, memorized them.

He turned the corner to the medical facility to see the doctors were already there, shouting questions, directing Dog to a gurney placed just inside the room.

"She's not moving," he growled, laying her gently on the bed. "Do something. She's not moving."

His hand stroked her face and he swore it was on the verge of trembling.

"You have to move, Dog." Sobolova ordered him firmly.

"She's not fucking moving." Rage filled the vicious snarl that left his lips as they pulled back from his canines and he glared down at the Coyote specialist.

"Dog, you have to let them get to her. They can't help her if you don't move," Dash snapped, pushing him back, fully expecting the powerful Coyote to attempt to take his throat out. Any touch other than a mate's could cause an extreme reaction in some male Breeds.

Styx and three of the Wolf Breed alphas who followed him from Colorado moved to restrain the Coyote, knowing the enraged scent pouring from Dog would result in an explosion of violence.

And it nearly did. Dog tensed, his arms bunching, the scent of the Coyote strengthening with unusual sharpness as the steel gray eyes that met Dash's flashed to a near black.

As their gazes met, the animal rose inside the other Dog

with such unusual strength that Dash paused. He watched the Coyote's gaze flicker, felt the battle waging inside him, before the black receded to gray and the animal slowly retreated, leaving the Breed tense but no longer in a killing fury.

"Let me go." That voice, though; Dash had heard a similar sound once or twice, though that Breed had been Feline, not Coyote.

And the Breed he'd heard it from was unlike any other he'd ever met.

"What are you?" Dash kept his voice low, nearly soundless. "What the fuck are you?"

But he had a feeling he knew.

"Her mate." Dog's head jerked in Cassie's direction as the gray of his eyes darkened, then lightened again. "Her fucking mate."

Dog jerked away from him, his gaze moving to Cassie again as Dash watched, and his expression tightened. Then his jaw bunched before he turned and stalked from the examination room, leaving Dash to stare after him in shock.

◆　◆　◆

Control. Never had it been so difficult to maintain, to leash the animal clawing at him. As he fought the rising fury he was aware of the ever-sharpening strength of his eye sight, his sense of smell. So much so that when he slammed out of the lobby doors, leaving a crack in the reinforced glass, he knew exactly where Mutt and Mongrel awaited him as well as the scent trail of Cassie's attackers.

Breeds and humans alike scattered out of his way, their wary looks and instinctive suspicion of danger rising at the sight of him.

His eyes would be black, the color threatening to bleed into the whites surrounding the pupil. His muscles were harder, his flesh tight, absorbing nuances of the air itself as the fine, nearly invisible hairs covering his body lifted, picking up the most subtle shifts in the air. Power infused him, filling him in ever-increasing waves, pushing at his mind, his flesh, clawing at his senses as the creature threatened to push past the human consciousness and take control.

He was aware of Mutt and Mongrel moving to his side, following silently, apprehension filling them as he followed the scent trail the two Wolf Breeds had left as they'd run.

Wolf. They were Breeds he'd often seen about the Bureau. They were known for their loyalty to the Breed cause and their strength. They were Breeds who would be sworn to Cassie's protection. Instead, they'd become her enemy, a threat he couldn't allow to remain living. They had struck his mate, harmed her; they could have killed her. The strength of those blows would have taken the life of a human, and they wouldn't have cared if their attack had taken her life.

"Dog, man, pull back," Mongrel muttered as they entered the corridor between the Bureau headquarters and the Enforcer apartments, separated by the parking areas. "You're going to give yourself away. That's only going to risk your mate."

Nothing mattered but his mate. Protecting her, surrounding her with his strength. Nothing mattered but ensuring the danger didn't touch her, that nothing, not human nor Breed, harmed her.

Without Cassie, he was nothing. His very existence was without meaning.

The creature acknowledged that as did the Breed. If his secrets were discovered then it could ensure her death.

He felt that knowledge, felt the enraged animal pull back just enough to avoid detection while still maintaining the power that hummed through his body.

"You can't kill them, Dog," Mutt warned him from his other side. "You'll risk your mate if they can enact Breed Law on you."

A growl tore from his throat, savage and enraged. Instantly, the Breeds at his side tensed further. He couldn't kill them? They attacked his mate. All bets were off as far as he was concerned.

As they pushed into the lobby of the Enforcer apartments he came to a stop, glaring at the elevators as they opened and half a dozen Coyote and Wolf Enforcers stepped out, flanking the two he'd come for himself. Leading them was Jonas Wyatt.

The silver mercury of the Lion Breed's eyes attested to the strength of the Primal he possessed and how close to the surface it walked. The Primal, the third force of Breed genetics. The human and animal genetics combining with such force that it became an animal all its own.

Dog pulled back further, pushing the creature within him to the depths of his consciousness, keeping it shadowed, hidden.

The Breeds who had attacked Cassie were in restraints, heads lowered, but he could feel the strength of their hatred for him, for Cassie. He had no choice but to allow them to live, for the moment. But he'd ensure that time came to an end soon.

Stepping aside, he watched as the Enforcers escorted the two Breeds from the building, leaving Jonas alone with them.

"I have this," he told Dog, the command in his voice firm. "They'll pay for what they did."

Dog merely grunted at the claim.

"Ensure they do, Director," he growled. "Because I'll be waiting for them. I promise you that. I'll be waiting for them."

· C H A P T E R   6 ·

"I'm fine!" It wasn't the first time Cassie made the statement in the four hours since she'd awakened in the Bureau's
medical lab, and she was getting damned tired of having
the demand ignored. "Would you stop poking at me?"

She glared at Dr. Sobolova as she came at her with yet
another pressure syringe. "I need some of my blood myself,
you know."

Her head was throbbing, the result of what the doctors
suggested was a fist to the back of her head. Her ribs were
tender from another blow. For some reason she'd gone to
her knees before collapsing and their contact with the cement hadn't been easy.

"Cassie, they're trying to help." Her mother's calm voice
wasn't helping. Nor were the worry and fear shadowing her
dark blue eyes.

It was a reminder of when she was a child and her knowledge of the strength it had taken for her mother to always
remain calm, no matter how hard, how fast, they had to
run, that ensured Cassie didn't give in to her own terror.

She hated what had happened to her mother during

those two years. The fear, the battle to stay one step ahead of the monster determined to take her daughter and the constant attacks had nearly destroyed Elizabeth."

Cassie remembered the night Dash had found them at that truck stop in the middle of a blizzard. The car they were in couldn't travel farther; the scent of her mother's blood, her hopelessness and her determination to fight to her last breath had been smothering Cassie.

Then there Dash had been, the letter she'd sent him in one hand, promising safety with the other. Now, fifteen years later, Elizabeth was stronger, well trained by her husband to defend herself and her children, and still fighting to protect her daughter.

From the corner of her eye she saw Sobolova advancing on her again.

"If they touch me one more time, I'm going to lose it," she muttered, looking up at her mother from beneath her lashes, fighting to hold back the anger building inside her.

Elizabeth was worried. Cassie could see it in her face, but even if she couldn't, she could sense the deepening concern filling her mother. Her dark blue eyes were shadowed, her expression somber.

It seemed that no matter her attempts, she couldn't give her mother any peace.

"I'm going to my suite." She eased from the gurney, thankful neither doctor protested too strenuously. "Do you think you or Dad could have some food delivered?"

Collecting her shoes from the metal shelf next to the bed, she hoped—no, prayed—Dog was still close by. She might need some help getting to her suite on her own two feet.

"I'll call," her mother agreed. "Give me your phone. I don't have the numbers here."

Oh yeah, right. No way in hell was she going to tell her mother about her phones. Elizabeth would erupt with fury and Dash would probably force Cassie back to Colorado.

"On second thought, I'm not hungry." She was starving. "Is Dog still with Jonas?"

Maybe she could get Dog to call. She really wasn't up to explaining the fact that her phones had been wiped. Remotely wiped. Whoever had ordered it hadn't even had the courtesy to ask for the phones or simply take the Bureau line.

As she considered whether she was actually able to walk to the elevators on her own, the door to the examination room opened and Dog strode in. Tall. Powerful. The sense of relief that swept over her was weakening.

"Going somewhere, halfling?" he growled a second before he swept her up into his arms.

She didn't have the strength to protest. Resting her head on his shoulder, she felt the breath she'd been holding slowly release.

"My suite," she sighed, feeling his warmth surrounding her.

She'd been unaware how cold she actually was until she felt his warmth, felt the beat of his heart, his arms encasing her.

He was moving before she spoke, though, pushing through the opened door and carrying her along the hall to the elevator.

"There are guards at our door," she told him as the elevator closed and they were alone.

"Really?" There was something in his voice that sounded just a little too self-satisfied. It was a warning she took to heart. Even if she hadn't known who he was, she'd heard of the Council Coyote, Dog, for years.

He was lethal. There wasn't a Breed she knew of who wasn't at least wary of him.

"Please don't fight." She simply couldn't deal with it. Not right now. "Not here."

The totally male grunt that vibrated in his chest was a mix of disgust and amusement.

"You're about to become high maintenance, darlin'. I enjoy a good fight," he told her as the elevator doors opened. "But this one time, I'll be a good boy."

She doubted Dog had been a good boy a day in his life.

As they neared her door, the scents of dislike and distaste reached her nostrils. They were Breeds; they were trained to better control such emotions. The fact that the scent of them was so strong was insulting.

It wasn't unexpected.

Whenever she moved about the Bureau's halls, whether on the residential floor or in other areas, she caught the scents reaching out to her, normally from the Wolf Breeds rather than felines, though she could rarely identify whom the emotions were coming from.

"Interesting," Dog muttered. "That normal?"

She knew what he meant and she could only shrug in reply. It wasn't unusual. At least she could identify the Breeds it was coming from this time.

"Open the door, assholes, then back off." Dog stopped several feet from the door leading to her suite.

The Breed Enforcers' expressions were bland, but the scent of their disgust grew despite the fact that the door was pushed open and the enforcers stepped back as ordered.

Did they really believe they were safe from him? That he wouldn't strike out at them simply because the emotions weren't directed at him? That he wouldn't take it as a personal challenge?

Dog strode into the room, caught the door with his heel and slammed it closed.

This would be dealt with, Dog assured himself as he carried Cassie to the bedroom and laid her on her bed. Very soon, and very painfully. At least, painfully for them. They had no fucking idea the animal they were screwing with or exactly how protective he truly was over his little mate. His halfling.

Cassie was too pale, and a sense of weariness emanated from her. But that weariness had been growing in her for more than a year now. Possibly two. No wonder if that was the bullshit she had to deal with.

"How often do they let their ignorance show like that, Cassie?" he asked her casually, careful to hold his anger at bay.

Once again, she shrugged, not looking at him as she dropped her shoes to the floor beside the bed and propped herself against the pillows.

"I think I'm hungry," she sighed, a statement meant to distract him.

He didn't distract easy. At least not that easy. She'd have to be naked and talking about more than food.

"Want me to go ask them?" Crossing his arms over his chest, he leaned back against the dresser and watched her, only allowing mild curiosity to show.

The glare she shot him assured him she wasn't fooled. What she couldn't smell, she was smart enough to know lay beneath the surface. She was smarter than they were; she sensed the animal he harbored, even if she didn't realize how very powerful it was.

"It's rarely that strong," she surprised him with the direct, firm answer. "But going out there and knocking a few heads together won't change it. They normally only allow me to sense it if I'm alone. They've learned not to show it at any other time."

Because the few times her father had sensed it in those first years, he'd erupted in such savagery on the Breeds who dared show it that it had taken some of them weeks to fully recover. But it hadn't made those who feared her like her any better. They'd only learned to hide it better.

"So because you can't knock their heads together, they refuse to show their respect when you're alone?" He didn't bother to hide the growl in his voice then. "And you haven't dealt with this yet?" That didn't sound like the woman, the Breed, he knew she was trained to be. Or the animal that lurked impatiently beneath the surface.

His little halfling gave an irritated roll of her eyes. "I could knock their heads together and they wouldn't dare strike back, but what's the point? The feeling would still be there. They don't strike back because they know Dad and Jonas would skin them out. That's not respect. It's fear."

And it wasn't her style. She was such a damned lady he doubted she ever gave in to that need to confront such stupidity. But the need to do it was there; he could sense it. It flowed through her with a hunger she refused to face and likely didn't even recognize.

He'd watched her over the years, studied her, paid attention to every expression, every scent, no matter how slight. His delicate little mate was a volcano kept tightly restrained.

He'd let that go for now. He'd deal with the two at the door and any others he sensed himself. Just as he'd been prepared to deal with the attack that morning. Mutt and Mongrel were on the trail of the third Wolf Breed who'd attacked her. The one Jonas was unaware of. The third, he'd have in custody soon and Dog would make certain the other two knew what awaited them.

He'd know who it was soon, and the bastard wouldn't live much longer. No Breed, no matter who he was, deserved to live after such a strike. Had they struck at Dog, he might have left them living, if he was in a good mood, but they'd struck his mate instead.

"It's been like that since I was a child, Dog." There was the weariness, the hurt. "I wasn't always as discreet as I could have been in things I knew. The felines for the most part were never bothered by it. Some were wary at times, but not distrustful. Coyotes take everything in stride." The irony in her tone couldn't be missed. "But Wolf Breeds, I think, react instinctively to the mixed scents of the DNA I possess as well as rumors concerning abilities I really don't possess. And they know the threat I represent to the lives they're building if I'm ever captured by the Council." She looked at him solemnly. "Felines, Father's Wolf Breeds, and Jonas personally would go to war if that happened. There wouldn't be a Breed alive who wouldn't be pulled into it."

She was making excuses for them? He couldn't believe what the hell he was hearing. But she was right. There wasn't a Feline Breed he knew of who had met her and didn't like her; many adored her. Coyotes were wary of her ability to argue Breed Law but, other than that, found her playfulness and charm enchanting.

He'd never heard that the Wolf Breeds felt any differently, but come to think of it, they rarely heard of any Wolf Breeds but her father's say anything kind about her either. And it had been a Wolf Breed who'd attacked her.

He'd been certain he was losing his mind as he watched her go to her knees, her eyes wide, dazed from the blows to her body. A haze of red had obliterated everything but the knowledge that she'd been attacked, hurt. And here she sat excusing them. Not just her attacker, but every Breed who dared show disrespect to her by allowing the scent of it free.

"Cassie, what right do they have to resent your genetics or your abilities? None of the other Coyote females experience this . . ."

It was the tiniest flinch of her expression that stopped him.

Evidently, the Coyote females were experiencing it. Ashley was tolerating it? The Coyote female even he would hesitate to meet in a dark alley, and Wolf Breeds were actually showing their disdain for her? They obviously had a suicidal wish.

"It's not all Wolf Breeds." Swinging her legs over the bed, she gripped the side of the mattress as she stared up at him. "Until the two at the door, I was never certain where it was coming from. Maybe it was just those two."

Bullshit.

She frowned up at him when he didn't say anything. "Don't glare at me like that. And sit down or something. I'm straining my neck."

He wondered if he could get away with paddling her ass. He knew the scent of her wariness combined with her Heat was about to make him crazy. From the moment he laid her on the bed, her arousal had been growing. And he'd been trying to ignore it. She'd been attacked, she had to be hurting, she didn't need to deal with his lust on top of it.

"Why did you leave the suite this morning?" And that was the uppermost question.

"I had things to do, Dog. I normally don't lie around in my suite all day. And I won't play the prisoner and begin doing it now." Steel will and determination filled her voice.

She began to rise from the bed after making that little declaration, as though the conversation were finished.

"Sit back down." He kept his tone polite, nice even.

He watched those odd blue eyes lighten just a hint and her expression tighten stubbornly.

"Excuse me?" Her tone, for all its pleasantness, held a note he rarely heard in a female's voice. That undercurrent that only alphas could actually pull off. Son of a bitch, he'd suspected it, but that moment of strength he sensed was surprising.

No damned wonder so many Wolves were having problems with her and Coyotes weren't. Coyotes loved the challenge an alpha female presented; Wolf Breeds tended to view it more suspiciously unless it was an acquired trait the mate of an alpha had developed.

"You heard me." He stared down at her, trying to fit together the pieces of the puzzle he knew about his intriguing little halfling. "What things did you have to do at daylight this morning that required leaving the building? Especially alone."

Her eyes narrowed on him. "Where were you, come to think of it? You were gone when I awoke."

She was deflecting. Now, this was interesting.

"Things to do," he murmured, barely controlling a grin. "Places to go. People to see."

"Council things?" The wave of anger that shot from her might have intimidated a lesser Coyote.

"Things that didn't cause an attack against you," he pointed out rather than answering her. "Unlike yours. Now, would you care to answer me?"

The scent that hit him when he finished speaking was so intriguing his cock hardened to iron and the glands beneath his tongue began throbbing with the need to kiss her. It caused such a punch of lust to hit his balls that it nearly stole his breath. Because that scent was one of such challenge, such daring, that the instincts he harbored in the darkest part of him nearly slipped free.

"Yes, your *things* did cause that attack." Rising to her feet, she faced him. Without her heels, shoulders straight, she stared up at him with narrow-eyed fury. "I was called a Council whore before that fist connected with my head. And I was out there because I was looking for a cab to take me to where I had stashed a secure mobile phone, because mine were wiped. Phones, tablet and laptop. I couldn't contact anyone and I had no access to any floor except this one, and there were guards to keep me from accessing the other hallways. I could use the elevator to go to the lobby. Period. Because of you." Delicate, graceful, a finger poked at his chest with imperious feminine anger. "And because of your Council *things*, I was unable to even contact the enforcers my father sent to see to my protection, let alone the ones Jonas assigned me."

Once he began killing, he might just start with Jonas.

There were few who could give the order to have her so restrained. Very few. And Jonas was at the top of that particular chain.

Straightening from his slouched position against the dresser, he looked at that little finger pointing at him before lifting his gaze to her eyes.

The Heat was building in her, but it was far slower than his, indicating her body was attempting to heal rather than mate. She hadn't been lying earlier when she said she was hungry, and beneath it all, he could sense the impotent fury that came from her belief that her mate was the enemy.

And that damnable pride he possessed wouldn't let him tell her the truth.

"Why don't you get out of those torn clothes and dress in something you can relax in. I'll order some food," he suggested.

Her eyes narrowed. "Your phone works?"

He couldn't help but grin. "I don't use a Bureau phone, sweetheart. And I use my own encryption. I have a spare I picked up for you this morning, though, to ensure the Bureau couldn't track any calls I made to you."

"I don't want one of your Council toys," she snarled back at him, striding past and heading for her closet. "I'll get my own."

"You're going to get fucked before you get fed if you don't watch all the little dares you're throwing out," he snapped, unable not to respond to the constant challenge. "Now, by God, do as I ask, just this once."

Before she could make another smart-ass reply, he turned and stalked from the room. But instead of making the call for dinner, he strode to the door, jerked it open, and before the Wolf Breeds guarding it could do more than jump, he was on them. The flat of his hand to the diaphragm put the nearest one to the floor, struggling to breathe. The other took a full punch to the face—lights fucking out— ensuring he was unconscious as he hit the floor.

As the first glared up at him, coughing, Dog pulled a cigar free of his shirt and lit it with lazy amusement.

"You know what that was for. Let it happen again, and you're dead." Turning, he reentered the room and found himself facing his mate's furious glare.

He closed the door and pulled his phone free of his belt and shot her a lazy grin. "I think steaks are called for. That work for you?"

CHAPTER 7

Dressed in gray cotton lounging pants and a matching camisole, Cassie sat back in her chair, the remains of dinner almost nonexistent. The steak, loaded potatoes, salad and yeast rolls had seemed far too much for her to finish when Dog unloaded the bags that were delivered.

Now replete, all she had to do was fight back the distracting arousal beginning to build inside her for just a while longer. She could feel a sense of imperative warning awakening as well. That warning had begun before the attack, though. It had begun the night her sister, Kenzi's, fear and panic had reached out to her.

It wouldn't be easy for her sister; she'd lost the foster parents who had sacrificed so much to protect her, only to ultimately lose their lives. And now she was having to finally face the parents she'd been kept from.

The threads of knowledge were dangling in her mind; she could feel them, sense them. They were all connected somehow; she just wasn't certain how, because that sense of impending warning still brewed inside her senses.

Though she and her father never spoke of it, as Cassie

had matured, her underlying paternal scent had begun emerging. It was faint because of the Coyote genetics she possessed, too faint for most Breeds to detect, but it was still there. Somehow, the Council had acquired Dash Sinclair's genetics and the scientist who performed the in-vitro procedure had created not just Cassie, but Kenzi as well.

"Here." Dog moved to her side, laying a phone and tablet on the table as he took her plate. "Both are encrypted and secured. I've programmed my number into the phone, and both devices are equipped with a nano-ghost. They're safe."

Her brows lifted. Nano-ghosts were even harder to build and program than nano-nits. Their encryption and ability to access the Internet through the wireless connections around them without leaving a trail made them highly valuable.

"How did you manage a nano-ghost?" Turning her head, she stared up at him suspiciously.

"Because I'm good like that." He grinned, flashing those canines he seemed so damned proud of.

Charm practically oozed out of him along with the arrogance and ever-present confidence. Unfortunately, that bad-boy charm only turned her on more. It had aroused her before he'd ever touched her. Six years of calls, messages, favors and ridiculous demands, and each time, she'd become more captivated by him. She'd always known he was part of the Council. She'd suspected he was a Coyote. And she'd still so rashly made that final bargain with him.

"I'm not certain how I feel about that," she admitted. "You're too damned good at the wrong things, Dog."

Rising from her chair, she wondered what that said about her, that she was so willing to break Bureau rules by accepting such a device. Not that she would be caught doing so. Detecting nano-nits was hard enough. Nano-ghosts were impossible to detect unless the programmer knew exactly what she or he was looking for.

"I try." His expression was both sensual and knowing.

"But you have a little bad inside you as well, halfling. Admit it."

A little bad? Sometimes she felt in danger of being possessed by instincts she had no idea how to handle. Jonas had once said he sensed the battle between the Wolf and the Coyote she was created from and he wondered which would win in the end.

She had walked away from the discussion, terrified that he had seen that inside her. That battle between the good and the bad.

"I can't exactly deny it." She lifted her shoulders negligently. "Those genetics aren't exactly hidden. Any Breed can smell them."

Dog was watching her too closely now, staring at her as though she were a puzzle he needed to put together.

"You think the Coyote genetics are responsible for the hellion you keep hidden?" A grunt of laughter followed the question. "I don't think so."

"There's no hellion hiding, Dog." Picking up the phone and tablet, she moved for her room. Both needed to go in the pack she kept ready in case she had to leave quickly. "Though sometimes being nice takes work."

Sometimes, she wanted to tear into those who allowed their hatred of her to mark their scent, who allowed their distaste to touch her. Sensing it and actually smelling it were two different things. Allowing another Breed to scent those feelings was considered the ultimate insult.

"And you think Wolf Breeds or felines are naturally nice?" He laughed at the idea. "Baby, you are so determined to deny the little Coyote crouched and ready to defend itself that you amaze everyone who really knows you. Breeds aren't nice. Doesn't matter their designation. Just as humans aren't really nice. They just hide it from one another better."

Crouched and ready to defend itself? No, the Coyote was crouched and straining to attack at all times. It was the impulse to slip up behind the guards outside her room and prove she was just as deadly as they. It was the need to snarl in fury at the enforcers who had worked beneath her when they questioned her every order, every decision. It was a lifetime of resisting the desire to run from the protection her parents put around her, to strike against her enemies with deceptive stealth.

How many times had she been forced to run and hide at Sanctuary with her brother while her parents faced danger? Her father had trained her to fight, he'd trained her to be deadly, but when she'd had to use that training, he'd stared at her with such disappointment, she'd cringed inside.

She agreed with Dog, though. Breeds weren't always nice. Not when dealing with the enemy or the prejudice that poured from humans. But they weren't cruel either. They took each situation as it came and dealt with it. They didn't bemoan their lives or whimper over the blood they had to shed, but neither did they want to shed that blood.

The need to shed blood was becoming harder and harder for her to dismiss, though.

"Cassie, aren't you tired of playing the perfect little Breed princess?" he asked as she passed him. "Haven't you gotten sick of being a good girl all the time? You're not human. You can't keep pretending you are."

He had no idea what he was talking about.

Flashing him a furious look, she passed him and strode into her bedroom to the closet. There, she stored the phone and tablet. Before she reclosed it, the hilt of her knife caught her eye, as did the small, old-fashioned handgun. There were a dozen clips for the gun, loaded with deadly bullets, at the bottom of the bag. The knife was sheathed in a holster made to fit her thigh.

She kept them hidden because carrying them felt too natural, and more than once, the need to use them had been overwhelming.

The good versus the bad.

Her fingers glanced over the leather hilt before she forced herself to pull back and secure the flap once again.

She was aware of Dog moving in behind her, watching her, daring her.

Yeah, that was another failing she shared with him. Passing up the challenges and dares so mockingly thrown out to her by the Wolf Breeds who regarded her with such suspicion and distaste. So many times the need to meet those challenges had been like a fever that refused to abate.

She could feel it now, the Coyote pacing, straining at her control, demanding release. As she'd matured, the Coyote and Wolf genetics had fought to outpace each other. Dr. Armani still studied the phenomenon and had drawn Sobolova into it when she'd joined the Breeds' medical and scientific community.

"You were eighteen," Dog stated, moving farther into the room. "I was in that fucking atrium waiting for Jonas when you walked in, that virgin's gown flowing around you. It wasn't the Wolf Breed you were called in the media that stepped in that room. You were wild and restrained. Like an enraged Coyote, caged. And I wanted nothing more than to mark you that night."

She'd wanted nothing more than to carry his mark that night, she realized. The restlessness that plagued her had been one of those periods when her Coyote genetics had reigned.

"I was caged," she told him coolly. "I'm still caged."

Rising to her feet, she closed the closet door, pushed back the needs tearing at her.

Dog chuckled behind her again. "What an intriguing scent," he murmured, the amused drawl causing her to stiffen. "Are you pissed off, little halfling? Does it offend you that I don't allow you to hide? To pretend you don't possess all those nasty Coyote genetics?"

She turned to him, her gaze raking over him derisively. "Stop trying to start a fight, Dog. Go attack the Wolf guards again if you can't control your need to be nasty."

"My need to be nasty?" His expression turned calculating. "You think I'm trying to be nasty, mate?"

"You're trying to be cruel and I don't like it," she stated, refusing to meet the dare in his eyes.

If she gave in, just once, then it would all be over. She'd never rein those impulses in again. She'd never regain control of herself or the creature all too willing to attack.

Dog scratched his cheek, regarding her quizzically as she went to move past him.

Before she could clear his side, he reached out to grab her, to restrain her. She felt him getting ready to move, felt his need to control her.

Before he could touch her, she jumped clear of him, twisting away in a perfect flip as he moved to counter her.

As she came to a crouch, she stared back at him through the curls that fell over her face, before straightening quickly to glare back at him.

And he laughed at her. His gray eyes gleamed with mirth, and the playfulness she sensed had her regarding him warily.

"I'm not in the mood to play," she snapped.

"No, you're not," he agreed easily. "You're in the mood to fuck and fuck hard." Taking the chair next to the door, he placed it in front of the closed panel, sat down and pulled off his boots. "And I like fucking you, mate. It's the only time you let that little bitch inside you free."

The heat flashed inside her, brilliant hot and all consuming. Her breasts became so swollen, so sensitive, her nipples actually ached. Between her thighs, her clit became engorged, her vagina clenched, and the silky slide of arousal spilled free.

Breathing hard, she glared back at him. It was Mating

Heat, she told herself furiously; that was all. Anger made it worse; she'd heard that for years.

That was all it was.

Dog watched those perfect lips curl at one side, flashing a delicate canine as a sensual challenge began to fill her expression. She was so desperate to be free, fighting herself with such strength he was amazed the animal inside her actually found a way to peek free.

But it was there, the she-Wolf and the Coyote female merged, wild and determined to prove he belonged to her. It wasn't that she was more one than the other. It was that each part of her dictated certain traits and strengths she possessed. It was the Coyote, though, who faced him now. The scent of her Heat was particularly potent, a narcotic to his senses. It was a punch of lust to his balls and had the glands beneath his tongue instantly filling with the mating hormone.

"You like that, don't you?" he growled, rising to his feet and releasing his belt. "When I talk dirty to you. And I do like talking dirty to you."

"You're crazy," she snapped.

He wondered if she even realized the pure strength that filled her voice, the way the animal slipped free to lend that hint of a growl.

A natural alpha female. The kind of female created to lead beside her mate, not behind him.

He chuckled at her declaration as he unbuttoned his shirt.

"I can smell your Heat, Cassie. You're burning alive. And when I get you down on that bed, the first thing I'm going to do is suck those hard little nipples pressed against that thin-assed shirt you're wearing. Then I'm going to tear those pants off your body and shove my tongue up that hot little pussy. I'm going to lick every fucking drop of cream I smell saturating it right now."

He swore he saw her eyes glaze over. Her face flushed and her nipples became impossibly tighter, poking against the material of the camisole in demand. Heat filled the air now, her spicy sweetness making his tongue ache to taste her.

He dropped the shirt to the floor, watching as her gaze jerked to it, then back to him warily.

"I'm going to mount you, mate," he growled, pushing the wild, barely restrained creature he sensed struggling free. "I'm going to flip you to your knees, mount you, and fuck you until I'm locked inside you and filling you with Coyote cum."

She attacked.

Dog couldn't hold back the satisfied snarl as he met her, caught her shoulders and flipped her around before that knee she was bracing went into his balls.

"Really, Cassie?" He laughed, pushing her away from him, watching as she whirled around, her hair flowing like a cape around her. "Watch that knee, halfling. I'd hate to spoil your fun once I get you on your knees."

She struck again, ducking at the last second in an attempt to sweep him from his feet. And she almost succeeded. God, he loved her.

Watching her jump to her feet and fly at him with a kick, he laughed in sheer joy, then grunted as her foot struck his chest, throwing him back against the wall.

"Well now, that's going to hurt later." He chuckled, keeping his eye on her as she fell back to a crouch.

He'd watched her train in the sparring room over the past months, thought he knew how she moved, how she liked to play with her sparring partners. Now, he'd show her how a Coyote male played.

"Why don't I just mount you and take your ass?" he suggested, the thought of that ultimate submission a temptation he could barely resist. "Teach you who's your alpha and who's your mate."

She liked that idea more than she'd ever admit, he guessed, because the growl that slipped free was a sound of pure anticipation.

"Yeah, I like the thought of that too," he decided, watching her body shift, the line of her shoulders, the tilt of her head. "And when we're finished, you can tell me how good it was having me buried there, submitting to me like a good little mate."

She jumped, prepared to kick again. This time, he caught her waist and tossed her to the bed, making certain to rip her shirt from her as he did. Before she could push that mass of hair from her face, he managed to shed his pants and rip hers from her hips.

He caught her hair, careful not to grip the strands near the area where she'd been struck, as he straddled her legs and held them closed with his knees. Jerking her head back, he bent his head, nipped her lips and growled when she tried to bite.

Releasing her hair he gripped her jaw, applying just enough pressure to keep her from biting, and covered her lips with his own, his tongue sweeping into her mouth, stroking hers.

The taste of her had him mindless.

The taste of him had her tongue stroking against his, the smell of her Heat a wave of lust-inducing pheromones that nearly had him coming against her thighs.

Pulling his head away, he released her jaw, gripped her hair again and pulled her head back once more.

Eyes narrowed in arousal, the blue gleaming like flames, her lips parted and moist. She was the most beautiful creature he'd ever seen in his life. Her fingers gripped his wrists, the one wrapped near her head, the one at her shoulder, her nails digging in, holding on to him.

"You're scared, Cassie," he mocked her, fighting the need to relent, to let her hide. "You want to be bad with me with a power that makes you shake, admit it."

"You're fucking crazy," she snarled up at him. "It's the Mating Heat and your insanity."

Bending his head lower, he teased her lips as he spoke. "You want to get nasty with me. I can sense it. Come on, it's just me. No one has to know you enjoy fucking your Coyote mate. I promise, I won't tell on you."

Her gaze lightened, then darkened. The scent of her Heat was so damned heady he could barely think for it.

"Let me see you be bad for just a minute. Play with those pretty nipples for me while I watch; then I'll suck them for you. Come on, give me a little of your bad, and I'll give you a whole lot of mine."

A moan whispered past her lips as she shook her head, desperation reflecting in her eyes along with the driving, furious need burning inside her.

"Come on, baby," he whispered, licking her lips teasingly before lifting his head again. "Show me what you did to yourself when you thought of me through the years and I'll show you how I can make it better."

She felt her fingers release him, as though forcing herself to let go one by one as he eased back, his dick throbbing as it rested in the seam of her thighs. The thick crest rested just below her clit, the heat of her slick moisture cushioning it.

Eyes narrowed, he watched as she slowly cupped her breasts, her fingertips at first ghosting over the stiff points, drawing a ragged sigh from her lips.

"Is that how you want me to suck them?" He was burning alive for her. "Nice and sweet and easy like that?"

She gripped the points, jerking in his hold, a wild gleam of anticipation filling her gaze as her thumbs and forefingers tightened on the tips. A cry tore past her lips, her body arched and the pink tips flushed, darkening as her fingers tightened, then released, plumping the little points as her hunger scented the air.

"If I suck those pretty nipples, then you're going to tease me a little bit, just to punish me," he suggested, lowering his head to whisper a breath over one tight point. "I'd go crazy if I saw those pretty fingers between your thighs, bringing yourself pleasure. You know how fucking possessive a Coyote can be of his partner's pleasure."

He glanced up in time to watch her gaze darken, felt the lash of overwhelming lust taking control of her.

"Let me have one, mate," he groaned. "Let me suck one of those sweet nipples."

Cassie felt the moment she lost control of her response to him or her ability to deny the greedy waves of demand rushing through her. She watched as his lips covered her nipple, felt him shift until he rested beside her while pushing her thighs apart with one hand.

Then flaming sexual need erupted through her body. The heat of his mouth, sucking, tugging at her nipple, his teeth rasping it, his tongue licking it as the hormone that spilled from his tongue sensitized the peak to almost painful awareness. She heard her own cry, felt the arch of her body and the grip of his fingers on her wrist, pushing them to her thighs.

And oh God, she needed. She needed to be touched there. Her clit was raging, so swollen and aching. The flesh between her thighs was slick with the rich moisture spilling from her.

"Dog, it's so good." The words tore past her lips as her fingers parted her folds. "Do it harder, suck me harder."

She was dying, arching. Her fingers found the tight bud of her clit, rasping against it in her desperation to find her release. When the stroke of her fingers against the sensitive little kernel didn't push her over the edge, she pushed them lower and found the entrance hidden there.

The growl that vibrated on her nipple was a primal warning to stop. And one she ignored. Lifting her hips, she speared her own fingers past the entrance, her head tossing as his lips moved to her other nipple and his fingers found her hand.

He pushed at it, driving her fingers deeper inside her. And still, it wasn't enough. It had never been enough in the past when she tried to pleasure herself. No matter what she did, she could never find the ease she needed.

Pulling back, she moved for her clit once again, then froze a breath before a cry tore from her.

His fingers pushed inside her, thrusting against the clenched tissue, parting it, calloused fingers stroking, working inside her as violent pleasure lashed at her.

She was only barely aware of his lips releasing her nipple, his kisses spreading down her stomach. When he pushed her fingers aside and his lips found her clit, her hands sank into his hair, desperate to hold him there.

She needed him right there. Licking, sucking. His tongue moved over it, then lower as his fingers slid free of her. His tongue pushed inside her then, filling her, licking her . . .

"Dog . . ." She cried out his name, twisting in his hold as his fingers moved lower and found the smaller, tighter entrance that awaited him.

She was so lost within the pleasure, the lust, that she could only cry out as his fingers eased inside her. Lubricated by the excess moisture spilling from her vagina, his fingers took her rear with an ease that rocked her. Stretching her, thrusting inside her, until she was pushing into each penetration and begging for more.

And just as suddenly, he was gone.

"No." She jackknifed up, reaching for him, only to find herself flipped to her stomach as he jerked her hips to him, forcing her knees beneath her.

The feel of the broad, iron-hard crest tucked against her rear entrance had her freezing.

"Submit." The growl in his voice was primal, demanding. "Submit to me, damn you."

A cry tore from her. She let her head and shoulders fall back to the bed, her fingers fisting in the blankets as she felt a pulse of heated pre-cum ejaculate against the entrance.

Instantly, the hormone-rich fluid began easing her, creating a sensual, insidious burn that demanded he satisfy it.

"Take it," he snarled, his body lowering, his lips at her shoulder. "Submit to me, mate. Take it."

She pushed back, feeling the pulse of heat as her muscles parted further for the crest. Lashing pleasure mixed with an unfamiliar pain as the hunger that filled her drove her to take more, to feel him taking her, to trust him to guide her through it.

With each press into the tightened muscles, another pulse of the hormonal pre-cum shot inside her; slick, heated, it built such a demanding pleasure she was shaking from the force of it.

With each thrust against her rear he took her deeper, stretching her as she burned higher and felt herself fall beneath the onslaught of sensations. With him buried to the hilt, his cock throbbing in a place so private she'd never imagined she'd allow it, Cassie knew something had changed inside her.

"Fuck, Cassie," he groaned.

A second later his teeth gripped the mark on her shoulder and he began to move. At first in long, slow thrusts, then harder, until he was driving inside her, pushing the flames inside her higher.

The powerful strokes drove him forcefully inside her as she screamed out his name, desperate for release, the pleasure tearing her apart until she felt herself melting.

It wasn't a true orgasm, because the need only rose as Dog slid from her, then gripped her hip with firm fingers.

"Don't move, Cassie. Move, and I swear I'll make you wait hours before I give you what you need," he growled when he thought she might protest.

Instead, instinct had her freezing in place. If she had to wait hours to orgasm, then he might as well kill her now.

She heard the bathroom door open, heard water running. A minute later the scent of the soap he'd washed with teased her nostrils as she felt him move onto the bed behind her once again. She was dazed with the needs still pulsing through her. Her clit was so swollen, the folds between her thighs sensitive and her vagina clenched in involuntary contractions.

"There, baby," he crooned, touching her thighs, angling her hips. "Go wild for me now, Cassie. Give me all of you now."

As he spoke, the feel of his cock invading her, pushing against the clenching tissue, working inside her, stole the last of her sanity. She pushed back, taking him deeper as pleasure and pain merged, creating such wild hunger she was helpless against it.

"Ah fuck. Your pussy's so sweet, Cassie. So fucking good . . ."

The words merged, explicit phrases, erotic demands as he thrust inside her, stroking over sensitive flesh, stretching it. She struggled to adapt to the thickness even as she craved more. She bucked into each impalement, driving herself harder on his cock, hearing his approval, his pleasure in his voice.

When he bent over her once again, his teeth locking on her shoulder, his thrusts driving his hardened flesh inside her, she felt herself dying. She knew she was dying. Nothing could explode through her with such force, with such shattering ecstasy, and let her actually survive it.

At the same time, she felt his release, felt the heavy swelling of the Breed knot locking inside her. Each pulse of the thickened extension triggered another explosion, the heat of his seed spilling inside her, the lash of his tongue at the mark on her shoulder, all converged until the final, violent wave of ecstasy shattered her.

What he had done to her, she wasn't entirely certain. It was beyond the physical pleasure; it went beyond anything she'd known with him before. And when it was over, when he finally pulled from her, all she could do was collapse on the bed, exhaustion weighing her down and dragging her into sleep.

Where she could hide. Just for a minute, she needed to hide from whatever he'd released inside her.

CHAPTER 8

Dog pulled his boots on his feet the next morning, tracking the hours before dawn and the update he was awaiting on the evacuation of his people. His gaze touched his sleeping mate when he sensed the Breed that entered the suite through the living room. Rubbing wearily at the back of his neck, he rose from the chair and strode to the bedroom door. Opening it silently, he stepped from the room before securing the door once again and facing the Breed.

Hell, he didn't need this right now. At least there were no longer guards on duty outside the room, though he expected more to show up soon. He hoped their replacements were a bit more polite. The next time, he might not be so nice himself.

"What do you want?" he growled, wondering why in the hell the director of Breed Affairs thought this was a good time to invade Cassie's suite.

"We need to talk." Jonas's voice remained low. "But not here. Across the hall if you have a minute."

Dog narrowed his gaze on the director. He liked to think he knew Jonas pretty well by now. The man was as deceptive and as calculating as any Coyote ever born, despite the fact that he was a Lion.

Jonas opened the door leading to the hall and tilted his head toward it. Following the other man from the residential suite, across the hall to another, matching suite, Dog forced himself to restrain an impatient growl.

Closing the door behind them, Jonas moved past him to the bar on the other side of the room, where he poured himself a drink. Considering the lateness of the hour, the fact that Jonas was drinking was an indication of his irritation level.

"Fuck, you picked a hell of a time to pull this shit. I wish to hell you'd warned me." The other Breed turned back to him, his silver eyes flashing in anger as he tossed back his drink.

His mate's apparent openness with Jonas could become a potential problem if she ever learned the truth of who and what her new mate truly represented.

"We've discussed this," he reminded the other Breed as he moved to the bar himself and accepted the drink Jonas handed him.

"Dammit, Dog," Jonas cursed, flashing him a look of brooding anger and frustration. "This situation is going to hell fast. When she came to work in this office, we ran hormonal tests with the Breeds she'd be working with. Those tests matched her to another Breed. All the initial mating signs were present—"

"She has no other mate." Training, years of control, every emotion, every possible chance of giving himself away, nearly failed him.

The creature he was in the darkest core of his soul gathered itself, filled with fury, with territorial possessiveness, threatened to break free, to emerge in a way Dog knew he could never pull back.

Jonas's look was intent, almost confused, as he stared back at him, as though he were trying to figure out a puzzle he'd never seen. This wasn't a game to Jonas. Dog knew he wasn't lying, because it was the reason he'd staked his claim as he had, before that son of a bitch he'd scented on his mate could make a claim.

"Those tests say otherwise. And the Coyote she matched with was aware of the possibility. I can't say he won't do as he's threatened and test the possibility that he could change the outcome." Jonas grimaced, rubbing at his neck wearily. "Son of a bitch. We don't need this right now."

"She was eighteen when I first realized she was my mate. And I would have waited until the time was more convenient had you not pushed that bastard at her." A growl slipped into his voice then, something that rarely happened. "Whatever fucked-up anomaly allowed his scent to cling to her was a false attempted mating. Let him attempt to challenge me and he'll die."

Rhyzan Brannigan. The son of a bitch Coyote Jonas had chosen as his assistant in the Federal Bureau of Breed Affairs. Dog had no doubt that was the Coyote she'd tested compatible to. The very fact that his scent had dared to cling to Cassie after they'd danced together several weeks before had ensured that Dog came for her, that he claimed her.

"You can't ignore the possibility, especially if Rhyzan takes the matter before the Breed Tribunal. And your habit of associating with the Genetics Council, openly working with them at times, won't endear your counterobjection to the Cabinet. Cassie will verify this." He glared at Dog as though a crime had been committed. "She knows the Breed statutes better than anyone alive. Rhyzan can demand further testing, and if those tests show the compatibility is still present, despite your mating, he can force you to stand aside and force her to allow him a chance to convince her to test a mating with him instead."

Jonas stalked from the bar to his desk, shaking his head before a furious growl left his throat.

"Then he'll die." Dog shrugged, feeling a shift in his

senses, in his awareness of the darkness he carried within him. "Rhyzan doesn't want to make that mistake. Cassie's mine. I won't let her go."

He wasn't some damned alpha leader forced to allow a separation from his mate because of Cassie's arguments on behalf of the human mate. Cassie wasn't a human with no awareness of Mating Heat or her Breed physiology. And Brannigan would know the rage he was tempting if he made such a move.

"Dog, your pride and stubbornness aside, you are not a member of the legitimate Breed community as far as anyone else knows, and until we have your people free, we can't disclose it. You aren't an alpha; you aren't aligned with an alpha. You have no rights where Breed Law is concerned. The only reason you're not in chains at the moment is because of Breed Law's statutes to the effect that no matter your crimes in the past, the fact that your mate is innocent of those crimes gives you another chance."

Dog's eyes narrowed on Jonas. "My mate."

"Doesn't matter." Jonas sighed, leaning against his desk as he crossed his arms over his chest and the warning in his gaze deepened. "If push comes to shove, support will go to Rhyzan. And Cassie's upset enough that you tricked her into this mating . . ."

"Bullshit, Jonas. No one tricks Cassie." Dog snorted. "She made a deal. She knew I was a Coyote. She knew the risks and she was warned of the risks. She simply thought she could control it."

But hadn't he thought the same?

"And if she thinks she can control a mating with Rhyzan instead?" Jonas tilted his head, watching him closely.

"Then blood will spill," Dog promised him. "Rhyzan's blood. Now, if you don't mind, I think I'll return to Cassie . . ."

"The moment your mating became known, Cassie lost

her place in the Bureau," Jonas said as Dog turned to leave. "Unless you align yourself with the Breed community immediately and take a stand against the Council, she'll have to leave the security of the suite and this Bureau."

Cassie had lost her place within the Bureau

Dog froze at that information. He knew she'd been locked out of her phone and tablet but he'd been unaware it was this extreme. Or perhaps he just hadn't considered what the electronic wipes had meant.

"Does she know this?" he asked.

Jonas nodded sharply. "Just as she knows she'll have to leave. I told you, Cassie understands Breed Law better than any of us. She knows what the mating means. For God's sake, let me go to the alphas at least and reveal what you've been doing."

Dog shook his head firmly. "It's too soon, Jonas. Far too soon. I want my people out first and I want the information they've gathered."

Now he knew the reason for the tears his mate was holding locked inside her, and the pain tearing her apart.

"She'll lose her life as she knows it unless you come in, Dog," Jonas warned him. "And she won't thank you for keeping this secret from her. I know Cassie. She may not forgive you."

Unless he came in.

Unless he revealed his secrets and gave up the battle he'd fought for so many damned years. Too many years.

"You are a risk to the security of this Bureau as far as the alphas are concerned, the agents as well as any sensitive information we hold. If it were anyone but Cassie, she wouldn't have been allowed to stay this long. But this is Cassie. For her, they've given me twenty-four hours to fix this; then she'll have to leave."

Protecting her wouldn't be a problem. Revealing any loyalties to the Breed community, even the smallest sign that he wasn't Council loyal, would unravel every fucking deception he'd worked to build for far too many years, though.

Could he protect her without that tie? Could he, Mutt and Mongrel protect her without the backing of the Breed community and the resources she could call upon until he had his own people in place?

"The alphas may fear you're willing to risk her life or even turn her over to the Council. According to those I've spoken to, they'd be willing to give Rhyzan a chance to test a possible mating for that reason alone," Jonas warned him.

Dog lifted his lip in a subtle sneer at the director's suggestion. He'd worked with Jonas over the years; he knew the Breed's complete dedication to the Breed community. Jonas was a man whose word one could trust, one that tested the temper, but one Dog knew would stand by a bargain.

Jonas wouldn't reveal his secrets, not unless Cassie's safety within the Breed community itself was threatened. He wanted that information as badly as Dog did, but Cassie was close to him. She was important to him. But Dog couldn't risk his people yet. They had to have time to get out. It was something he couldn't yet reveal.

And there wasn't a chance in hell he was giving away his mate either.

"Jonas, you don't want to push me where Cassie's concerned. Not you, Rhyzan or her parents. Attempt to take what's mine, and the hell I'll rain down on you will be apocalyptic."

He could do it. He'd hate to do it. It would make a few enemies for damned sure, but he'd do it to keep Cassie.

He met the silver gaze locked on him, let the Lion sense his own determination and the truth of his word. Jonas liked to think he knew everything, everyone's secrets, everyone's inner core. When it came to him, though, the other man didn't know shit.

A frown edged Jonas's brow then, the strange silver gaze deepening as the primal animal he harbored peeked out. No doubt, claws were pricking at the tips of his fingers as the animal rose close to the skin.

Dog let a grin tip his lips. As a Breed, Jonas was one of the more powerful ones, but as a Coyote, Dog had an edge on him.

"Twelve hours, Dog," Jonas reminded him when Dog said nothing more. "Or allow me to discuss this with the alphas on the Cabinet and reveal the work you've been doing. Think beyond yourself on this. Think about Cassie."

"I'll be sure to ask my little mate how that's done," he drawled. "Seems to me she's spent too much time thinking about a bunch of dumb-ass Breeds who are all too willing to toss her out when she does something that displeases them. Maybe she can give me some pointers there."

A hard growl rumbled from Jonas's chest, one similar to Dog's when he was getting ready to kick insubordinate ass.

He gave a low, mocking chuckle. "Don't make that mistake, Director. You don't want to go head-to-head with me without backup. You don't like my opinions? I really don't give a fuck, because I think yours are bullshit as well. Now, if you'll excuse me, I think I'll head out for breakfast for my mate."

And to make plans.

Where the fuck was Dane Vanderale when he needed him?

◆   ◆   ◆

Dressed in a soft black lounging set and matching slippers, Cassie stood in the center of her sitting room and faced not just her father, but also the assistant director of the Federal Bureau of Breed Affairs, Rhyzan Brannigan. Her father she'd actually expected at some point that morning, just not this early. And damned sure not with the Coyote Rhyzan.

"Why do I feel ambushed?" she asked her father as she faced him and Rhyzan. "And where's Mom?"

"Your mother's with Kenzi. She finally agreed to talk to her," her father told her, his voice gentle as he moved to the couch. "I wanted to see you now rather than waiting till later this afternoon and asked Rhyzan to bring me up."

Yeah, that one really made sense. Her father knew exactly where her suite was and he knew how to get there. He didn't need Rhyzan.

"Kenzi's doing well, then? Can I see her?" She was dying to see her sister.

So many years of sensing that connection, uncertain what it was, who it was, only to learn she had a twin, had left her with a hunger to see the other woman.

"Kenzi's still upset," her father answered as he took the chair next to her, his gaze somber.

Cassie nodded at that as she sat next to him, clasping her hands in her lap. "Yes. I imagine she is."

She glanced at Rhyzan as he pulled the other wingback chair from its position against the wall and parked it on the other side of her, far too close for comfort. She suddenly felt hemmed in.

"How long have you known about Kenzi?" her father asked her, drawing her attention back. "Why didn't you tell your mother and me?"

She blinked at him in surprise. "You think I've known about her?" Her chest clenched painfully. "But I didn't, Dad. Not until hours before she was found in the desert. I contacted Dog as soon as I knew and asked him to make certain she was safe."

Her father thought she'd betray her own sister and leave her in danger?

"Cassie," he whispered painfully. "You know Dog's a Council Coyote. You contacted him and met with him. Do you have any idea how dangerous that was?"

She could feel her heart racing now, an ominous warning beginning to tingle through her. Rather than allowing them to sense so much as a hint of her uncertainty, she met their gazes with cool calm as she restrained any emotion that might slip free.

"As a consultant for the Bureau, I can't be penalized for making contact with any Council associate in my effort to protect or rescue any Breed, whether Council or under Breed protection," she reminded him as well as Rhyzan. "I had very little time to do what had to be done."

"Cassie, do you think I'd lead you into admitting something that would hurt you?" her father chastised her gently. "Rhyzan isn't here to censure you for anything you may or may not have done where Breed Law is concerned."

She watched her father, hating the fact that she felt she should guard herself against him. She kept Rhyzan in her periphery, her senses protesting this meeting, warning her to get away from it. Escape wasn't nearly so easy, though.

"I was merely reminding you I know the boundaries within my job. I'm not a child any longer and I've been working for the Bureau for quite some time," she pointed out.

"And per your discussion with Jonas, you've been in contact with the Council Breed, Dog, for several years as well, haven't you?" Rhyzan questioned her, his tone interrogating.

"Why is he here?" she asked her father, barely restraining her anger now. Her father might not be trying to set her up, but she wasn't so certain about the Coyote.

She had no idea what the hell was going on here, but she knew she didn't like it. She felt pinned by their gazes, judged. For a moment she had to force herself to hold back the displeased rumble of sound that rose to her throat and tightened it warningly. The instincts and shifting power she could feel far too close to the surface now were proving impossible to push back.

"Cassie, sweetheart." Her father grimaced, glanced at Rhyzan, then turned his gaze back to hers. "Did you know you and Rhyzan were tested compatible to Mating Heat?"

She wanted to escape. The need to jump and run was

nearly overwhelming, but the way her father and Rhyzan were positioned, she'd never get past them.

Where the hell was her mate when she needed him?

For a moment, meeting Rhyzan's gaze, she wished she had her knife rather than her mate, though.

"Don't do this," she whispered, turning back to her father and meeting his gaze. "Please, Dad. Don't do this."

"Cassie, listen to me." He leaned forward intently. "Dog is a Council Coyote. You can lie to your mother, but not to me. I know this isn't what you want."

"Stop," she demanded. "Before this goes any further, before something's said that can't be taken back. Just stop."

"There could be an anomaly that would allow a mating with Rhyzan instead," he told her somberly.

"And why wasn't I told this before?" She glared at Rhyzan, then her father. "Why didn't you tell me when the tests were done? Like you were supposed to?"

He breathed out heavily, the sound rife with regret. "I wanted to be certain. I was waiting for the tests to be completed with the unmated Wolf Breeds. I wanted to be sure there wasn't a match to your Wolf genetics before I told you."

He hadn't wanted her to mate with a Coyote. The words were unsaid, but there all the same. Just as Dog had said, the fact that she was a Cross Breed had been deliberately left unsaid for so many years that sometimes she wondered if anyone but her even remembered. Evidently, her father had remembered.

"But now that there's no time left, you can tell me about Rhyzan? Any Coyote's better than the one I chose, right?" she demanded.

Surprise glittered in her father's brown eyes before they narrowed reprovingly. "You know better than that, Cassie."

"The point is moot anyway." Anger and hurt raged inside her as she shot Rhyzan a glare. "Any other test doesn't matter. I have a mate now."

"Not necessarily," Rhyzan contradicted, his voice holding a vein of satisfaction that only pissed her off further. "You know Breed Law, Cassie. Possible anomalies were built into the Mating Laws. One of those possibilities was—"

"A Reconsideration?" she exclaimed in disbelief. "Are you insane?"

A Petition for Reconsideration stated that if another Breed tested as a match to a mated Breed or human, then that Breed could petition the Breed Cabinet to separate the two mates and give the possible mate a chance to convince the one his tests were compatible with that he or she would be the better choice if they proved compatible.

"Insanity isn't one of my genetic anomalies." Rhyzan grinned as though amused. "But I'm entirely serious. I want a chance to see if the tests were correct and we could be mates."

"I have a mate," she snapped.

"Cassie, Dog will get you killed. Or worse. He's a known Council Coyote. He could turn you over to them . . . ," her father protested.

"He's not insane," she sneered. "He knows they'd take him as well and he'd suffer the same fate. He hasn't survived in that world by being stupid, Father."

Everything inside her was screaming out in denial, in pain. She could see her father's disappointment and it was killing her. He hadn't told her Rhyzan could be her mate because he wanted to see if she could mate a Wolf instead. Anything other than a Coyote.

"Cassie." Rhyzan drew her gaze back to him. "Wouldn't you prefer a mate with honor—"

"How many times do I have to reject one of your advances? For God's sake, Rhyzan. Whenever I've been in your company I can feel your contempt and distrust. Why would I want you for a mate?" She jumped to her feet, smothered between the combined disappointment and disapproval of her father and Jonas's assistant director.

God, Rhyzan's arrogance had made her crazy even before she'd mated with Dog. He was damned fine to look at, and she would even have considered sleeping with him once or twice if his contempt hadn't been a complete turn-off, but whenever she thought of anyone as a potential mate, the memory of the mysterious contact that had fascinated her for years interfered.

Her father and Rhyzan rose to their feet as she rushed between them. Where the hell was her mate? He was supposed to be here; he was supposed to keep this from happening, at least until she could handle the hormones raging through her.

"You have yet to reject me," Rhyzan stated with his ever-present confident prickishness.

She shot him a furious glance. "You're damned good to look at, Rhyzan, but that's about it. And if you had gotten that little sneer on your face one more time when someone was overheard calling me the psychic Breed, then I would have had to smack it off your face."

It wasn't just the sneer; it was the feeling that the thought of her former abilities was seen in contempt. He saw *her* with an edge of contempt.

"Cassie, my formal Petition for Reconsideration will be sent electronically to the Breed Cabinet at first light. I won't allow that bastard to take my mate." Ice filled his voice, his gaze.

That was it. He was cold. The Breed had an ice cube for a heart and she didn't think she'd enjoy frostbite.

"Have you forgotten who you're fucking with, asshole?" she snarled, ignoring her father as she faced a Breed she was beginning to see as the enemy now. "I'll twist your petition in so many damned directions so fast, you'll get whiplash."

She'd never cared much for Rhyzan, had never liked his lack of compassion or his hard-line approach to Breed Law. He was a Breed who saw everything in black and white.

The rule book was all that mattered, not the law broken or the reasons why.

"You're not the only one who knows Breed Law," he stated, assurance settling over his expression.

She turned to her father, seeing the speculation in his gaze as he watched her now. Could he sense the chill invading her? she wondered. The fear?

"How dare you do this?" she snarled, seeing her father's and Rhyzan's start of surprise at the sound of her voice. "You come to this room, the scent of my mate marking it, as well as me, and dare to suggest you're strong enough to replace it?" A sneer curled at her lips as she raked Rhyzan with a contemptuous glare. "And then to suggest you can force it? I'd slit your throat if you even tried and I'd get away with it."

"Cassie," her father whispered, pain contorting his face. "Dog will get you killed."

The slamming of the suite's door had them all swinging around.

Terror raced through her. If he'd been standing outside the door, he could have heard everything said. She hadn't completely closed the door; she remembered that now. Some warning, some inset kernel of knowledge, had made her stop just shy of securing it.

And that may have been a very big mistake.

She watched in fascination as Dog stepped over to where he'd carelessly tossed his pack earlier. Not taking his eyes off them, he reached into the side, drew a slender cigar free and placed it between his lips, lit it.

The flame from the old-fashioned match cast his features into an eerie glow before he lowered it, shook the flame out and slowly blew out a cloud of fragrant tobacco smoke.

It took precious seconds to realize she was slowly shaking her head as she stared back at him, anger still raging like a storm inside her. This couldn't happen. She couldn't let blood be shed here. God help her, nothing could happen to her dad, and if Dog attacked Rhyzan, her father would feel honor bound to stand with the assistant director.

"Mate," he drawled softly. "Come here."

She'd taken a step toward him when her father's hand touched her arm with but a whisper of discomfort, pulling her gaze to him.

"I love you, Cassie," he said gently. "And I'll do whatever necessary to protect you. Even from your mate."

And he would. Whatever he felt he had to do.

Her head lifted as she forced back the sharp words that wanted to escape.

"I chose him," she assured him firmly. "I contacted him. I asked him to be my lover, knowing he was a Coyote, knowing there was a chance that he was my mate." She flashed Rhyzan a killing look. "If I had wanted anyone else, I could have chosen them instead."

No bloodshed. No war. The only way to fight a Reconsideration was to stay firm, confident, and let no one suspect for even a second that he wasn't the mate she would have chosen if she had known.

Turning, she moved across the room to Dog's side, expecting him to make some show of ownership or dominance.

Instead, his hand merely settled at her back, warm, strangely comforting.

"Alpha Sinclair, I actually have some measure of respect for you," he stated, his tone reasonably respectful. "Because of that, I assure you that getting my mate killed or captured is the last thing you need to fear. But make the mistake of attempting to use her love for you, and your disappointment in her choice, then that will change. I don't think either of us wants to hurt Cassie in such a way."

Her father's expression didn't change, but the animosity pouring from him seemed to thin, as though Dog's response surprised him.

"As for you." Dog turned to Rhyzan. "Get the hell out of here. The scent of your self-righteousness is pissing me off."

Cassie was aware of her father watching, his expression bland, but he was analyzing every word, every undercurrent and emotion in the air, she knew. And he was amazingly perceptive.

"I'd like to see Kenzi soon." She turned to her father.

"Your security is no longer active and Kenzi's under Bureau protection," Rhyzan stated, moving for the door. "As a matter of fact, you have twelve hours before you'll be asked to leave if you insist on remaining with him."

He left the room as Cassie fought to control the hard strike of pain she felt lance her chest.

That was her sister, and because she refused to consider an attempt to switch mates, he'd use Kenzi as a weapon?

She didn't look at her father then. She wouldn't beg, not Rhyzan and not her father. She wouldn't put him in the position of having to hurt her because he couldn't overrule Rhyzan.

"I'm sorry, baby," he said softly as he drew to her side and lowered his head to kiss the top of hers. "I love you. If you need me, you have only to call. You know that."

She nodded quickly. "I know. I love you too, Dad."

Her heart was breaking. She could feel it shredding in her chest and fought to keep the pain buried, to keep the tears from filling her eyes.

He left the room, closing the door gently behind him as he did.

She stepped away from Dog, a strange, hollow chill moving through her as she headed for the bedroom. "I guess I better start packing. It appears we're being evicted."

· C H A P T E R   9 ·

Cassie managed to talk to Ashley and several of the other agents she'd been working with and updated them as to her new status, or lack thereof. She hadn't met with Jonas, but each time she considered it, she rejected the idea just as quickly. Some instinct warned her that now wasn't the time.

Her mother had arrived several hours after her father and Rhyzan left, clearly upset. Cassie had refused to discuss the earlier meeting with her, despite the fact that her mother obviously knew what had happened. Just as she knew Cassie had been given notice to leave.

Finally, that evening, there was nothing left to do but pack. Not that she had a lot to pack. Her clothes and shoes for the most part. She hadn't brought much else besides a few pieces of jewelry when she'd come to Window Rock.

Dog had left and returned several times, his expression forbidding each time he'd come back to the room. What his plans were when they left, she had no idea. What his plans were while he'd been in the Bureau's residence with her, she still didn't know. All she knew was that whatever he was working on, he was determined to keep it to himself.

Council business? she wondered, but something in that thought simply didn't feel right. That, or she was just trying to fool herself.

Aware of him moving around in the other room, she placed her luggage on the bed and began packing. She had her apartment; they could always go there. Or that was where she intended to go. Someplace reasonably safe while she and her mate battled out a few choices he needed to make quickly.

"How confident are you that you can block the Petition for Reconsideration?" Dog asked her from the bedroom doorway as she pulled clothes from her closet and carried them to the bed.

Placing the hangers of clothing on the bed, she straightened and stared back at him, her stomach sinking at the hard expression on his face and the brooding anger in his eyes.

"I can't block it. I'd have to be able to access the articles of Mating Law. My security access was rescinded, as well as any ability to file the proper paperwork without going through the Breed Tribunal to gain permission to access it." She frowned as she considered the options she had. "All I can do is refuse to see him until the BRC agrees to hear my arguments. But they can still force me away from you until that time."

Could she bear that? Even now, the need for him was a heated ache in her core, distracting at best, but she knew it could be much worse. Mating Heat and the need for one's mate were an ever-present hunger until the hormonal changes that occurred in both the male and female ran their course or pregnancy occurred. According to Dr. Sobolova, the injection she administered would halt conception, but nothing could halt the Heat itself. It was unknown until recently that the Coyote Breed's DNA hadn't been coded with the mutation to block conception. That mutation was one of the reasons Wolf and Feline Breed female mates experienced such extremes in their arousal and needs.

"You have five minutes to change and grab your pack." He stepped into the bedroom, his glance taking in her clothes. "Brannigan filed his petition and I'd prefer not to give that bastard a chance to die today."

Cassie could feel the blood draining from her face.

She could feel the knowledge that such a move would turn into a war. If Rhyzan actually managed to separate her and Dog, blood would spill. And that blood would stain the Breeds and Mating Heat forever.

She couldn't allow this to happen.

If Dog killed Rhyzan for attempting to separate them, it would tear the Breed community apart, no matter the law that allowed it. Mating Law was filled with addendums, statutes and, in some places, vague language to allow for later clarifications on a case-by-case basis. Such as this one. But it firmly established the fact that mates couldn't be separated by order or decree.

There wasn't a Breed alive who was aware of Mating Law who would stand for even Dog to be separated from his mate. It was unthinkable. It would divide the Breeds as nothing else ever had.

"We can't leave without being seen . . ."

"Let me take care of that. Four minutes, Cassie." His expression hardened further. "The second he has confirmation that he can separate us, he'll head up here with enough Enforcers to fill this suite. And trust me, I will die to keep my mate, and I'll make damned sure I take a hell of a lot of them with me."

It was his tone, the strength in it, the faint growl that rose from his throat, the wave of possession and determination that suddenly filled the room.

If he would die to keep Rhyzan from taking her, then he'd never allow the Council to take her either. The fear of that had been one she hadn't been able to push aside, until now. That preternatural sense of coming events or possibilities woke inside her long enough that she knew whatever he was, whoever he worked for, he wasn't loyal enough to them to turn her over.

Grabbing the clothes she needed, she quickly removed her slacks and silk blouse before redressing. Jeans, a dark T-shirt and overshirt and hiking boots.

Damn Rhyzan. What the hell was he trying to do? One thing was for certain: His blood was going to spill if he kept on this course.

As she hurriedly braided her hair, Dog strapped his weapon to his thigh. While she was securing the braid he was lifting the pack and looping one of the straps over his shoulder.

"It won't take long for him to receive an answer." She kept her voice low as she took the hand he held out to her.

"Then let's not waste time. Stay behind me, stay quiet." He led her through the suite, but rather than going to the exit, he pulled her into the spare room behind the small kitchen.

She watched in amazement as they entered the small walk-in closet there. Pausing at the back of the closet, she watched as the wall slowly slid back, revealing a narrow corridor.

God bless Jonas's heart, but how in the hell had Dog known about the hidden access?

Following silently, she was aware of the access door closing behind them as her night vision kicked in, allowing her to see her way through the dark corridor.

It took only minutes to find a stairwell. Dog moved quickly, silently, despite his size, down the sound-absorbing steps until they reached another long corridor. Pausing, listening for long seconds, he then led her to the door at the far end.

The exit led to a cement tunnel that came out several

blocks away from the Bureau into a parking garage. There, she watched as two Coyote Breeds separated themselves from the shadows to meet him.

She knew the two Breeds. His partners, Mutt and Mongrel. God, she was going to have to discuss names with them.

"Brannigan just received confirmation of receipt of the petition and was given the go-ahead to have your mate taken to the doctors until the Breed Ruling Cabinet could convene," Mutt reported as Dog opened the back of the Desert Dragoon and threw his pack inside. "The order was given for retesting alone, but I doubt Rhyzan will pay much attention to it."

"Why the labs?" Cassie questioned them. "There's no reason that I'd be kept there."

"He gave Sobolova and Armani orders to come up with a hormone that would counteract what he called your infection," Mutt said, sneering. "He wants to give whatever hormone he carries a chance to ensure a mating."

Disbelief filled her. That wasn't possible. In all the years of mating, nothing had been found that could counteract Mating Heat.

"He's insane," she hissed, her gaze going to Dog as he watched her quietly. "That's not possible."

"Not with Wolves or Felines," Mongrel drawled. "Seems they think it might be possible for a short amount of time with Coyote DNA. Though it seems Sobolova and Armani are currently threatening Rule Breaker and Jonas Wyatt with formal protests for attempting it."

"Let's go." Dog jerked open the passenger door of the four-seat armored desert all-terrain vehicle and all but pushed her inside.

The other two climbed into the back while Dog strode around to the driver's side and slid inside. Within seconds, the Dragoon was pulling out of the garage and heading away from Window Rock.

"Where are we going?" God, she prayed she wasn't making a mistake.

She was alone with three of the most notorious Council Breeds she knew of. She was a mate as well as the one Breed the Genetics Council had been attempting to snatch since she was nine years old.

"Where Rhyzan can't touch you," Dog said with a grunt, watching the night as the Dragoon's lights cut a swath through the darkness.

"And where would that be?" she asked, staring at him, trying to hold on to his earlier declaration that he would die before being separated from her.

A chuckle from the back seemed to mock her fear.

"She thinks you're going to turn her over to the Council, Dog," Mutt announced, far too amused.

"She knows better," Dog muttered, but she saw the narrow-eyed look he shot her. "She'd be with Rhyzan if that's what she thought. Wouldn't you?"

She tried to swallow past the uncertainty tightening her throat.

"I would," she answered him firmly, rather than giving voice to that uncertainty. "That doesn't mean I don't expect to know what the hell you're going to do. I'm not a child or a simpleton and I'm fully capable of contributing to whatever you have planned if I know what the plan is."

Being kept in the dark just made her crazy now. Before, the answers she'd needed had always been available, and if not the answers, at least an assurance of safety or danger. Those ghostly forms no longer came to her, though, and the uncertainty of what was coming was about to break her control.

"Well, it's not exactly a plan." He flashed her a grin, leaned back in his seat and extracted a cigar from his shirt pocket and lit it. "You could say we're flying by our asses here."

The scent of the tobacco wasn't harsh or acrid, and if she

wasn't mistaken it was the same type of cigar and tobacco that Dane Vanderale smoked. And Dane exclusively smoked the slender rolled tobacco that one of the Vanderale companies made in Africa.

He was smoking Vanderale cigars. How the hell did he get them? She knew for a fact that particular brand of tobacco was made for Dane exclusively. It wasn't imported and couldn't be bought. And Dane didn't supply just anyone with them, especially Council Breeds.

"It's not exactly a plan," she repeated quietly. "Do you know exactly where we're going?"

"Pretty much," he drawled, that amusement in his tone becoming irritating. "Is this a guessing game?" she snapped, reaching out and snagging the cigar long enough to take a draw herself to confirm her suspicions about where it had come from.

It was smooth; the hint of cherry mixed with a flavor that reminded her of cognac flowed over her senses. Holding the cylinder between two fingers, she placed it between his lips once again, ignoring the surprise that had obviously rendered the three men silent.

Lifting his hand, he pulled the cigar free long enough to glance at it, then suddenly grinned again before returning it between his lips and increasing the speed of the Dragoon.

"Did you guess?" He shot her a knowing look.

The two Breeds behind them were completely silent, completely intent on what was going on in front of them.

He shouldn't have those cigars, just as he shouldn't have known about Jonas's escape route.

"Will Jonas be there, or Dane?" she asked, narrowing her gaze on him as he exhaled, the smoky scent wrapping around her senses.

"Jonas is going to be rather busy for a while," he said, grunting. "I warned him Rhyzan was a sneaky bastard; he didn't want to listen. Though what makes him think he can take my mate, I have yet to figure out."

Yeah, that one was damned confusing.

"Rhyzan is playing some game." She exhaled roughly, able to think more clearly now that they were away from the Bureau and the threat of Rhyzan's interference behind them. "But I think he's aware of the fact that I'm not his mate."

That had bothered her, why she and the other Breed had tested compatible. It didn't make sense and it shouldn't have happened.

Rhyzan was incredibly hard to read, though. He kept his thoughts to himself and rarely shared his opinions. During the time she'd spent with him over the past months, she'd had the impression that she actually bored him.

"Well, I'll just make certain it's nothing personal when I kill his ass," Dog assured her. "Because I will kill him, Cassie, if he continues on this course."

She shook her head at the promise. "Receiving permission from the Breed Tribunal to separate mates is just the first step. Even in Coyote mates it's been established that after that time the mating hormones begin mutating and then mates begin bonding on the genetic level. The idea that Mating Heat can be counteracted before that is just a supposition at this point. But even with that done, the final decision is with the Breed Ruling Cabinet, not a Tribunal."

"So, it takes how long for that to happen?" He shot her a quick look.

"Three to seven days," she sighed heavily. "It varies."

"They've discovered the two of you are gone. Rhyzan's ordered the heli-jet in the air," Mutt broke in. "This bastard is going to piss me off, Dog, ya know?"

"What direction?" Dog growled as Cassie felt her heart begin racing.

"No word yet. I doubt we have much time. We need to hurry. We're still several miles from the second Dragoon." The tension in the Coyote's voice deepened. "I told you we should have killed him when Jonas refused to back down on placing him in the Bureau."

"We're not far from Graeme and Cat's." The Bengal Breed was crazier than hell, but she knew he would help them if he knew what was going on.

"I got this, mate." Sheer confidence filled Dog's voice. "Hang on, this will be a fast stop." He glanced over his shoulder at the two Breeds behind him. "Get ready to bail."

Literally. A minute later Dog swung the Dragoon off the road alongside a deserted building. Before the vehicle rocked to a stop, the two Coyotes were jumping from the vehicle, doors slamming behind them.

Dog then hit the gas again, pulling back onto the road, and within seconds another Dragoon was racing behind them.

"Where are we going?" She hardened her voice as she stared at him demandingly. "Don't keep me in the dark. You won't like how well I don't deal with it."

A low, playful chuckle whispered over her senses as he looked at her. The look was approving, challenging.

"I have a place about ten miles from here," he answered as the other vehicle shot past them. "Mutt and Mongrel will make certain it's still secure before we arrive. With any luck, we'll be there safe and sound before Rhyzan turns his heli-jet this way."

"And if we aren't lucky?" Her fists clenched in her lap at the thought of having yet another choice taken away from her.

"Then things go from sugar to shit real fast," he growled. "Because if that stupid bastard keeps fucking with me, Cassie, I'll kill him. There's a reason why Jonas and I didn't reveal exactly what I've been doing over the years or who I am. And if just one of my people ends up dead because of Rhyzan's ignorance, then I promise you, he won't survive my rage."

He was a double agent, a plant within the Council's ranks. She'd known Jonas had several within the Breed ranks the Genetics Council still controlled, but this was a hell of a coup for the director.

"Who are you, then?" At least her genetics hadn't led her completely astray, she thought wearily. He wasn't the scourge everyone thought he was, but he'd still lied to her for years, and he was still a Coyote.

"That's a discussion for a later time." He sighed before taking another draw on the cigar. "When we're safe. When my people are safe. Until then, I'm just what everyone thinks I am. A Council war dog with a dumb-ass sense of humor and the Breed princess for a mate." He shot her another mocking grin. "I haven't changed, Cassie."

"I never imagined you had. So why couldn't you tell me all this after we mated? Why wait until now?" It would have been easier for her if she'd known at least part of what she was dealing with.

He was silent for long moments, his gaze thoughtful, before he glanced over at her.

"You didn't hesitate when I told you Rhyzan had filed those papers. You didn't ask how I knew or demand proof. You followed me. You trusted me. Why?"

"You could have betrayed me at any time over the past six years," she admitted to herself as well as to him. "You've known we were mates, yet you still waited to claim me. You wouldn't have done that if you were loyal to the Council. But you didn't answer my question."

"I wanted your trust, simply because I'm your mate," he finally answered her quietly. "I didn't want it because I was suddenly more than I seemed. I wanted it the same way I gave it."

The same way he gave it.

And he had given it. Any other Breed would have been enraged with her father when he overheard that conversation, but Dog had known a strike against Cassie's father would have destroyed her. And a strike against Rhyzan would have forced her father to defend the other man.

For six years, Dog had done everything she'd asked of him, no matter how difficult, and often the payment was such a blatant effort to draw her interest that she couldn't help but agree to it.

Sunbathing in a bikini that had her parents scolding her for weeks when they caught her on the roof of the house in it. A scarf she had worn to a party left behind. Once he'd demanded that she merely talk to him for several hours on a secure sat phone he'd left for her. She'd been up half the night on that damned sat phone, listening to his voice, laughing at his often ribald humor.

"If I hadn't trusted you, I wouldn't have played that asinine game with you for six years and I damned sure wouldn't have met you at the hotel," she told him quietly as the Dragoon took a fast turn from the highway onto private land. "But that doesn't mean I trust you with anything other than my life, Dog. And keeping more secrets, keeping me in the dark about what's going on now, will only make it harder for me."

He slowed as a sprawling ranch house materialized from the darkness and the wide door of a garage slowly opened. The Dragoon shot inside and shut off.

"Come on, in the house. That heli-jet is only a minute or so away working in a sweep pattern, and Mutt and Mongrel need to cool the vehicles down in a hurry." She scooted across the console and took his hand, jumping from the vehicle and hurrying behind him as the two Coyotes worked to quickly pull the heat-masking covers over the Dragoons.

Damn Rhyzan.

Whatever his problem was, it was beginning to piss her off. God help him if she got access to the secure Mating Statutes again. Because if she wasn't mistaken, there was definitely a way to turn the tables on him and ensure the

Breed Ruling Cabinet clarified that little Reconsideration Petition.

Then she was going to make his life hell.

◆ ◆ ◆

Dog couldn't explain exactly what he was feeling, or what the hell it was that softened in his chest the moment Cassie had followed him without question. She hadn't hesitated, hadn't balked once. She hadn't demanded to call her father or Jonas; she'd trusted her mate.

She'd had no reason to trust him, not really. Six years of messages and infrequent calls whenever she needed something wasn't a friendship; it wasn't a relationship. It was all that had kept him sane, though. From the moment his lips had brushed hers in that damned hospital after he'd been forced to wound her on Seth Lawrence's island, no more than a whisper against petal-soft lips, he'd lived in hell.

Whoever thought Coyotes had it easier with Mating Heat had obviously not been talking to the males. It was ice in his gut, a chill that went to the bone, a need for his mate's warmth that felt like talons raking beneath his flesh. Until he was close to her.

The simplest touch, his hand against her back, the warmth of her sinking into his palm through her clothes, and he was warm. Being near her would have been enough, but touching her, sharing her kiss, her lips on his flesh, his against hers . . . it was like life itself.

As he showed her through the single-story home, then led her to the master bedroom, he could see the weariness in her pale features, the worry in her pretty blue eyes. And the hunger. The scent of her need was like a drug hitting his senses and spurring his own.

"I need to check with Mutt and Mongrel before we turn in for the night." He cleared his throat as she turned to look at him, her expression somber. "I won't be long."

Dammit, emotions weren't his strong suit, and he was damned if he knew how to handle them.

"That works." She nodded as she sat down in the chair positioned close to the bed and began unlacing her boots. "I didn't pack anything to sleep in."

"Grab a shirt from my pack. I have extras in there," he told her. "I shouldn't be too long, but I need to keep up with Rhyzan's movements for a while."

"I just want to go back to sleep anyway." She sighed. "Rhyzan's little meeting woke me up."

The sexual excess earlier with her mate had exhausted her. Dragging her ass out of the bed when the chime of the doorbell sounded had been almost impossible. Now that she was coming down from the adrenaline caused by her anger and then their flight, that weariness was washing over her once again.

She undressed quickly after he left the room, then pulled a T-shirt free of Dog's pack as he'd offered. It almost swallowed her smaller frame, but it beat being naked.

She brushed her teeth, washed her face and, taking a deep breath, returned to the bedroom. A silent, empty bedroom. Pulling down the blankets, she slid into the bed and turned off the lamp next to the bed.

She wished there was an electric blanket. She was cold and alone. And far too uncertain about the Breed she had accepted as her mate. Or the future awaiting them now.

She hadn't marked her mate.

That thought penetrated her sleep, filled her mind as she felt Dog slide into the bed beside her, his powerful body warm as he pulled her against him. She hadn't known how chilled she felt until he wrapped around her, or how aroused until she felt his hardened shaft against her belly.

"Hmm, you're warm," she whispered, caressing his chest with her hand as she slid her leg along his.

"So are you." Amusement rumbled in his voice, but she could sense the disquiet beneath.

"Ever'thing okay?" She pressed a kiss to his chest, feeling the muscles tighten beneath his flesh.

His hand slid along her back to her buttocks, calloused flesh rasping her skin and awakening pleasure centers beneath her skin that fed the arousal already beginning to burn.

"It is now." He groaned as her tongue licked over a flat, hard nipple.

One hand tightened in her hair, tugging at the strands sensually as she rasped the small disc with her teeth.

She pushed against his shoulder, a lazy sensuality taking hold of her. It was unlike anything she'd experienced so far with him. It was deeper, overtaking her, but without the imperative race for fulfillment. It was wild, hungry, but with a need to relish every taste, every nuance of touch.

"What do you need, little halfling?" he whispered, turning to his back as she lifted herself next to him, her head lifting and lowering to his.

"My mate." Her lips brushed against his, then her tongue. "All of him."

"Then take him. I dare you." His lips parted, taking her tongue as it slipped against him, his lips closing on it, suckling at it for brief seconds before giving her his in return.

The kiss was slow, deep. His taste and hers merging through her senses as the mating hormone began to infuse the pleasure they shared.

When she pulled back, her lips slid down his neck, nipping at the tough skin over his jugular, licking his Adam's apple and then laving a path back to his chest. Her hands stroked over his shoulders, his sides. The need to touch as well as taste, to pleasure as well as take, folding over her like an erotic storm.

Dog stared down at her in wonder, the scent of her pleasure overwhelming him. It wasn't the pleasure he'd sensed from her before. This was both wilder and lazier, her pleasure drawing from his as she kissed and stroked her way slowly to the engorged length of his cock.

His fingers tightened in her hair as he bit off a ragged groan and restrained the need to push her to her back and come over her, to give her the same pleasure she was giving him. At the same time he just wanted to lie there and soak in the sleepy need and rising emotions he sensed beginning to flow from her.

He hadn't sensed this before. This ebb and flow of emotions, both fierce and gentle, like the woman herself. And never before had he sensed both the woman and the animal instincts she possessed reaching out to him as they were now.

Lowering his hands to the sheets beneath him, he clenched his fingers in the material and eased the control he kept on the inner beast fighting to rise to meet her hunger. Just a little, he told himself. He could sense the creature she hid as well reaching out, searching, and he knew what it sought. That connection on a level never known before.

Breed to Breed, mate to mate, man to woman. Animal to animal. That dark core of a Breed's soul where the animal waited, watched, content to lounge until needed. Or when called free by its mate.

As he let those instincts free, he felt hers leap, surge closer. Suddenly, his skin was more sensitive, his cock harder if possible, throbbing desperately to bury inside her.

He could feel her pleasure mounting as well, the scent of it infusing the air, merging with his own. And when her tongue swiped over the head of his cock, it was pure, undiluted rapture.

The growl that tore from him was met with a feminine one of her own. Her hands stroked along his abdomen to his thighs, her lips parted over his cock head, sucked it inside the wet heat, only to release it moments later.

His thighs tightened, his lips pulling back in a snarl of denial, then one of pure pleasure as she licked her way down the shaft to his balls. There, she laved, played, kissed and sucked at the sensitive flesh until the need for her was agony.

"Oh hell, Cassie," he groaned as she licked her way up his hard flesh again. "That hot little tongue is going to make me insane."

She rolled it over the engorged crest, licking free the pulse of pre-cum before drawing the head into her mouth again.

As her lips lifted seconds later, he had to restrain the need to force her mouth back.

"I love how you taste," she sighed against the sensitive skin of the crest. "The feel of you taking my mouth, taking my pussy."

His entire body jerked at the sensual whisper. Ah fuck yeah, he loved hearing her talk dirty.

"And I love fucking your mouth and pussy," he groaned, staring down at her as her mouth covered him again, sucking him deep, tongue lashing at the underside and straining his control.

"Fuck. I'm going to come in your mouth." His voice was a tortured rasp.

She released him then, rising beside him before she shocked him, blew his mind as she threw her leg over his hips. Reaching down he gripped the shaft and lined it up with her slick inner lips. Rubbing it in the sensitive slit as a whimpering gasp fell from her mouth.

"Are you gonna ride me, baby?" He tucked the wide crest at the opening to her body and felt the hormonal pre-cum pulse from the head to the ultra-snug channel awaiting him. "Take what's yours."

She pressed into the penetration, moaning as the crest began stretching her, parting and exciting the slick inner muscles as he felt them close over the tip of his cock.

"Fuck. So sweet and tight. Go ahead, baby, take my dick."

A cry whispered from her lips as her hips jerked, taking more of him. With each increment she forced inside her, the pulse of the hormone filled her, easing the muscles, sensitizing them, making her pleasure hotter, brighter, as it sensitized his own flesh.

She was tighter than a fist wrapped around the head of his cock. Her hips rocked, shifted, lifted, then lowered again, working him inside her until Dog was sure he'd die from the incredible pleasure. It was like sinking into the center of an ecstasy so pure he could feel it against his skin, taste it against his tongue.

His hands jerked from the sheet to her hips, gripping them as he felt her trembling above him.

"Scared, baby?" he whispered up at her as her head tossed, her hands suddenly gripping his wrists as she levered herself straighter, her hips rocking against his. "You're so fucking tight. It's pleasure and pain at once."

Her juices spilled along the head lodged inside her as another harder, fuller pulse of his pre-cum ejaculated inside her. Her muscles clenched and rippled, tightening on him and sucking his erection deeper inside her.

"Harder, baby," he groaned. "Work yourself on my cock harder. Take it. Let me hear you cry for it."

She was trying to restrain her cries as well as the hunger building inside her.

"Let the fuck go," he snarled up at her. "Damn you, don't you pull back now."

Levering his upper body up, he caught a hard nipple in his mouth, sucked it in deep, hard. His mouth closed around it, tongue lashing at it as she froze for one timeless second.

Then, the wild, inner core of her jerked free of her control, surged inside her. Her hips bucked, one hand locked in his hair, bearing down, taking him deeper, deeper . . .

Ah fuck. He was buried full length inside her, throbbing, her grip on his cock so tight several ejaculations of the hormone filled her, one after the other. He released her breast and his back hit the bed, hips arching as he forced his eyes to stay open, just to watch her.

Her cries washed over him. Straightening, she tipped her head back and began to move, rocking, lifting and falling as her hair caressed his thighs, licked over his balls. His fantasy come to life, his wild little halfling riding him as those sensual curls teased his flesh with the lightest touch.

It was the most erotic experience, the most sensual pleasure, he'd ever known in his life, and he wanted nothing more than to hold her there forever. Just let the world recede and do nothing but spend his life buried in the heat and acceptance this one woman wrapped him in.

But the world wouldn't recede, and as her flesh milked and stroked over his cock, the pleasure tightened, rose, began straining at his senses with the need to come. His teeth clenched, hips arched to her, a growl rumbling in his chest.

Then he felt her stiffen, felt her losing her breath. Gripping her hips, he gave her what she needed, moving beneath her, thrusting hard and deep inside her as he felt her unraveling. Her pussy locked around his shuttling cock, so fucking tight, rippling, sucking at his erection as her orgasm exploded through her.

The intensity of her release, the pleasure whipping through him, sent his own senses exploding, his seed shooting inside her as he felt his cock swell halfway up the shaft, locking him inside as his release gained momentum and he swore took the top of his head off.

Son of a bitch . . .

It was like fucking dying in ecstasy. He heard her cries echoing around him, felt her collapse against him, and all he could do was hold her to him as his hips jerked between her thighs, each ejaculation milking him dry.

When it was over, he had to fight to breathe. His breaths were sawing from his chest, his teeth locked in her shoulder, and hers locked at his chest.

He could feel her canines piercing his flesh, her tongue spilling the heat of her mating hormone to the small wounds, marking him as no other woman ever could.

She was marking *him*.

The primal satisfaction that raced through him was nearly as heady as the physical release. She was his. Completely, irrevocably. God help the man or Breed who thought he'd steal her from his arms.

◆ ◆ ◆

The room was still dark when Cassie found herself suddenly awake. She lay against Dog's side, his arm beneath her head and his body curved over her, holding her to him. Her hand laying at his heart, his covering it. And he was sleeping. Funny, but in the time they'd spent together, she'd only known him to nap.

Frowning, she blinked, lifted her gaze, then froze.

At first, she thought she had to be dreaming. In all the years she'd watched spirits walk around her, she'd never had an occasion to actually have a male visit her. And he was definitely a spirit. Tall, broad, so obviously Dog's father given the fact that they shared the same features, the same coloring.

The spirit stood, military straight, his arms crossed over his chest, his expression curiously gentle despite the savage cast of his features. He was dressed in military fatigues, the shirt stained with blood. His blood if the torn cloth at the chest was any indication.

He laughed when he was a boy, the spirit said softly, the voice filled with regret. *He had a coyote pup that would come out of its mother's den and play with him. His laughter always reminded me of his mother.*

Pain flickered across those hard features, and though he spoke to her, he never took his gaze from Dog.

I lost her, in childbirth. He glanced at her, but only for a second. *She was too weak, from the damage to her body days before, when they'd found us again, to survive it. As she held our baby, she slipped from me.*

Cassie didn't speak; she didn't think he expected her to speak.

He was ten when they found me. I'd left him in the mountains while I went for supplies. He looked at his chest and sighed before looking at Dog once again. *I'd tried to train him to survive in case I didn't return at some point, but ten is so very young for a child to be left alone. Even one trained to survive.*

Ten was far too young, she agreed silently.

I swore to his mother I would always watch over him, so she could go peacefully to the other side. That I wouldn't desert him until his mate found him, as mine found me. A thread of amusement touched his whispery voice. *He's a stubborn boy. Getting him to that island and getting him into place so I could draw you to the balcony that day took considerable effort, you know?*

It was his presence she had sensed all those years ago, she realized. Hidden from sight but pushing her all the same. He was the reason she had agreed to those deals over the years, trusting Dog when logic told her it was insane. Because he was there, assuring her that Dog could be trusted.

You knew. I didn't have to tell you. Though sometimes, I admit, I may have whispered assurances to the creature inside you. Your animal listens far better than you when it comes to my boy. He tilted his head as Dog shifted in his sleep, his hold tightening around her.

He survived, he whispered, once again somber. *A boy, no more than ten. Alone. And until you, he never forgot he was alone. With you, he found hope.*

And he'd given her hope. But her heart ached for the spirit who stood watching over his grown son even as he must have watched over him as a boy.

You should accept your animal, girl. It's not truly Wolf, not truly Coyote, but a being as unique as your creation. It's one creature, instinctive, accepting as no other could ever be. To survive, you must accept it as it accepted you, he warned her, taking his eyes from Dog only long enough to level a demanding look her way.

I named him Cainis, I called him Cain, the spirit told her, turning back to his son. *I didn't know how to be a fa-*

ther, but as I held my son and watched my mate die, I knew that small being was all that mattered. And as I died, unable to reach him, I couldn't leave him. I'd sworn.

She felt a tear slip down her cheek, hurting for this Breed and for his loss, as well as Dog's.

Now his mate has found him, and mine's calling to me, he told her, his expression gentling as Dog's hand gripped hers, holding it to his heart.

The spirit turned his gaze to her, his expression hardening then. *Warn him, Cassie. Before you leave this place, warn him. His enemy knows him for who he is, for what he is now. The princess consorts with the enemy, it's whispered, and Cain's image has reached him . . .* The voice trailed off, and fury flashed in eyes nearly black as the image wavered.

She could see him talking, his lips moving, his gaze fierce as he faded from sight, leaving only his regret and his fear for his son behind.

"Cassie?" Dog whispered her name, his voice scratchy, his hand stroking her arm as she realized she'd jerked upright, staring at the image as it faded, trying to read lips that she couldn't see clearly to begin with. "What do you see, baby?"

Her head jerked around, staring down at him, and she realized she was shaking, trembling in reaction.

"Cainis, he called you Cain," she whispered, her voice strangled as she fought to breathe. "It's said the princess consorts with the enemy, and your image has reached him. He knows. He knows who and what you are . . ."

Fear tightened in her chest, a cold sweat breaking out across her flesh as Dog jerked upright and pulled the quilt around her before dragging her to the warmth of his chest.

She was so cold. Brutally cold. Ice flowed through her veins and she swore she could feel death breathing over her shoulder.

"It's okay. Shhh. It's okay, Cassie." Dog kissed his mate's brow and tried to warm her as he drew her back to lie against his chest. "It's okay. Let me get you warm."

It took long minutes to calm her breathing, to warm her, to convince her to just lie against him. It took even longer for her to drift back into a restless sleep. And all he could do was stare into the dark, the hairs at the back of his neck stiff with warning.

Cainis, though the spelling was different, meant the same thing. Dog. But his father had called him Cain. He barely remembered the father who'd raised him, who'd trained him to survive in a harsh wilderness. But he'd always remembered the warnings. If he was ever caught, his name was Cainis. He was created in Red Lab Three, but it was destroyed the year of his creation and he was rescued by a nurse who had since died. Always remember his enemy was Major. His mother was an angel. The warnings were always clear, repeated to him daily, and he'd repeated them back.

Until the day the man he called father hadn't returned to the wilderness.

Cain. His father had called him Cain, but he was to never, ever allow the shortened version of his name to be known. If he was ever asked his name, he was Cainis. He was Dog. He was to beware of Major, and his mother was an angel.

He still carried the picture of his mother that his father had kept in the cabin. Blond, eyes a pretty blue, she'd stood tall, close to five-seven, and she'd stared up at her human mate dressed in military fatigues and glaring at the camera as though it were the enemy.

That picture was tucked in his pack, hidden in a slit he'd cut in the leather.

And the only way she could have known any of this was if the ghost of one of his parents had come to her.

It would have been his father, he decided, remembering

the somber, taciturn man who had raised him. He hadn't been one to give hugs; he'd avoided them. But he'd often found ways for Dog to have a reason to laugh. At some point, Dog had realized his childish laughter eased the pain he sensed coming from his father.

Fuck.

It was said the princess consorted with the enemy and his image had reached *him*. Because of *him*, his parents were dead. Someone he knew only as Major. And this faceless, unknown threat now knew who and what he was. He was a hybrid, born of a Breed mother, a human father. And now someone knew. And they would know he'd mated another hybrid.

Goddamn.

Cassie watched Dog warily the next day. As she worked on the tablet he'd provided her, using a back door in the Bureau's files to get into the Articles of Mating Law, she was always aware of him.

Even her animal instincts were wary, rising inside her, conscious of every move, every word he said as he, Mutt and Mongrel kept up on the search Rhyzan was conducting for them.

The two Coyotes he so often fought with sensed something within him too. They would look between her and Dog, their expressions sometimes thoughtful, sometimes confused.

She put up with it until evening fell and she finished downloading the files she needed and double-checking to see if there was anything else she had missed.

She'd wanted to sneak into her sister's file, check on Kenzi's debriefing and see what information she had, how she felt about the family she hadn't known existed, but Cassie didn't dare slip into that particular database. If Jonas caught her in the Breed Law database, he'd recognize the back door she'd used and ignore it. Rhyzan wouldn't do the same with his personal files.

Finishing up her work, she shut the tablet down, refreshed her coffee and finished the stew she'd started earlier for dinner. Once she washed the dishes, she walked to the wide doorway separating the living area and watched the three Breeds silently for long moments as they went over maps and discussed the progress of the escape Dog's people had made.

She remained silent, simply watching her mate. His expression was closed, and she could feel the tension emanating from him, growing tighter the longer she stood watching him.

"There's nothing else we can do, for now," he announced, rising from the chair and closing his own tablet as Mutt and Mongrel glanced at him.

They rose slowly to their feet, their gazes sliding her way, those same thoughtful, considering looks on their faces.

"We'll just, uhh, go check things outside." Mongrel cleared his throat as Mutt gave an energetic nod.

The two hurried to the door leading to the garage and closed it quickly behind them.

"Everyone made it out okay?" she asked, tucking her hands into the pockets of the loose casual pants she wore and propping one sock-covered foot atop the other as she leaned against the door frame.

"We're a few hours behind in terms of information." He pushed his fingers through his hair in irritation before he paced past her and went to the coffeepot. "There have been several lags in reports, though, so everything should be fine."

But he was worried. The disconnect from the real-time reports made him edgier than he was to begin with.

Turning, she watched as he filled his coffee cup, his back to her.

"Are we going to keep ignoring it?" she asked him,

crossing her arms over her breasts and holding back the knowledge that Dog was now just as wary of her as everyone else was.

As a child, she hadn't always been as careful as she should have been in regards to the Breeds who were followed by spirits or by the images of their own inner demons. That had begun the dislike that many of the Wolf Breeds felt for her. Generally, though, Coyote Breeds had always thought it was "kinda cool," as one had expressed. It was nice to know he wasn't alone.

"Now's not the time to discuss it." He kept his back to her and sipped at his coffee. "Later."

"Okay." She breathed in slowly. "Would you at least tell me who Major is?"

He shook his head. "Fuck if I know, and I've been trying to figure it out since I was ten. I guess we'll know soon enough, won't we?"

"If we could go over anything you remembered together, maybe we could figure it out—"

"I said not now, goddammit," he snapped, his voice low, filled with fury. "Just not now, Cassie."

Her lips parted, anger surging through her, to slap back at him for the sharp tone of voice.

"Well, love, didn't you go and pick a surly bastard to mate?" The South African accent was tinged with amusement and affection as Dane Vanderale stepped into the room behind them.

Cassie swung around, facing the Breed who most of the world believed was no more than a Breed benefactor and philanthropist. They had no idea about the Breed crouched and ready to spring forward inside him.

Hybrids were so far a mystery to the scientists. Their genetics rarely came forward until their teens, and it seemed the animal and human senses they possessed were far more integrated than those of Breeds created by scientists.

Tossing Dog a small pack he carried as Dog stepped past her, Dane strode to the bar, poured himself a drink, then turned back to them. She caught the faint scent that reached her from the box, which indicated it held the slim cigars he provided certain Breeds.

Dane himself was a master of control, but along with the scent of the cigars was one of pure, unmatched fury barely contained.

Dressed in gray silk slacks and a white long-sleeved shirt, the sleeves of which were rolled back to his elbows, he looked less like a hybrid Breed and more like the businessman he portrayed himself to be. That is, if one overlooked the shaggy hair the color of desert sand and didn't detect the animal lurking behind those emerald green eyes. Eyes he usually toned down with colored contacts.

Cassie narrowed her gaze on the hybrid, seeing far more than the mockery, easygoing charm and latent danger that she always picked up. For the first time since she'd known him, Dane was almost close to losing control of that inner animal he harbored.

"The parents, mine that is, are joining Callan and Jonas in Window Rock, by the way." He lifted his glass in a silent toast to Cassie. "Dash and Callan have both called the Leo, requesting he and Mother assist you in this. It appears your father may have attempted to kill Rhyzan when he filed that petition after your disappearance." He lifted the drink to his lips. "Don't bloody well fuckin' blame him."

Dane tossed back the drink, then slapped the glass to the bar and refilled it.

"Is Dad okay?" Cassie breathed out wearily, watching the hybrid as he sipped at his drink now. She was surprised. She was under the impression her father would approve of Rhyzan's actions.

"In excellent condition." His grin was hard. "I believe they may have had to pull him off Rhyzan, though. I heard he tried to beat him to death. Near succeeded too. Bastard's nose is slightly out of line, and I hear there may be a canine he's in danger of losing due to the blows your father got in."

This was a mess.

"Why did Dad and Callan ask Leo for help?" Cassie shook her head.

"Mother's research in Mating Heat," Dane pointed out. "And it appears Rhyzan is being rather an ass in regard to rescinding the Petition for Reconsideration, despite your father's insistence. Father, along with Seth Lawrence, who's arrived with his mate, by the way, is attempting to get to the bottom of Rhyzan's stubbornness. Mother's going to run the tests herself. As she stated, in all her decades of work with Mating Heat, she's never seen a Breed acquire two mates."

Two mates.

Rhyzan wasn't her mate and she knew it, but their tests had shown a compatibility . . .

"Oh God," she whispered, turning back to Dane in shock. "Kenzi. If he's Kenzi's mate, then it would make sense that I showed a compatibility but no true mating."

Dog's irritated growl had her wanting to roll her eyes.

Dane inclined his head, unsurprised. "That was Mother's thought as well. But Rhyzan should be aware of that. He's been with Kenzi quite a bit, debriefing her. Which begs the question, why is he holding firm in wanting you and your mate separated before the mating mutation completes within you and Dog?"

Rhyzan was playing a game, and Cassie knew it, Jonas knew it, but what that game was she couldn't guess. It made no sense that even with compatibility he'd attempt something like this. He had pride in surplus. He'd never admit that another Breed, especially a Council Coyote, had taken his potential mate. Or that he'd allowed it.

"It won't matter once I locate him." Dog's smile was a Grim Reaper's curve as he turned back to Dane. "What's the status on my people?" The fact that he was furious wasn't hidden. "I lost the connection with the team hours ago."

Dane stared at the floor, that rage beginning to burn inside him once again.

"We lost one," Dane finally said, sighing wearily as Dog snarled furiously. "One of the children. And perhaps one of my Lions as well. The wounds as he tried to protect the boy with his own body are pretty severe. We were forced to go dark just before that when we realized they'd found a way to track us. We found out just before the attack that they'd managed to slip a nano-tracker on one of the vehicles as we passed the gates."

Cassie sat down slowly in the chair behind her and stared at Dane in shock. What was he talking about? Children?

"There were children?" Dog hadn't told her there were children. He'd only said his people had to get out of a mission they were involved in before his status as a spy was revealed.

Dane nodded heavily. "Most of them were children. That was the information Dog and his teams have been working on within the Council ranks. The location of several dozen Breed children. Some still babes . . ."

"They're still doing it?" Horror filled her voice.

They were still creating Breeds?

"Do you really believe they'll stop?" Dane asked gently despite the fury pulsing beneath his voice. "They're always certain the answer to whatever they're seeking will come with the next one they create. Though what they're seeking we're not exactly certain of anymore. But they have come up with an interesting way of destroying the Breeds they've created now."

She turned to Dog, disbelief pouring through her, tightening her throat and chest.

"What is he talking about?" The grief she could sense pouring from Dog had her stomach clenching in dread.

"While the Breed rescues were deemed complete, we knew it wasn't over." Dog sighed, rubbing at the back of his neck as he moved to the bar and accepted the drink Dane poured for him. "Our first indication that there was a problem was when a young man showed up at Sanctuary about ten years ago. He said he'd learned a Breed child had been killed to provide the heart that he'd been given as a transplant when he was younger. As he began to mature, and the heart matured, his parents were killed in an effort to get to him and destroy him before anyone learned of the changes he was going through from that transplant."

"He died of his injuries a few days later." Dane grimaced. "Fucking brave as hell he was, but the wounds were too severe to save him."

Children. A Breed child had been killed to provide a human child with a heart?

"What changes?" The horror creeping through her was destructive. The monsters that were still operating as men of science were going beyond the evil they'd originally begun with.

"Breed changes." Dog finished his drink before pacing to the other side of the room. "He was beginning to show anomalies at the DNA level. It's taken me years to find the right people in the right place or to get the right people in place and locate the labs holding the Breeds being used for the transplants. Amazing what a person will agree to in an effort to live. That kid's parents knew a Breed child would die to supply that heart and they allowed it. Paid a small fortune for it."

Cassie pressed one hand to her stomach, sick inside at the thought of the horrors Breed children had faced. What had happened to science that some of the world's most intelligent minds were involved in this?

"We located the final lab several months ago, but access and the ability to infiltrate took a while. We finally managed to identify several scientists and techs willing to help us. We were preparing a plan when Kenzi was taken, just after Rhyzan stated his intent to Jonas to push the chance of a mating to you."

And a child had been lost because Rhyzan had decided to force something that he would have sensed wasn't a true mating. A compatibility showed up on many tests, but so far, the tests were highly unreliable when it came to an actual Heat rising between the Breeds tested.

"You'll have your teams back within twenty-four hours," Dane promised. "The children are being taken to the Leo's estate; the lab techs who aided in their rescues are with them. Jonas is having the scientists who cooperated with us transferred to Sanctuary. Those who didn't will be dealt with."

Jonas was amazingly practical. If he couldn't use the scientists in one way, he'd do so in another. He rarely executed the scientists if it was possible to apply their abilities to the survival of the Breed community as a whole.

"What do we have in terms of information?" Dog's voice was a terrible rasp of fury.

And Dane's smile was savage. "Top-level scientists, Dog. The cream of the Council crop. My teams are moving into place to grab as many as possible who escaped, kill those we can't acquire. With any luck, we're getting closer to the bastards funding this. Jonas's enforcers are joining my teams within the hour to begin downloading information and gathering evidence within the labs. Everything they had. They didn't have time to destroy anything. Their soldiers followed the escapees, deserted the labs. My teams moved in and secured them, thinking there was no way they could track the others. We were wrong."

The Genetics Council. The twelve-member Council hadn't been identified; even pinning down suspects had proven impossible in the eighteen years since the Breeds had announced themselves to the world.

In all the years since the world had learned of the

Breeds, every time a new lab had been discovered, records and information storage had been damaged before the Breed Enforcers could get to it. They'd never managed to acquire a facility with all records and information storage undamaged.

"Rhyzan's been apprised of all this?" Dog asked; then at Dane's nod Cassie watched Dog's eyes narrow warningly. "And he's still determined to enforce his petition? Even with the knowledge that I'm no rogue, but a member of the Bureau instead?"

"So it would seem. Hence Dash Sinclair's rage." Evidently, that made no sense to Dane any more than it made any sense to her or to Dog. "Rhyzan has demanded a full Cabinet meeting at the Window Rock Bureau for tomorrow afternoon. Jonas is having the required Cabinet members flown in tonight." He turned to Cassie. "Determined chap, isn't he?"

"Looks like it." Rising to her feet, Cassie rubbed at her arms, frowning in confusion as she left Dog and Dane to continue discussing the mission that had played out as Dog fought to hold his place in her life. The very fact that Rhyzan was still alive amazed her.

Dog wasn't known for his patience in the face of anyone attempting to steal so much as a cigar. The fact that he hadn't killed the assistant federal director himself amazed her.

There had to be a way to neutralize him short of killing him, because hiding didn't sit well with her.

Sitting back in her chair as she tapped the fingers of one hand on the upholstered arm, she narrowed her eyes on the old-fashioned clock hanging on the wall across the room.

There was too much going on right now to stay hidden like this, not just for Dog but for herself as well. And it wasn't as if Rhyzan's stand would hold with the knowledge of Dog's position. Besides, it wasn't the first time compatibility had shown between siblings to a single mate. It had occurred several years ago—two Bengal brothers, but only one had been the mate . . .

She stilled, frowning at that thought, information suddenly connecting, forming the answer she hadn't been able to come up with since learning of the compatibility tests.

She sat up, the answers pouring into her mind as she quickly went through each angle, each objection Rhyzan could make, each counterobjection. And still, there was only a single conclusion to draw.

"Cassie?" Dane's voice filtered through her thoughts.

"We need to go back—"

"Like hell," Dog grunted.

"If we stay hidden I won't be able to argue clarification on the Reconsideration and I won't be able to argue for another mate if this happens again. They'll always call into argument the fact that I hid myself rather than following the articles of Breed Mating Law." That she wouldn't allow.

"Fuck Breed Law," Dog growled. "Cassie, that assistant director will die if he attempts to take you out of my sight."

Oh, she had no doubt Rhyzan would die if he attempted that.

"I have to file a counterpetition." The answer came so quickly she was amazed she hadn't thought of it before. She turned quickly back to Dane. "Contact Callan. I need the form for counterpetitions sent to Dog's tablet as well as the form for a Petition for Restraint. He can access those for me if, as pride leader, he disagrees with actions being taken. I have them, but I need to show a paper trail to keep my back door into the files open."

"You're not part of his pride; your father will need to lodge that protest," Dane pointed out. "And he's considered prejudiced in your favor."

She smiled slowly. "Dane, I was made part of Callan's pride when I was nine years old, before Dad instituted his own pack. That induction was never rescinded because I visited so often." She turned to Dog. "Are you considered alpha to your teams or do you answer to someone else?"

As if she didn't know that answer.

"I answer to no one but you, halfling," he assured her, satisfaction suddenly gleaming in his gaze.

"I'll need the forms to file pack status as well," she informed Dane as he pulled his mobile phone from the leather holster at his side. "We'll go to my apartment rather than the Bureau tonight and arrive in time for the Cabinet to convene tomorrow evening."

"You have an apartment?" Dog's brows arched with curious amusement.

"Of course. I've had one near the Bureau for months." Didn't everyone have their own place?

She'd just never had reason to use it.

"Of course," he murmured, his lips still quirked with that odd smile. "So we're going to that little meeting and facing Rhyzan?"

"We are. I'll fill out the forms when Callan sends them and shoot them to all the required parties. All I need is Callan's verification and acceptance of the protest to ensure Rhyzan's hands are tied until my mother can complete the mating tests with Kenzi, which will be before the meeting." She shook her head. "I should have thought of that, dammit. I would have if you didn't keep my brain messed up."

His brow arched as Dane chuckled at the accusation.

"Message sent," the hybrid announced. "And confirmation of agreement received. Dog will have the forms within the hour." He looked between them, a dark blond brow raised inquisitively. "Shall we go, then?"

She slid him a considering look. "May we borrow a few of your Breeds? They're not required to follow Bureau dictates, correct?"

"Correct." She could see the laughter gleaming in his green eyes. "They are not."

"We need a security detail that's not required to obey Rhyzan's orders if he somehow manages to throw a wrench in the works. I'll be ready to leave within the hour." Turning, she hurried to the bedroom.

She had a lot to do in that hour.

◆   ◆   ◆

There she was.

It was all Dog could do to force himself not to follow her, to bend her over the bed and assure himself he was still alpha in this mating. He'd be damned if she wouldn't challenge that position every chance she had.

"That look on your face is almost envious," Dane drawled, pulling Dog's attention from the fact that the bedroom door was closed and his little mate was hidden from view.

The undertone of regret in his friend's voice was a reminder that the woman Dane believed should have been his mate was another's, something the hybrid had never stopped regretting.

"She makes me complete." Dog sighed, shaking his head. "Hell, I never knew I was incomplete until the mating."

The problem was, he wasn't so certain she felt the same way. He knew she was determined to make the mating work. It wasn't her determination he wanted, though; the hunger for her heart was growing by the day.

He wanted her love.

"Her life hasn't been easy, has it?" Dane remarked. "She's too damned intelligent, sees too much, senses too much for others' comfort. That woman could rule the world if she set her mind to it."

The world, or the Coyote Breeds Dog led. Over the years he'd drawn several dozen beneath his command. More than six alphas in their own right and Breeds hungry for a home, for a life that didn't include living among the monsters they'd worked to destroy.

"I'm going to petition for Coy status when this is over," he informed Dane, referring to the title given to a Coyote alpha who commanded more than a single pack. "Lobo's Wolf Breeds are the only Breed force in the area, but it's small and very secular. I have over sixty Coyotes that follow me with accompanied alphas ready to pledge their loyalty to the Breed Ruling Cabinet. I think there's enough room among the Nation here for a Coyote community."

He had far more support for it than even he had imagined until the Bengal who worked with Lobo had informed him of the backing he'd have. It would take that backing too, if he was going to pull off his plans.

Hell, come to think of it, all he needed was Cassie fighting for him. The halfling with the siren's voice and an ability to argue Breed Law as though she had written it herself.

"Your teams will be a benefit to the community," Dane agreed. "Once you've finalized your plans, contact me and I'll make certain you have whatever you need for security."

Dog's gaze sharpened on his friend. "Callan's and Wolfe's Breeds are making a mark with their military and rescue teams. Del Rey's Coyotes are aligned with the Wolf Breeds in Colorado and their own security forces and are in high demand. I've discussed this with the alphas. I think we're going to look more in the private sector rather than military or strike."

"Whatever you need to set up, Vanderale will be there for you." Dane nodded. "As it appears we're going to party tonight, I'll notify my men of the change in plans and prepare to move out. Shall we use the heli-jet to transport your mate back to town? I believe we can land behind her apartment building. It would make a statement."

A statement Rhyzan wouldn't miss.

"Let's slip in," Dog suggested instead. "Keep it quiet, everything under wraps until we arrive at the ball. Let's not give Rhyzan a chance to consider any options he may have."

Not until he knew his own backers were in place. Which meant he needed to make a few calls of his own and pull in a favor or two. And the support he had in mind would definitely make a statement.

And then he'd have to face a past he'd tried to ignore for far too many years but had never forgotten.

His father had always warned him that Major was in a position to know who Dog was, know he was a hybrid if Dog was ever in the public eye. As long as he stayed under the radar, then he'd been safe.

Not that safety had been his concern for a lot of years. Now it was of the highest importance. Because of his mate. Nothing could endanger his mate.

· CHAPTER 12 ·

DC Insider News

CONSORTING WITH THE ENEMY?

If the heading hadn't caught his attention as he sat down with his morning coffee, the picture of the rough-hewn, powerful male would have.

> Pictures were attained of the Breed princess, Cassandra Sinclair, in the arms of who insiders are claiming to be her lover.
>
> Known only as Dog, and according to several unidentified sources to be a known Genetics Council associate, the powerful Coyote Breed is listed as "rogue" within the national Breed database, meaning he's declared no affiliation with the legitimate Breed community and is suspected of crimes against Breed Law.
>
> Ms. Sinclair, known as the Breed's foremost legal expert where Breed Law is concerned, and a consultant for the Federal Bureau of Breed Affairs, couldn't be

reached for comment, but other sources within the Breed community claim the affair to be no more than a fling or possibly a hoax. They say a news release is expected soon announcing the engagement of Ms. Sinclair to none other than the assistant director of the Federal Bureau of Breed Affairs, Rhyzan Brannigan.

Ms. Sinclair, a known companion of Deputy Director Brannigan, is rumored to have already committed to the engagement. So why then was the Genetics Council Dog seen carrying Ms. Sinclair through the entrance of the Western Bureau of Breed Affairs in Window Rock?

The spokesperson for the Bureau of Breed Affairs, Tanner Reynolds, is promising a press release soon, and the arrival of Breed leaders Lupine Gunnar, Coy Delgado and Prime Lyons, along with their wives, has already been noted. Alphas of the largest packs and prides, as well as Ms. Sinclair's parents, Dash and Elizabeth Sinclair, are also known to be in attendance . . .

Senator Aaron C. Ryder's attention shifted from the article. He didn't give a goddamn about the Breed goings-on in general. It was like watching an animal shelter fucking free-for-all. And the damned masses were still so stupid over the animals that no matter their actions, the Breeds waltzed through the public like they owned it.

No, it wasn't the gossip or the lovefest googly-eyed article that had him shuddering. It was the picture.

The young Breed female was sheltered in the Coyote Breed's arms, her head resting on his shoulder. It was that Coyote's face that held him, had him tracking every plane and angle of the imposing features.

Sharp, gunmetal gray eyes were piercing behind thick, sand-colored lashes. A high forehead, an aristocratic nose, and an imposing chin. Generations had gone into perfecting those features and building the tall, powerful body. The Breed DNA that now marred them only sharpened them, made the body more powerful, stronger.

But still, an abomination.

Yet he couldn't take his eyes off the Breed's face. He'd suspected he existed—hell no, a part of him had known he'd existed. When his father's body had been returned, there hadn't been so much as a whisper of a child, but there was no doubt a child had been born of the mother.

Her body had been found nearly a year after the escape. The scientists who oversaw the autopsy were certain she'd died just after whelping the bastard.

His fist clenched in fury as he scrolled down, finding several other pictures of the Breed. Most were fuzzy, the features not really clear. The Coyote was called reclusive, secretive, never allowing pictures to be taken. He shouldn't have allowed that picture to be taken.

Because what he was could be revealed, and surely he didn't want that. No, no one wanted that, and it had to be stopped before it happened. It had to be stopped before the world learned that Ms. Sinclair could possibly whelp his child. A child no test on earth would reveal as a Breed. A child who could infect the world if it bred.

"Hey, Grandpa." The cheerful young woman who took her seat at the breakfast table had his head lifting, regret shaming him as he stared at her despite his return smile.

Those generations of careful selection had somehow bypassed this sweet girl. Her hair was a soft, nondescript brown, her eyes an unremarkable hazel. She was barely five-five, a little on the plump side, which he detested, but she loved him.

He was quite fond of her, just sorely disappointed in both her looks and her bearing. Finding her a husband should have been easy, would have been easy, but somehow it never quite worked out.

Not that he often regretted it, except for the fact that it still left him with no male heir. There was no way he could leave his fortune to this flighty, often forgetful child.

"Good morning, dear." He shuttered his tablet and laid it aside. "Tell me, how do you feel about a little trip out west with your grandfather . . ."

She was dressed in her customary slim black silk skirt, a sleeveless white silk blouse buttoned and tucked into the waistband, a thin black belt cinching her waist. The blouse was buttoned to just above the vee of her breasts, the tailored fit not snug, but complimenting her breasts, while the sleeveless cut displayed the silken flesh of her arms.

She wore stockings nearly the color of her skin, and the black four-inch heels that added to her height and, sometimes, her confidence. The long, rioting curls that normally tumbled around her were now pulled back from her face and woven into a loose braid, compliments of Dog.

As she walked across the hardwood floor of her apartment's living area and went over her arguments displayed on the tablet, she felt energized. She felt strong. She could feel that energy surging through her and welcomed it, knowing that when she stepped into that meeting, she'd be a force to be reckoned with.

Breed Law statutes danced within her head, all the various pieces fitting together and displaying each loophole to allow her to present a scathing, censorious statement against the actions taken by the assistant director of the Bureau of Breed Affairs.

As she worked, her focus was sharper than it had ever been before, her awareness of Dog somehow heightened. He'd worked with her through the night, going over the individual articles of the law and finding several areas she'd missed. She'd known he was highly intelligent, calculating and logical, but as they argued back and forth, tested each other against each argument, she realized he was also amazingly intuitive and possessed an understanding of law she hadn't expected.

He waited patiently now, leaning against the framed doorway leading into the bedroom. She'd had to threaten him with all manner of bodily harm to get him into the black silk slacks and gray shirt Dane had arrived with earlier. He'd glared at her, growled at her, swore he was going to spank her when he got her back to the apartment. He was wearing them, though, along with a pair of black leather boots that were possibly new as well.

His dark blond hair was combed back from his face, a little neater than his normally shaggy appearance, though she did like that rough bad-boy look, she had to admit. It wasn't just a look; he was indeed a bad boy, and he was hers.

She almost paused at that thought before she let it sink inside her, let herself accept it. Whatever the future held, whatever came from the meeting with the Cabinet, she knew he was hers, just as she belonged to him. She'd belonged to him since she'd stepped out on that balcony of Seth Lawrence's guest suite and felt Dog's crosshairs land on her.

And he belonged to her as well.

"Halfling, that look on your face is making me hard." The sexy rumble in his voice had her lifting her gaze from the tablet and fighting a grin.

"You're always hard. Wouldn't be a mating otherwise." She almost laughed at the mock glare he shot her.

Sometime that morning, she'd realized that many of the contradictory and confusing emotions that had been roiling inside her had merely been a process of acceptance. The Mating Heat ensured that mates had to work through those beginning conflicts, the changes and different views they held, to find that place where something deeper, something more enduring, was just waiting for them to find it.

They were finding it, she thought. She was certain of it.

"Keep it up and I'll do something about it again," he promised her, glancing at the digital display on the clock hanging on the wall. "And then we'll be late."

Again. He'd done something about it twice through the night. Once, bent over the back of the couch while he powered inside her, his voice hoarse as he whispered her name. Then, when they showered, his powerful arms holding her to him as her knees gripped his hips and she rode him with delirious pleasure.

For a second she considered letting him, before regretfully rejecting the idea.

"We need to leave." Turning from him, she strode to the dining table and the leather case bulging with files and exhibits in Breed Law statutes that backed her arguments.

"I'll get that." He reached around her and gripped the handle of the case, lifting it effortlessly from the table.

"Dog." She stopped him, laying her hand on his arm as he looked down at her, his gaze somber. "On that island, when I was eighteen," she said softly. "That night in the atrium." She paused, feeling something rush through her heart and causing it to race. "I knew you'd be there, waiting for me. Just as I knew over the years after that I belonged to you. I was frightened . . ."

He laid a finger against her lips, his expression softening, his lips quirking with a grin that was in no way mocking.

"You fight so many parts of yourself, Cassie," he said softly. "I've always known that, just as I knew you'd need time before dealing with a mating. Stop fighting everything so hard, baby. Don't you know, I'll always be here, watching over you. I won't let you get lost."

Tears pricked at her eyes before she quickly blinked them back.

"I won't let you get lost either, Dog." Did he know that? Did he really know he wasn't alone anymore?

"I haven't been lost since a halfling met my crosshairs and threw out her little dare." His head lowered, his lips brushing against hers in the lightest caress. "Now, let's go whip Brannigan's ass."

Stepping back from her, he held his hand out to her, and it was natural, it was just right, when his fingers clasped hers and he led her to the door.

No matter what came of the Cabinet hearing, no matter the decisions of others, she wouldn't stop fighting for what she was finding with him. Now, if she could just do something about that prickle against her skin, that inner knowledge that the danger wasn't necessarily the Cabinet meeting, or Brannigan.

Whoever the unidentified Major was was the true threat. And that threat was growing closer.

Western Bureau of Breed Affairs
Breed Cabinet Inquiry

The Breed Cabinet was made up twelve Breed members, including Prime and Prima Lyons, Lupine and Lupina Gunnar, and Coy and Coya Delgado, as well as Jonas Wyatt and Dash Sinclair; the newest Wolf pack alpha, Lobo Reever; a Bengal Breed representing the Navajo Nation, Graeme Parker; and Rule Breaker, the director of the Western Bureau of Breed Affairs.

Unlike the twenty-four-member Breed Ruling Cabinet, there was no one in the Breed Tribunal not affiliated with the Breed community, either a Breed or a Breed mate. There was no senatorial presence, though there were several senators in residence at the offices to oversee federal mandates as the new Bureau office established itself.

The drive from her apartment to the Bureau was a short one, though the accompanying Feline force Dane had loaned them had required extra time. As she stepped from the secured Dragoon into the underground parking garage, twelve cold-eyed, heavily armed Lion Breeds had surrounded them, along with Dane, and escorted them into the lower level of the offices.

During the brief drive, a message from Dr. Sobolova had been returned stating the mating capability tests with Rhyzan had come back negative, but the assistant director was still refusing to drop his petition. He demanded that the inquiry proceed.

Cassie made a mental note to make certain she scheduled time with the Breed Ruling Cabinet in the coming months to ensure this particular statute was changed. She felt as though she were being held hostage in a way, her future with her mate no longer under her and Dog's control.

Ahead, the wide double doors to the meeting room swung open and the Lion Breeds escorting them parted at the entrance to allow Dog, Cassie, then Dane to step inside.

The Cabinet members were waiting on the raised benches at the head of the room. Below, on each side of the room, two podiums waited next to accompanying tables.

Behind that and stretching five rows deep to the double doors were bench seats, though those behind Rhyzan were deserted. To the right, Drs. Armani and Sobolova were in the front row; behind them was Cassie's mother, and along with her were the Leo, Leo Vanderale, and his wife, Elizabeth, as well as the Coyote females Ashley and Emma Truing.

Cassie moved to the right of the room and stepped to the podium, Dog next to her behind a chair at the table, Dane to his left.

Rhyzan rose from the table where he waited and moved to his podium as well. His face was bruised, one eye black, his cheek swollen and his nose just slightly off-center as Dane had said.

The deputy director was an impressive figure despite his injuries; she'd always admitted that. Six and a half feet tall, long straight black hair and Celtic green eyes. The eyes were rather an unusual color for a Coyote, though. Like all Breeds, he was strong, genetically designed for rugged good looks and a powerful physique. Though she was beginning to think his genetics, unlike others', also leaned toward insanity.

With everyone present, Jonas rose from his seat placed at the center of the bench, and stared back at them.

"Are all parties present?" he asked.

"Present for the petition," Rhyzan answered him.

"Present for the objection." Cassie spoke clearly, a relaxed calm descending over her even as her senses became sharper, stronger.

Her head turned slowly toward Rhyzan as she inhaled slowly, her eyes narrowing on the Coyote as he stared back coolly.

His lips tilted into an icy, mocking smile as he turned back to Jonas. "Before we proceed, Director, I'd like to formally rescind my Petition for Reconsideration in light of the new mating tests that have come through. Though, as all parties are present, I request that the Coyote known as Dog be taken in for questioning regarding the disappearance of a Breed child present during the landing of the Council transport that held Ms. Sinclair's sister, Kenzi. According to her, there was a child between three and five years of age when she was placed in the transport but that child had disappeared by the time she regained consciousness."

Cassie froze.

No.

He couldn't do this.

"Dog?" Jonas asked as every member of the Cabinet stared back at him.

"There was no child present," Dog answered, and Cassie could feel his confusion.

Her jaw clenched at Rhyzan's demand as she glared up at Jonas, their gazes meeting for a long moment.

"According to Kenzi, the child was there. She's been questioned by three other interrogators and deemed to be telling the truth. In that at least." The amusement in Rhyzan's tone was unmistakable. "All parties present that night who are still living have been interrogated except Ms. Sinclair's mate."

He was ruining everything.

Damn him.

The son of a bitch was destroying her, and she hadn't even known it was coming.

She inhaled slowly, her gaze still locked with Jonas's.

"I suggest we adjourn . . . ," Jonas began.

"And I respectfully disagree," Rhyzan spoke up, causing Jonas to swing toward him as his lip lifted in a snarl. "Director Wyatt, you have consistently upheld Ms. Sinclair's actions within the Bureau, even when they've been questionable more than once."

"At what time have my actions or any decision I've made in my capacity with the Bureau been deemed questionable?" she asked, keeping her tone pleasant, nonconfrontational.

Rhyzan turned to her slowly, that icy gaze piercing. "We can discuss that during a review of your position. We're here to discuss your mate."

"Wrong." Turning back to the Cabinet, she faced them, her gaze sweeping over the members. "This Cabinet was convened to discuss Deputy Director Brannigan's Petition for Reconsideration. As that matter has been resolved, hopefully to everyone's satisfaction, then Deputy Director

Brannigan can file the proper paperwork to question my mate. Those requests can be sent directly to me, as I am his legal counsel. I will then file my requests and we can begin this farce he seems so determined to play out."

"Are you in agreement?" Jonas sounded as though the words were grinding from between his teeth as he turned to Brannigan.

"A waste of time," the Coyote objected, of course. "He's here now, as are the interrogators. An additional request will be made to question Ms. Sinclair, as she was apparently aware of her sister, Kenzi's, location before the transport landed in the desert that night. I'd like to know how."

Cassie turned, met Brannigan's gaze and smiled sweetly.

"That one's easy enough. I'll answer it now." She shrugged. "A ghost told me. Any other questions?"

Dislike. It suddenly shimmered in the air around him. Disgust. Why, the deputy director was a shade prejudiced against her. And evidently, he didn't care much for her flippancy either.

"A ghost told you?" he sneered. "Aren't you tired of playing that card, Ms. Sinclair? I believe your mate, in his capacity within the Council, informed you of the abduction and transportation of your sister and the other child that night. Just as I believe you've conspired with him in the past, especially concerning the minor child who was on that transport."

"Director Wyatt, your assistant's about to get an attitude adjustment." It was Graeme who spoke up, the lazy feline drawl rumbling with menace. "He isn't even attempting to hide the scent of his distaste or unfounded prejudice. Does that give all Breeds leave to foul the halls with their petty dislikes?"

It was the ultimate form of disrespect among Breeds and considered unacceptable where Breeds gathered together. Even Council Breeds kept that under control whenever they met other Breeds in public.

There was something more in Graeme's voice, though, something Cassie couldn't put her finger on, but she could sense it.

"Deputy Director Brannigan, it's also my understanding"—Graeme leaned forward, lazily playing with the pen he held as he stared down at the Coyote—"that two of the Wolf Breeds at your command were dismissed by Director Wyatt for the same infraction. Is this true?"

"My feelings, or total lack thereof, for Ms. Sinclair, are not the issue. Her disregard for Breed Law, as well as her mate's, is, though. And must be addressed," he argued with steely calm.

And he was good, damned good; she had to give him credit. Unfortunately, he really didn't have a leg to stand on with the Cabinet. They knew her; most there had practically raised her.

"It's almost my position that the Ruling Cabinet should be convened for this, considering the strong ties Ms. Sinclair has with each of you, and your overwhelming bias toward her," he finished.

Yeah, he was really good.

"I must admit, I've barely met Ms. Sinclair." Alpha Reever shot her a polite smile before turning back to Brannigan. "And I believe Alpha Parker and Ms. Sinclair have no more than been introduced. Yet I believe we'd agree that your request is outlandish, just as it was my opinion that your petition was. I agreed to hear the case out of disbelief that Wyatt allowed it."

"And as her alpha, I and my Prima have loudly protested it," Callan stated as an aside before turning to Coy Delgado.

Coy Del Rey Delgado let a mocking smile twist his lips. "I'm not much of a fan of Ms. Sinclair's, as it was her argument that separated me from my mate, at my mate's request, for nearly a year. But even I found the petition, and now this request to ignore protocol, outlandish. If the deputy director wants to interrogate Ms. Sinclair's mate, then he can file the proper requests. As for interrogating Ms. Sinclair?" He shook his head slowly. "I'd vote against it. Her ability to know things she shouldn't know, as I understand it, is one she's had since she was a child. And I rather doubt she conspired with her mate at age nine."

Each of the Cabinet members was given a chance to weigh in, and each agreed, as she'd known they would. As they spoke, she opened her senses, those instincts she'd always fought before, and allowed the ebb and flow of emotion in the room to drift through her.

Rhyzan was furious. But how could he have expected anything different?

"You know," Dog finally spoke up, a mocking, condescending drawl that had her gaze jerking around to him. "This is damned interesting." He took his seat, then sat back in his chair rather lazily. "All this protocol and opinion stating." He turned to Rhyzan. "Why don't you and I settle this like Breeds rather than wasting everyone's time like this? The last one still standing decides."

Dane lowered his head, shaking it slowly as he so obviously tried to control a grin.

"Works for me." Rhyzan's agreement was rather a surprise. "Now?"

"Not unless both of you want to be locked up." Jonas came to his feet once again, the demand in his voice unmistakable. "The laws drafted for this society were done so for a reason. Now, by God, you can adhere to them." He turned to Rhyzan, flashing him a savage look. "This Cabinet is adjourned, the petition that brought us here rescinded. Should you have other matters to bring before it, file the proper fucking paperwork."

Slamming his chair back, Jonas stalked from the bench, wrenched open the door leading back to a private room and slammed it closed furiously.

Cassie turned, watching as Rhyzan gathered his files

calmly, for all appearances not in the least concerned. But she could feel his fury, barely contained, boiling beneath the surface.

"He's going to be a problem," Dog stated, not bothering to lower his voice. "One I'll delight in taking care of." As he spoke, he slid a note her way.

Jonas is having Kenzi moved as we speak—Dane.

Thank God. Nodding, she turned around, her gaze finding her mother.

Elizabeth was watching her in concern, her dark blue eyes shadowed and worried. Whatever Rhyzan was up to, he'd picked a hell of a time to hit them with it. And now she had an additional worry. Someone else knew Lizette was alive.

Breathing out heavily, she turned back to Dog, her gaze glancing over the other Cabinet members as they stood talking, when it was snared by the Bengal's. She stared back at him, seeing a warning shifting in his gaze before he turned away from her and spoke to his mate.

She didn't know Graeme, but she knew Cat. Not well, but enough to know the other woman was more than a little concerned.

"I'm of the opinion that your life is far more interesting than I ever believed, halfling," Dog stated, drawing a cigar from his shirt.

"You can't smoke in here," she told him absently, looking around, watching, sensing some undefined message as it drifted about the room. A warning she couldn't decipher, a dark emotion so well hidden she couldn't locate it.

"Really?" A match flared, and the scent of tobacco lighting drew her attention back to him.

He was more than simply furious. Drawing on the cigar, he slid his gaze toward Rhyzan again before coming back to her. She could only shrug at his unspoken question. Hell, she had no clue what the other Breed's gripe against her was.

From the corner of her eye she watched as Rhyzan

gathered his briefcase and moved in their direction, finally stopping next to the table. Laying her hand on Dog's shoulder, she stared back silently.

"I've filed a request that you and your mate not leave the area," he stated, doing a good job of holding back a sneer. "The Cabinet will have the proper filings before the hour is out."

Dog's shoulders bunched, tension gathering in him as a growl rumbled in his chest.

Leo chose that moment to step to the table, his gaze locking on Rhyzan, the pure power of the demand in that look impossible for the Breed to miss.

Rhyzan inclined his head to the first Leo, then strode for the doors leading from the meeting room.

"He's a problem, that one," Leo stated as the doors closed behind the Coyote. "And he's not finished with this."

Dog snorted at the statement. "He better get finished, because there was no kid there that night." He rose to his feet slowly, his arm sliding around Cassie and pulling her to him. "But he keeps on in this direction, he's going to find himself in a mess of trouble he sure as hell doesn't want, and I'm going to make certain of it."

Stepping into his residential suite several hours later, Rhyzan closed the door slowly, all too aware that he hadn't
closed the curtains over the balcony doors when he'd left
that morning. The lights were out, leaving the room nearly
pitch-dark. Not that he needed lights, no more than the
Breed sitting across from him in the large easy chair
needed them.

Setting his briefcase aside, he walked to the bar and
poured himself a drink.

"Drink, Director Wyatt?" he asked.

"I helped myself." Jonas lifted the glass when Rhyzan
turned back to him.

He'd known Jonas for a lot of years, had seen him in a
variety of moods, and he'd thought he'd seen him at his
most furious. It was possible he'd been mistaken in that,
because what he was facing now went far beyond furious.

Sipping at his drink, Rhyzan stared across the room,
watching the Breed carefully, all too aware that the low rasping sound was claws against the upholstered arm of the chair,
the glow of those eerie silver eyes like pinpoints of light.

"Do you have a suicide wish?" The low, Feline sound of wrath whispered through the room. "Sinclair may not care much for his daughter's mate, but he is her mate. He'll kill you."

Yeah, he'd guessed that the day before when Sinclair tried to beat the hell out him. He'd taken that beating. He hadn't struck back, because he understood, he even expected it.

"If I don't beat him to it." The rasp deepened, the sound of the primal, fully emerged, causing the hairs at the back of his nape to lift in warning.

"The request wasn't intended as an insult," Rhyzan assured the other Breed.

"You stank of your prejudice, your dislike and disgust toward her." Those demon eyes flared as Jonas spoke. "You stood in front of an innocent young woman, one who has known nothing but danger, nothing but the risk of the horrors that could await her since she was a child, and insulted her with such base disregard that every Breed on that Cabinet was thirsting for your blood."

Yeah, he'd gotten that before he left. It would have been damned hard to miss. Unfortunately, it was exactly what he'd intended. He'd had no choice in what he'd done, though.

"The missing child—"

"There is no missing child." The growl deepened; canines flashed along with silver eyes. "Kenzi told you she thought she heard the guards discuss a child. There might have been a child. You lied."

Oh, there had been a child—Rhyzan had no doubt of that—but it really wasn't the child who concerned him. His initial investigation assured him that the girl was safe, possibly better protected than any of them.

The girl was a weapon, nothing more. A weapon he needed to threaten the freedom of the Coyote Dog and draw out an enemy he'd been stalking for years.

"I lied," he agreed. "But I'll continue to lie if I must. If

I have to, I'll have Dog dragged into a cell in chains and his mate languishing beside him if that's what it takes. I'd hate it," he assured the animal tensing to attack. "Believe that, Jonas, it wouldn't be a choice I made unless I'm left no other recourse. And all I can do is pray to God it doesn't come to that."

He wouldn't have a chance against a Primal Breed without some hellacious luck, Rhyzan admitted silently. Jonas could move with incredible speed when that creature came out to play, and avoiding those claws would be next to impossible.

When Jonas didn't speak, didn't move, Rhyzan blew out a weary breath.

"The disrespect you and the Cabinet scented was forced," he admitted. "I have the highest regard for Cassie and hated doing it. Just as I hated messing with the mating compatibility tests after she mated with Dog." Grimacing, he felt the tension rising, felt the Primal gathering itself to attack. "I suspect his grandfather is one of the twelve who head the Genetics Council. And his spies are here, in Window Rock."

Stepping across the room carefully, he strode to the safe inset in the wall, activated the panel that hid it and pushed in the digital code. Opening it, he retrieved the file he kept there and tossed it to the coffee table in front of the director.

"I've followed them for years," he told Jonas as one claw-tipped finger flipped the folder open. "The grandfather, then Dog and Cassie." There were pictures, many pictures.

"Sit," Jonas growled, with a jerk of his head to the couch next to him.

Stepping to the couch, Rhyzan sat down and leaned forward as Jonas placed three of the pictures next to one another.

The first, an army officer, the second a navy SEAL officer, and the third, the Breed Dog. Lifting a fourth picture,

Jonas laid it above Dog's and sat staring intently at the collage he'd made.

"Light." The growl was still a harsh rasp, but it no longer had Rhyzan's hackles raised.

Reaching to the lamp on the table next to them, Rhyzan flipped it on, watching the glow spill over the pictures.

"Why didn't you bring this to my attention?" Still rough, but easing a fraction more, the voice rumbled with displeasure.

"I would have, if I hadn't needed your anger, as well as Sinclair's, to lend credence to my supposed threat." Balancing his arms on his knees, he stared at the pictures. "I found reason to suspect some of the Wolf Breeds here at the Bureau feared Cassie, that their prejudice toward her genetics was making her a target. When word hit that she'd mated Dog, a transmission was picked up from the Bureau to his residence." He stabbed his finger at the army officer. "He showed up here at the Bureau yesterday, but before he arrived he met with the two Wolf Breeds Dog confronted outside her suite. He left when he learned Dog was back in town after having run with Cassie."

From the corner of his eye, he saw the claws tipping Jonas's fingers slowly ease back beneath the perfectly manicured nails and had to fight a breath of relief.

"He's a hybrid." Jonas glanced to him, his expression thoughtful.

"He's a hybrid." Rhyzan nodded. "And he's mated a hybrid. According to the belief many scientists share, hybrids will give birth to Breeds that can't be identified even with the deepest genetic testing. There will be no way to tell them from a human, and no way to eradicate Breeds completely if that happens."

"A true Cross Breed," Jonas murmured.

"He was here, Jonas." Rhyzan stared at him intently. "And the interest he's showing in the accusations against

Dog and Cassie isn't normal. Just because he left doesn't mean he's going to let his grandson go."

Rhyzan turned his gaze to the pictures. When laid side by side, it was impossible to deny they were related. Grandfather, father, son, and above them, a young, blond Coyote female.

"What happened to the parents?" Jonas asked.

"The Breed mother died from wounds sustained when they were nearly captured, just hours after giving birth to their son. The father disappeared, and the grandfather spent thousands trying to find him. Ten years later he was killed by a Coyote team that tracked him to Washington State. According to what I learned, they spent several weeks attempting to learn if he'd been seen with a child but found no evidence to support it."

Jonas closed the folder slowly over the pictures.

"Anyone else know your suspicions?" he asked.

"No one," he answered. "He's slick. He's on the Breed Ruling Cabinet, plays the Breed benefactor and manages to get information he should never have access to."

"What proof do you have he's one of the twelve?" Jonas pinned him with those eerie eyes again.

"The father." Rhyzan gestured to the file with one hand. "He had a sister. When he disappeared, she managed to wire him a couple hundred thousand when he contacted her. About a year after his death, as the Breed rescues were at their height, she received a letter he'd had arranged to be sent if something happened to him. She was killed several months later, but her daughter recently found that letter and contacted me."

A fucking stroke of luck. He'd been in shock for weeks after he'd met with her and she'd turned it over to him.

Opening the file, Rhyzan pulled the envelope free and laid it on top of the pictures.

"He knows Dog is his grandson," he said softly, laying

his finger against the envelope and staring at Jonas as the Breed turned his head slowly, their gazes meeting. "He has no heir now. He knows that hybrids can possibly breed a child that can't be identified as a Breed. And he knows they've mated."

"Cassie hasn't conceived," Jonas pointed out softly.

"Yet . . ."

Reaching out, Jonas once again closed the file. "Do you have digital copies?"

Rhyzan nodded in a short, tight movement.

"I'll take this, then." Picking up the file, he rose to his feet and walked toward the door. "Stay away from Cassie and Dog until I finish this, or I'll kill you."

The door closed quietly behind him.

Rhyzan rubbed his hands over his face, shook his head and rose to his feet to collect his briefcase. He'd file the requests to interrogate Dog. The last thing Senator Ryder would want was for his grandson to be convicted under Breed Law. That would draw far too much notice.

He didn't care much for his granddaughter, according to the girl. He tolerated her, he'd raised her after her mother's death, but she'd always suspected her mother had been murdered. She'd drowned in the family pool. An excellent swimmer who rarely drank, yet she'd been found facedown in the pool and the autopsy revealed a high level of alcohol in her system.

She'd loved her brother, worried about him. He was her big brother. The fact that he'd disappeared and ordered her not to tell their father he'd contacted her when he'd disappeared had led her to suspect her father was behind her mother's death.

Senator Ryder. He'd bought his way into politics and used his influence and good-ole-boy façade to engender a level of trust, even among some Breeds. He played Breed benefactor without even a whiff of his murderous hatred for them. He was the ultimate liar, the ultimate monster.

And Rhyzan was determined to unmask him. With or without Jonas's help.

❖   ❖   ❖

"You want to tell me what the hell happened down there?" Dog closed the door to the suite he and his mate were shown to after the hearing, watching her as she paced across the room, rubbing at her arms as she stared at the floor.

During the time he'd sat and listened to Rhyzan's bullshit, he'd decided he was going right out and buying a fucking cape and some goddamned blue tights, because when it came to sheer self-control, he was fucking Superman.

"I'm not quite certain." She shook her head, her confusion genuine as she said the words, her bafflement growing.

Dropping her leather case on the chair next to the bar, he unlocked his jaw, a sound of pure aggravation rasping from his throat. Pouring himself a drink, he considered the liquor for a moment, tossed it back and promised himself he was going to get something stronger real damned soon.

"So we're just going to stay here and let him serve me up to a few interrogators without so much as a protest?" He snorted at that thought, anticipation rising inside him. "I've not had a good fight in a while. Might be fun."

He'd kill the bastards with his bare hands.

She was silent, not even protesting the threat. She stood next to the balcony doors just behind one side of the curtains and stared out at the sun-drenched landscape.

"Jonas won't allow it," she said quietly. "And even if he did, the Cabinet members wouldn't."

"You put too much faith in them," he warned her, wondering what the hell that look on her face was all about.

It was the same look she'd gotten when Rhyzan had asked about that kid who didn't exist. Haunted, almost fearful.

He narrowed his eyes on her, poured himself another drink and considered her for long moments.

He'd always known Cassie kept a lot of secrets locked

inside her. It showed sometimes in the weariness of her expression, the haunted shadows in her eyes. He had a feeling that this time, though, the secret Cassie was keeping could burn both of them.

"Where's the kid, Cassie?" He asked the question, wondering if she would lie to him.

She froze for a second, then with a heavy sigh, shook her head. "I don't know. I don't know where she is."

At least she was honest with him.

"But there was a kid, wasn't there? When that transport landed, Kenzi wasn't alone." He stalked across the room as she faced him, glowering down at her.

"I don't know." The barely smothered cry was filled with pain, with confusion. "All I knew then, and now, was if she wasn't there when Kenzi was found, then she was safe and where she was supposed to be. I don't know anything else."

As she pushed past him, the scent of all those bottled emotions, fears, unshed tears and pain lashed at his senses. Turning, he watched as she faced him again, her lips tight, her exotic eyes gleaming with moisture.

"How did you know about her and Kenzi to begin with? Who came to you?" Which spirit, ghost of whoever, whatever the hell it was?

When she turned back to him, he could see the torment on her face. "I've felt Kenzi for a couple of years, felt this coming. I didn't know who she was, not until the night I contacted you. For years events have interconnected, always drawing me toward her. And I knew she was important." Her fists clenched as emotion tightened her face. "I didn't know it was my sister."

Cassie stared back at Dog as he stood near the window, watched his expression, the almost calculated look in his narrowed eyes.

"How did you know those events were connected? Walk me through this, Cassie. Make me understand it before Rhyzan hangs me out to dry here."

And the assistant would do it too. Whatever he wanted, whatever he was after, he was more than willing to use her and Dog however he had to, to get to it.

When had it begun?

That summer on Seth Lawrence's island, she realized. It was that first knowledge that the successful mating of Seth Lawrence and the cougar Breed Dawn Daniels was so integral to her future.

From there, smaller events, people who had come into her life, and odd occurrences, until she'd found herself in Window Rock the year before accepting Jonas's offer that she head the Breed Underground Information Network. The division of the Bureau was created to pull in information and track the movements of Genetics Council sympathizers and supporters and those groups that followed them.

Odd flashes of knowledge, a feeling of connection, of knowledge that someone so integral to her own freedom was waiting for her, that they needed her.

As she spoke, trying to find the words to make Dog understand that it hadn't been a matter of something telling her, or even showing her. It was that connection. It was a sudden flash of intuition, a meeting, looking into someone's eyes and knowing where they should be.

"The night you contacted me, you knew where that transport would be and when," he reminded her. "How did you know?"

She licked her dry lips, knowing he'd ask that question. She'd known that question was coming.

"Chelsea Martinez, mate to Graeme's brother Cullen, was part of the Breed Underground Network," she said faintly. "The day I met her, the year before, I knew who her mate was, and I knew she was integral to my freedom. When the emergency alert her bodyguard, Tobias, managed to activate the night I contacted you sounded in the Network's central command, I felt Kenzi slam into my senses, begging me for help."

That sudden connection had nearly taken her to her knees. Cassie barely remembered rushing to her office, fumbling, fighting to find Dog's contact information on her phone and send that message.

She'd been on the verge of sobbing in terror when suddenly the connection to her sister had severed just as quickly as it had come to her.

"The kid was there with her?" Dog was watching her closely.

Cassie nodded as her gaze slipped, drawn to the window behind him. Why her attention moved, she wasn't certain. The sun-drenched desert was always beautiful, but it wasn't the beauty that had her glancing from his eyes to the scene beyond. And it wasn't the beauty of that tranquil scene that had the window popping, a baseball-sized fault suddenly appearing.

She heard Dog curse, felt him slam into her and take her to the floor as a steady *pop-pop-pop* could be heard just below the alarms suddenly screeching through the Bureau's intercom system. Dog's curses were ringing in her ears as they hit the floor, close to the door as it exploded open.

"Move!" the shouted order came as Dog dragged her through the door at the same time that the sound of the window shattering behind them could be heard.

She came to her feet, kicking off one shoe, uncertain what happened to the other as Breed Enforcers surrounded them and rushed them along the halls.

"Teams are heading out," the Coyote Breed, Mordecai, yelled as alarms continued to blast through the halls. "Security has a location narrowed down; our enforcers are flying in."

She could feel Dog's arm around her waist as he raced down the hall, nearly lifting her off her feet at times as he kept her close to him. They pushed through the basement doors and within minutes they were on the basement floor and pushing through the doors to Information Command.

"Stay here." Dog swung her around to face him, glaring down at her as he hurriedly strapped on a weapon, his gray eyes cold, hard. "Right here until I get back."

"Make sure you come back, Dog," she ordered him. "Don't you leave me alone. Don't you dare leave me alone."

The very thought that he wouldn't come back wasn't something she could bear. She couldn't face it.

"Not even for a heartbeat." His hand curved around the back of her neck, his head lowering, his lips suddenly catching hers in a kiss that rocked her entire body despite its brevity.

And in that heartbeat, he was gone, pushing through the doors of the room and barking out orders. Savage, hard. Determined.

Her mate.

◆   ◆   ◆

Dark had fallen before Dog made it back to the Bureau. They'd found the sniper's nest, but the only scent to be found was a faint human scent and that of the weapon used. High-grade sniper rifle and matching ammo. The shooter had come on a dirt bike and left the same way just minutes after the satellite that watched over the Bureau began read-justing position.

Someone knew the right time to be there, and exactly where the teams patrolling the desert would be. It was just a matter of timing, but what made them think that bullet would penetrate a window rated to take a much more powerful strike?

They'd known the window would fail, which meant someone had already sabotaged the window's high-grade electronics.

By the time they returned to the Bureau, the Breed investigators had already gone over the shattered debris, found the corrupted electronics and had the evidence in one of the labs. Now the apartment he and Cassie were being given instead was being checked for similar defects in the windows and balcony doors.

And the question remained. Was it a strike against him or against his mate?

Stepping into Cassie's former room, he came to a hard stop just inside the door, eyes narrowing on the two unfamiliar visitors. The two Wolf Breeds standing next to the window weren't the investigators Jonas had assigned to go over the room and the window's electronics.

"Can I help you boys?" he drawled as he stopped just inside the door and allowed Mutt and Mongrel to move around him, flanking him carefully.

The two Breeds, both tall, one with hints of auburn in his brown hair, the other black-haired with hints of dark gray and pale blond strands, tensed at his entrance. They faced him silently, their eyes moving from Mutt and Mongrel back to him.

"We were just looking," the darker Breed assured him, quiet confidence echoing in his voice as his pale green eyes met Dog's.

Dog's brow lifted, his gaze dropping to the shards of the window beneath their feet.

"You're not the investigators," he pointed out.

"True." The Breed inclined his head, the scent of confidence, of inner strength and control, never shifting. "Merely curious."

Hmm. Curiosity was a Breed fault, he admitted. He had plenty of it himself. Still, this didn't feel like mere curiosity; this felt more like an agenda to him.

"Satisfied that curiosity yet?" he inquired, moving farther into the room, drawing in the scents he found there as he kept his gaze on the two Breeds.

"Not really." The Breed sighed and looked around slowly before meeting Dog's gaze once again. "But we'll go now. Pardon the intrusion."

Now, who said Breeds couldn't be polite? Not that they were, but this proved this one knew how to be.

Dog didn't move. He remained in front of the doorway, watching as the Breed stopped several feet from him.

There might have been a gleam of amusement in the hard features as their gazes met again.

"Names," he stated softly, one hand settling on the weapon strapped to his thigh.

The Breed's lips tilted in a wry curve. "John Kodiak." His head tilted toward the more watchful Breed. "Troy Rain."

Then they waited.

The air of steady watchfulness never shifted. Not once was there a hint of aggression, hatred or conflict. They just stood there, all patient and easygoing, waiting on Dog to shift.

"Not going to happen." He grinned, his hand gripping the holstered weapon as Mutt and Mongrel did the same. "So, tell me, John Kodiak and Troy Rain. What's the sudden interest in my window that failed electronics don't explain?"

The two Wolf Breeds stared back for long moments.

"Warned ya," Rain muttered, amused and irritated at the same time, as Kodiak shifted a look his way.

Dog arched his brow and kept his attention on the more silent Breed. If danger came, it would be from this one, he knew. That air of calm that surrounded the Breed had to be a shield of sorts. There wasn't a Breed alive that calm and centered.

"We're no danger to you or to your mate," Kodiak assured him. "As I said, we were just checking it out."

"Hmm." Dog pursed his lips. He was highly doubtful of that. "You know I don't believe you, right?" he pointed out.

Kodiak nodded slowly. "Yeah. I was getting that feeling."

"Want to tell me something I'll believe?" he asked. "Or do you want to fight your way out?"

Kodiak gave him an ironic grin. "That our only choice? Hell of a day when a Breed can't even be a little curious. It's not like you and your mate haven't been moved out of here."

He had a point, Dog admitted silently.

"Fight or talk," Dog suggested.

The Breed stared back at him thoughtfully, his body shifting but not in preparation to fight. Or if he was, Dog was damned if he could sense it.

That damned air of complete nonconflict was fucking freaking him the hell out just to begin with. Any Breed that right with himself and who and what he was needed to die, just for the safety of all Breeds everywhere.

"Tell me," Kodiak finally asked softly, his voice lower, his gaze thoughtful. "What do you know about your father?"

CHAPTER 15

Nothing.

Cassie glared at the reports coming in on the tablet she carried as she and Ashley stepped from the elevator and headed up the hall to the apartment she and Dog had been assigned.

Her irritation level was rising along with the Heat sizzling in her body, and she wasn't dealing with it well . The message she'd received from Dog more than an hour before informing her that he was delayed wasn't sitting well with her either.

She knew he'd returned to the building long before that. The diagnostics on the remains of the window had come through even before he'd returned, so he couldn't be waiting on that. Jonas and Rule along with the deputy director, Rhyzan Brannigan, were currently in a meeting with Seth Lawrence and his mate, Dawn, in regard to the window. Lawrence Industries manufactured the glass and electronics that reinforced the windows the Bureau used.

The disquiet she could feel gathering in the pit of her stomach was making her off-balance, the irritation was growing, and the Heat was so damned uncomfortable she swore she was going to break out in a sweat.

"All reports are in, Cassie," Ashley stated as she followed her. "Even those from the dark web, and there's not so much as a whisper of a Breed strike from anyone."

Not even a whisper. There was a whisper, there always was; she just had to find it. And normally, she was damned good at finding those all-but-silent murmurings. But then, normally, her body wasn't rioting for a mate's touch either.

"Tell them to keep looking," she ordered the other Breed, frowning as she tried to make sense of what she was feeling. "I want to know who that shooter was and who hired them. And I want that information now."

"Well, now is a little illogical," Ashley drawled, the Russian accent filled with mirth. "How 'bout quickly?"

Smart-ass Coyote.

Stopping at the door to the apartment, Cassie slapped her hand to the biometric plate, waited for the door to disengage, then strode into the room.

"Fine, *quickly*," she snapped, the heels of her shoes clicking across the tile entryway. "Real quick if you don't mind."

"Cassie, really, we'll work our Coyote asses off to find it, if it's out there," the Breed assured her with a vein of flippant amusement. "But so far, there's nothing."

There was always something. There had to be more than they'd found so far.

Laying her tablet on the counter separating the roomy kitchen and living area, she turned to the Coyote as her hands propped on her hips and fought for patience.

"Do you know how many times one of the windows created by Lawrence Industries has failed due to a strike such as the one today?" The back of her neck was tingling, her stomach tight with worry.

"That I could find. The only failures were those caused by outside interference. Three, I believe." Cocking a hip, the petite blond Coyote Breed consulted her own tablet. "Each was due to interference to the electronic shielding." She looked up, gray eyes regarding Cassie in understanding. "Diagnostics found the jamming chip and Jonas and Rule will find the shooter."

The confidence Ashley displayed was starting to piss her off.

"Not without a direction to look," she forced out between gritted teeth. "That's our job."

"And we will do our job." Ashley flipped her hair behind her shoulder with a little shrug. "While we do our job, you need to jump your mate's bones and relax a little. You know this will take a minute."

A minute? They'd been at it for hours.

Unfortunately, Ashley was right. Cassie couldn't think clearly, not like this. Not when everything inside her was rioting with the need for Dog.

"I'll go and harass Coyote ass to work faster." Ashley turned for the door as Dog's scent reached Cassie, drawing her, sending the need spiraling as she pivoted toward the doorway to the far side of the room.

He stood, leaning against the door frame, regarding her quietly, his gaze somber rather than amused. He was bare chested, his feet naked. He'd showered if the dampness of his hair was an indication. The dun-colored pants he wore were zipped but not buttoned, and beneath them she could see the heavy bulge that indicated his erection.

The door closed behind Ashley with a quiet *snick*, leaving them alone, staring across the distance that separated them.

That disquiet she could feel had her stomach in knots now.

"Did you find anything at the site?" She knew the reports so far said they hadn't, but sometimes there were holes in the reports, she knew.

"Just what we sent you." He shook his head, grimacing. "Rule sent trackers out searching for the dirt bike, but he's not optimistic. Once it hits the highway, it'll be impossible to track."

She wanted to go to him. She needed to touch him. There was something that held her back, though, something that didn't make sense. Swallowing, she glanced to the curtains closed over the balcony doors and rubbed at her arms nervously.

"Southern view." She turned back to him. "There's no satellite gap there. They won't be able to make the same attempt."

He followed her gaze but didn't respond. When his gaze met hers once again, she could feel her heart beginning to race with a sense of fear.

"What's wrong?" she whispered, unable to bear the tension rising inside her any longer.

Where were the spirits, the vague images that once guided her, that helped her when she so desperately needed answers? For the first time since they'd mated, she felt a distance in Dog, despite the mating bond that had been strengthening between them.

And it had been strengthening, building, binding them together and giving her a sense of hope that it would be more than just a physical mating for him.

"Nothing's wrong." He finally shook his head, holding his hand out to her. "I need my mate, though."

She stared at his hand, moving slowly to him, hating the fear rising inside her and the uncertainty building like a premonition of danger humming in her head.

Reaching out, she took his hand and let him lead her into the bedroom. A low light glowed from the table next to the king-sized bed. The comforter and sheet were pulled back invitingly. Despite the arousal burning inside her, a chill raced up her spine as he drew her to the bed.

"Something's wrong," she whispered as he sat on the side of the bed and drew her between his knees. "I can feel it, Dog."

Her hands rested on his shoulders, the warmth of his flesh sinking into her palms.

"Nothing's wrong, baby," he whispered.

Releasing the braid and pulling apart the sections of her hair, he arranged them gently before turning to her clothes.

The zipper at the back of her skirt slid free, the silk caressing as it slid over the tops of her stockings to the floor. When it pooled at her feet, he began unbuttoning her blouse unhurriedly.

"I was so damned hard watching you in that Cabinet meeting I couldn't decide if I should rip Rhyzan's throat out or drag you out of there and fuck you." His lips quirked ruefully as he pushed the blouse over her shoulders, forcing her to move her arms to allow the material to follow the skirt.

"Look how pretty," he crooned, his gaze moving from the white lace of her bra to the matching high-cut panties.

His hands framed her breasts, his touch sending a wave of weakening pleasure and need to rush over her, almost obliterating the fear that had been building inside her.

His thumbs rubbed over her nipples, rasping the lace against the tight points and drawing an involuntary groan from her as she fought to breathe.

"You make me weak," she whispered, trembling at the pleasure rushing through her and pushing the need higher.

"You make me strong."

Before the surprise, the shock of his statement, could race through her, his hand cupped the back of her neck as he gripped her hip and pulled her to him.

His lips covered hers, parting them in a kiss she realized she'd been dying for. As her senses were whirling from the sudden rush of the mating hormone burning through her, he lifted her from her feet, bringing her to her back and coming over her.

Deep, drugging kisses, nips of her lips, his tongue stroking hers, hers stroking his. Fear, disquiet, dissipated beneath the extraordinary pleasure and the sense of his complete attention centered on her.

They'd battled, argued. When they'd come together, conflict and uncertainty had filled it before. There was no conflict, no uncertainty. There was just his complete attention centered on nothing but her, and hers followed suit.

He released the cups of her bra, drawing it from her, but when her hands returned to stroke his shoulders, his back, her nails flexing against the tough skin, a groan rumbled in his chest. He cupped her breast, his lips moving along her neck, burning kisses, the scrape of his teeth.

Their legs twined together, reminding her that he still wore pants. She wanted him naked against her, wanted his flesh stroking hers, the feel of his erection against her.

She pushed at the band of his pants, crying out when his lips covered the tight peak of her nipple. Arching, swamped with the sharp arcs of exquisite sensation, she was only barely aware of him releasing the pants and working them over his hips, down his thighs until he kicked them free.

His lips drew on first one sensitive nipple, then the other, drawing it in his mouth, sucking it firmly, his tongue rubbing at it, the hormone spilling from him sensitizing it further.

"I love your taste." The guttural pleasure in his voice had her breath catching.

His kisses moved lower. Soft licks as his lips smoothed beneath the mounds of her breasts, then moving along her stomach as he slid her panties down her thighs, revealing the slick, swollen folds of her sex.

Pushing her thighs apart, he moved between them, those diabolical kisses moving to her mound.

"So fucking pretty," he groaned, his fingers caressing her inner thighs, his breath caressing the swollen bud of her clit. "All I can think about is touching you, tasting you. From the minute I saw you on that damned balcony six years ago, Cassie. I dreamed of this."

Her breath caught, a cry escaping as he delivered a heated kiss to her clit. Each brief, firm caress caused the bundle of nerves to swell further, to throb with overwhelming pleasure. Flares of brilliant, white-hot sensation rushed through her, clenching her muscles in desperate need.

Those kisses turned from her clit to her thigh, teeth raking, rasping her flesh. She jerked at the additional sensation, moaning, her hands locked in his hair as her hips arched.

"Don't tease me," she gasped, her head tossing against the mattress as those kisses moved to her other thigh.

"Not teasing, halfling," he promised, his voice rougher, deeper with lust. "Enjoying you. Pleasuring you."

He was killing her with pleasure.

His kisses moved to her hip, where he nipped, licked, leaving a burning brand against her flesh that had her crying in pleasure. Heat built and expanded, drawing a fine film of perspiration over her flesh. He moved her hands from his hair, pressed them to the bed, growling with erotic command when she tried to lift them to him again.

She couldn't bear this slow, blissful pleasure. As his lips and tongue caressed her, his hands stroked her thighs, pushing them farther apart as she tried to close them to trap his touch between them.

He chuckled when his lips brushed over her clit and she arched, trying to capture a firmer touch.

"Dog, please." She wasn't above begging. "I can't stand it."

She was dying for more. The heated slide of moisture spilling from her was a tormenting caress. The involuntary clenching of her vagina only made the need deepen.

Dog was determined to love her, to touch her, to draw every nuance of her inside him.

Just in case.

Just in case he lost her. Just in case he never had the chance to touch her like this again.

He touched, stroked. He tasted.

The taste of her was exquisite. He knew no matter what tomorrow brought, the taste of her would infuse his senses as long as he lived. It would live inside him, torment him if he never tasted her again.

He could feel her losing herself in him, and he'd dreamed of it happening. Dreamed of the day when his little halfling was so lost in the pleasure he gave her she could only lie beneath him, her cries filling the air around them.

The sweet heated scent of her pussy filled his head as his kisses moved back to her thighs. Her clit peeked out from the slick folds, a moist little pearl swollen and shimmering with the need for his touch.

He was so damned hungry for her, desperate to taste the need spilling from her. Knowing once his lips returned to those wet folds he'd be lost. There would be no controlling his lust for her then, no controlling the hunger surging through his senses.

But as his lips brushed against the sweet taste of her again, he knew he was lost. He had to taste.

His tongue swiped through the narrow slit, circled the swollen bud, and he groaned in defeat. Spicy feminine need exploded through his senses, the underlying sweetness tempting his taste buds. A temptation he couldn't fight.

The first stroke of his tongue through the sensitive folds between her thighs stole her breath. Cassie gasped, her body drawing at the agonizing pleasure that rushed through her on a sharp wave of building sensation.

He circled her clit, sucked it into his mouth and stroked it with his tongue. Pushing his hands beneath her rear he lifted her closer, that wicked tongue sliding lower once again, rimming the entrance and pushing inside her in a stroke of such pleasure she would have screamed if she'd had the breath.

Each impalement sent her senses screaming with the building sensation, drowning in the ecstasy she could almost reach, almost feel exploding through her.

"That's it, baby," he groaned, pulling back, his voice serrated. "Do it again, Cassie. Ride my tongue."

The thrust inside her had her vagina tightening, rippling with a ferocity of need that had her hips arching, mindlessly doing as he demanded, riding each thrust, fighting to reach that edge of madness where only ecstasy existed.

Just as she was certain she could reach it, certain she'd explode into shards of pleasure, his head jerked back.

"No. No . . ." Reaching for him, desperate now, need whipping through her in a storm of such sensation she didn't know if there was a way to survive it.

Her eyes came open as he jackknifed between her thighs. Pulling her up, he flipped her to her stomach, his hands gripping her hips, lifting them until her knees were beneath her as he came over her.

His teeth locked in the mark at her shoulder as the head of his cock parted the folds of her sex and began pressing inside her. The steady, stretching penetration had her back arching, whipping, agonizing pleasure radiating from the steady impalement.

A growl vibrated at her back, his teeth holding her still, keeping her in place as he worked his erection inside her. She couldn't survive this. Her eyes closed as a smothered wail left her lips and he drove in to the hilt.

She could feel her vagina struggling to ease despite the steady throb of his cock and each pulse of pre-cum that spilled inside her. He didn't give her a chance to catch her breath, to find herself within the storm of sensation tearing through her body.

Holding her to him with one hand beneath her hips, his teeth at her shoulder, he began thrusting inside her, his groans mixing with her cries as she gripped him, her muscles rippling in contracting pleasure with each stroke inside her.

It was killing her. He was killing her with the steady building sensations, pushing her higher with each thrust inside her until she was sobbing, begging.

"Please . . ." She tried to scream, but the sound was a gasp, agonized, as she shuddered, shaking with need. "Oh God, Dog, please . . . please . . ."

The snarling growl at her shoulder had her tensing. His thighs bunched and the thrusts drove inside her then. Deep, hard, penetrating her fully with each stroke and pushing her over that agonizing edge straight into rapture.

A rapture that refused to end. Hard, blinding explosions ripped through her body in an orgasm that seemed never ending. The feel of his release, the pressure of his cock swelling inside her, locking him to her, stole the last measure of reality.

The emotions that tore through her in that moment were like a kaleidoscope of color whipping through her, mixing with the blinding ecstasy, throwing her into a place that made no sense. A place filled with such love, so much love and devotion, and riding those soul-deep feelings was a pain she couldn't define.

How long it lasted, she didn't know. Reality was something that didn't exist, didn't matter, as she was rocked with ecstasy and emotion. She was aware of collapsing beneath him, his body still locked with hers.

His teeth released her shoulder as his head rested against hers, his breathing as harsh as her own.

"You carry my soul," he whispered as she felt exhaustion dragging her down. "My sweet, beautiful little halfling, you're all that's good inside me."

And she could have sworn she heard grief echo in his vow.

CHAPTER 16

God help him but he loved her.

As he stared down at her, memories of the battles he'd fought to claim her drifted through his head.

Hell, how many times had he nearly been caught just trying to get close to her? To hear her laughter, see her smile, to smell the unique, tempting scent of her. She'd been his dream and he'd become better for her.

A lifetime of living in the shadows, believing he lived only for the day that he'd find the man responsible for his parents' deaths, had changed the day his gunsights had landed on her.

The little halfling the Council was willing to pay a fortune no man could spend to attain. They wanted her unmated, a virgin, her unique genetics unspoiled by the hormone that would tip the scales in either direction and allow them to use her to further experiment.

Mated, her only value was that of any other mate, unless she conceived. And having mated a Coyote, she would be of even less value to them. It was generally agreed that the Coyotes were even more of a failure than the other Breeds.

Shiftless and lazy, they were called. Good only for killing, and at the end of the day, they rarely did even that as they were ordered.

More than a century and a half of genetic mutations, alterations, countless deaths and horrors, and still, they continued as though what they searched for actually existed. Though only God knew what they actually searched for.

They wouldn't find it with his mate now. Though they'd likely never realize just what they had truly created and what her life had finally allowed to emerge. A natural female alpha. Son of a bitch, he'd mated not just the only halfling living, but the only known emerging natural female alpha.

All Breed females were strong, but just as in the wild, females normally didn't lead, and it wasn't just due to physical strength. They lacked the sheer cunning and ability to instantly size up the males' weaknesses and use those against them. But it was also that unnamed something—a natural presence that radiated from the core of an alpha—that created leaders.

Cassie possessed all of the above. She would have stood at his side, never behind him. As those genetics matured and the inherent intelligence and quick wit grew within her, she'd become a force for the Breed society unlike any other.

Hell, she was already that, he admitted. They called her the Breed princess for a reason. She was the beauty, innocence, intelligence and inner strength that Breeds and humans both found impossible to resist.

And she was his mate.

For such a very short time, he'd held her.

Dog couldn't remember a time in his life when he'd cried. He couldn't even remember a time when he'd wanted to cry. He'd known regret, lost friends in the battle to survive, seen horrors that he still relived in his nightmares. But at no time in his life had he wanted to shed tears until he lay next to his mate and knew that when he forced himself from the bed, he was leaving her.

Staring into her delicate face, he traced the slope of her brow, the stubborn curve of her chin, that endearing tilt of her nose. The playful curve of her lips.

He'd watched her smile often, heard her laughter. She found hope in the world, in their world, despite the fact that so many would steal that hope if they could.

She fought for the Breeds with fierce determination, but as she stood in that Cabinet meeting defending him, he'd felt something reaching out from her that he'd never felt from anyone else. Determined, fierce, she'd reached out to everyone in that room with a silent declaration of loyalty. Loyalty for him.

His halfling.

What the hell was he going to do without her? Because God knew when this night was over, he'd be dead or brought up on charges for murder. And the murder of a United States senator wasn't something that could be hidden.

It was funny. He could remember when he was ten, hours spent with his father in the mountains of Washington. Dog had never known his father's name; he'd just been Father, a somber, hardened SEAL. But when he'd gazed at Dog, the ten-year-old he'd been had known his father's love.

He didn't hug the son he called Cain; he'd been damned hard on him to ensure that Dog knew how to survive during the times his father was forced to leave him for supplies. Dog hadn't realized until he was older that his father couldn't afford to be seen with a child, just in case he was found. Because if Dog had been found with the man he knew as his father, then the hell he faced, he might not have survived.

A hybrid Breed hadn't been heard of then, but scientists had dreamed of overcoming the original genetic model to see one born. They hadn't realized that Breeds needed far more than humans did to conceive. Breeds needed that one person, that one heart and soul that belonged only to them.

And Dog had thought he could finally claim his.

Now, staring at his mate, Dog found himself doing something else he'd never done. Regretting the choice he had to make.

He'd thought he could finally claim his mate, that he could finally carve out a chance at a future with this woman. He'd watched her grow from an uncertain eighteen-year-old to a strong, determined young woman. He'd watched her cry and laugh and he'd seen her play, and he'd wanted a chance to do all those things with her.

The realization that it was something he'd never have sliced through his soul with razor sharpness.

His halfling.

The inner strength and incredibly determined will rising inside her would make her a force to be reckoned with. The Wolf and Coyote genetics were fully merging as she reached maturity, at which point the aging would slow to a crawl.

She'd begin adapting, strengthening, and he'd thought he'd be there to watch it, to learn how to play with her, how to show her how he loved her.

There was so much he'd wanted to show her. Cassie had never been free. She'd never had the freedom to see the world as she should have, without a wall of bodyguards surrounding her. Not that she'd ever be able to be without security, even with him, but he could have given her a measure of freedom as well.

Dane would take care of the Breeds that had followed him for so many years. They were natural spies, able to adapt and become who and what they needed to be. They'd survive without him. Dr. Sobolova could ease the symptoms of the Mating Heat with the treatments she'd refined for the Coyote Breeds.

Cassie wouldn't suffer and that was all that mattered.

Touching the curls that rioted along the side of her face,

he tested one, watched it spring back into place and wanted to howl in rage. His fingers fisted in the silky curls, the warmth of them like a brand against his palm.

He had to force himself to release her, and it took every ounce of strength he possessed to make himself leave the bed. To separate himself from the heat of her body and the comfort he found just lying next to her.

He'd waited six years, waited for her to grow up, until he knew she could handle her emerging strength. And he thought he'd be there to guide her through it.

Hatred welled inside him as he dressed, never taking his eyes from his sleeping mate. When he finished, he grabbed up his pack and slipped from the bedroom, then from the apartment.

Closing the door silently behind him he paused, hanging his head to stare at the floor as grief swept over him.

"Love you, halfling," he whispered. "More than life, I love you."

He had one more stop to make, and that one was going to suck. He might end up dead before he managed to make his own kill. And at the moment, he was highly anticipating his own kill.

◆　◆　◆

Cassie, it's time to wake up. Come on, now. You haven't much time . . .

It was a voice from the past, one she hadn't heard for so many years. The spirit she called her fairy.

Opening her eyes, she stared at the misty figure, watching her wavering expression, the beauty of her face, the gentleness that filled it.

Get dressed, Cassie, you don't have much time. You have to hurry . . .

She was out of the bed, her gaze going around the room.

"Dog," she whispered, turning back to the spirit, fear rising sharp inside her.

You have to save him from himself . . . The spirit glanced at the bedroom doorway, clearly worried. *Hurry, Cassie, you don't have much time.*

She grabbed her pack from the corner of the room and tore jeans, boots and a T-shirt from inside. Dressing quickly, she laced her boots on her feet, then collected her holstered weapon, snapped the belt to her hips and secured the Velcro at her thigh.

The sheathed knife was strapped to the opposite thigh, extra ammo clips were shoved in her back pockets.

"Where is he?" she muttered. "What happened?"

He's found Major. The spirit was wringing her hands now, clearly upset as she looked to the door again.

Cassie had never, ever seen the spirit upset. When she was a child, the misty form of the woman had been imperative, urging her to hurry, but never so upset.

"Who the hell is Major?" she hissed, rushing for the door, aware of the presence floating behind her, following.

His grandfather.

Cassie froze at the apartment doorway, swinging around to face the vision.

Blond-haired, pale eyes, she watched Cassie with such sadness.

I came to you when I knew the danger you faced, the presence whispered. *Cain's mate. My son's mate. You have to save him, Cassie. As I saved you and your mother, you must save my son.*

Shock raced through her, nearly making her dizzy as she fought to make sense of what the spirit said.

Go. Fear filled the pale vision. *You have to hurry. Come . . .*

She floated past Cassie, moving through the door as though it didn't exist, as Cassie bit back a curse and jerked open the door, following her.

Dog's mother? The fairy had been Dog's mother.

All those years it had been Dog's mother coming to her,

leading her from danger, guiding her through her child-hood?

For Cain to survive, you had to survive, the form stated, her melodic voice whispering around Cassie as she raced through the halls of the Bureau behind it. *For him to find happiness, to flourish, for my and his father's deaths to have not been in vain, you had to survive, Cassie . . .*

All this time, the ghost of a conniving, manipulating mother had been leading her to her equally conniving son? Oh, this was one she was definitely not going to forget for a long time.

When all is well, and the time is right, the spirit promised as Cassie pushed through the stairwell doors, *I'll come to you. I'll tell you of his father, and of a love so perfect a killer found a soul and the Breed he loved learned joy. Later, Cassie, when Dog is safe . . .*

"What is he doing?" she panted, tearing down the stairs, holding the rail and jumping from one level to the next to keep up with the spirit. "Where did he find Major?"

Breeds believing they were righting a wrong. The spirit's sigh whispered around her. *They held the key to the puzzle and did not know it. I tried to keep them from Cain, but Cain is stubborn. Determined. I could not turn him away when he found them.*

"Go figure," she said with a snort as they reached the garage level. The spirit passed through the door as Cassie slammed it open and raced into the secured underground lobby.

Hurry, Cassie, the spirit urged, waiting at the doors leading into the garage. *You must hurry.*

She burst through the doors, heard the snarl that ripped from her throat as she heard the vehicle, saw the lights heading for the down ramp. Pushing herself, her lungs burning, she vaulted over the hood of a car veering to cut her off and sprinted the final distance, jumped over the cement barrier. She came to a crouch, one hand braced on the asphalt as she planted herself in front of the limousine, glaring at the oncoming lights.

Brakes screamed, the tires laying black marks as the vehicle came to a hard stop, the grille only inches from her face. Coming slowly to her feet, her weapon in both hands and leveled at the driver, she snarled again.

"Dog, you mangy fucking Coyote," she screamed, furious at whatever he was trying to do. "Get your god-damned ass out here."

◆   ◆   ◆

She was amazing.

Enraged and wild, black hair flying around her as she vaulted over the barrier, landed in a perfect crouch and forced Mongrel to bring the vehicle to a stop.

"Let her go," the senator's aide advised him, his voice quiet. It wasn't a warning; it was a reminder. "You don't want her there, Cain."

"Mutt." He clenched his fingers into fists, rage burning in his gut at the order he knew he had to give.

"Aw, come on, man," Mutt muttered, the low tone doing nothing to disguise the plea. "Don't make me do this."

"Now."

"Dog, you mangy fucking Coyote. Get your goddamned ass out here!" Her scream, so filled with anger, with confusion, ripped at his guts.

"Now, Mutt." He'd gone too far to turn back now.

"I fucking hate you," Mutt growled, but he pushed the door open and exited the vehicle.

Not more than he hated himself.

◆   ◆   ◆

Cassie watched the door open, her heart racing, the beat of it tightening her throat in horror as Mutt closed the door slowly and walked toward her.

Swinging the weapon on him, she bared her teeth, her breaths strangling her at the regret she saw in his face.

She could feel his determination to stop her and knew her mate had sent him to do so. Her mate. He was leaving her and he couldn't even face her himself. The rage she'd felt building inside her all her life began beating in her head, flooding her veins and tearing aside the shields she'd used to hold it back.

"Cassie, let him go." The Coyote lifted his hands as he moved closer. "Come on, no one's forcing him to leave."

"Get back, Mutt. I swear to God I'll shoot you," she warned him.

"I can't do that, Cassie. Dog's going to go no matter what you say or do. Let him go . . ."

She fired.

"Goddamn! Fuck!" His shoulder jerked as the bullet tore into it, but it wasn't enough.

She should have shot his knee out.

He jumped for her, his arm going around her waist, one hand gripping her wrists together as she fired, and fired and fired, screaming in agony and rage at his touch as the limo shot past.

"No . . . ," she screamed again, watching Dog staring straight ahead as the limo passed.

Mutt released her the second the limo disappeared from the garage, and she was ready for him. She lashed out as she turned, her fist burying in his balls. His eyes jerked wide, his breath a gasp, and her fist slammed beneath his jaw in a second blow, leaving him lying as she turned and ran.

She raced from the garage exit, her screams tearing from her throat, moving as fast as she could, fighting, fighting to get to him. He couldn't leave. He couldn't leave her.

He was her mate.

He was hers . . .

And he was gone.

The strength left her legs, slowing her until she felt her knees hit the pavement and heard an enraged animal's scream explode from her. Her head tipped back, a demented sound, not a scream, not a howl, exploding from her, the gun dropping from her fingers as she felt herself sobbing, heard the scream erupt from her throat again.

She was barely aware of her father yelling, her mother falling beside her, her arms going around her, the pain of the touch only blending with the agony tearing from her soul now. She had no idea what they were saying, there were so many voices, so many demands, and all she could do was scream Dog's name.

He'd left her.

He'd let another Coyote restrain her. Touch her. And he'd left her.

The betrayal was slicing her to ribbons, tearing through her so deep, with such force, that the agony was horrendous. It was tearing her apart, ripping something from her very soul that she knew she could never replace without him.

He'd been with her for so many years. The hazy form of the Coyote he harbored had followed her, always just out of sight, and even that was gone now.

He was gone.

❖   ❖   ❖

Jonas stood in shock, staring as Dash and Elizabeth fought to hold on to Cassie as she knelt in the center of the road leading from the garage. Her screams were the sound of an animal tortured, agonized and brutal as they erupted from her throat.

Long, riotous black hair whipped around her and tears ran from her eyes. All the control Cassie had fought for all her life was gone, shattered, wiped away as she fought like an animal to be free of her parents.

But it was what he sensed pouring from her that shocked

him the most. There were no longer the separate scents of
the Coyote and the Wolf howling in grief. They'd merged,
and as he watched her struggles slowly ease, watched as the
tears and the screams were silenced, he sensed the strength
forging inside her.

Whatever pain she should have felt at her parents' touch
receded, sinking inside her, merging with the now silent
howls he could feel echoing inside her.

"Come on, baby. Come on . . ." Dash lifted her in his
arms, cradling her against him as he came to his feet, his
gaze filled with agony as she lay limply in his arms.

Elizabeth's face was wet with tears, as was Ashley's as
she trailed behind them and followed them into the Bureau.
Breeds stood around the area staring, still in shock, weapons held ready with no idea what to fight, what to kill, to
ease the horror and enraged pain that still filled the air.

Alpha leaders had always watched her warily, put off by
her calm, by her air of steady strength. Distrustful of the
shy smiles and overtures of friendship from the young
Breed who always seemed to lack the dark-edged nightmares that most Breeds held.

Now her nightmares were free. A lifetime of them, and
one had just been added. And the realization that the calm
she had always projected—which, though they distrusted
it, had still given them a glimpse of peace whenever she
was near—was shattered.

"Find out who was in that limo . . ."

"It was Dog."

Jonas swung around to face Mutt, seeing the blood at his
shoulder, the limp in his walk.

"Council . . ."

Mutt shook his head. "Cassie shot me."

Jonas blinked back at him. He couldn't have heard right.

"I need a Dragoon, Jonas." Mutt stood before him, his
eyes damned near hollow with the regret pouring from
him. "I have to meet Dog."

"What the fuck happened?" Jonas snarled, grabbing the Coyote's shirt in one fist and jerking him closer. "What happened to her?"

"Dog left her," he breathed out wearily, pain and regret filling his expression. "He wasn't taken, he wasn't forced, and I don't fucking know why. I just went along with him until I could figure out what the fuck was going on. Now, let me go, so I can do that."

Jonas released him slowly and stepped back, shaking his head, certain he couldn't have heard him right.

"He left her?"

Mutt nodded slowly. "He filed a Separation and Disavowal before he left. When I know more, I'll contact you."

Blood dripped from the Breed's shoulder as he hurried to the nearest Dragoon, dragged himself into it and shot from the parking lot with a squeal of tires.

Dog had filed a Separation and Disavowal from his mate? What the fuck was going on?

CHAPTER 17

The spirit was silent, but she hadn't left. The tall, broad form of her mate, Dog's father, had joined her. They didn't speak. They were hazy, barely there, and they weren't speaking. They had no answers for her, they didn't know where Dog was, but his father knew he was with Major.

His grandfather. The same man who'd had his son and his son's mate hunted down like animals and killed. A grandfather with no male heirs now. Dog's father was certain that somehow, Major had convinced Dog to come home, so to speak. The order that had gone out on the parents hadn't been the same order that had gone out on the child. Major had demanded that the child he suspected had been born be delivered to him.

So, her mate had decided, in essence, that his grandfather was more important than his mate.

Wild fury filled her at the thought. It burned inside her, searing her soul with the knowledge. Well, he hadn't married a female willing to allow him to ride off into the sunset and live happily ever after with his grandfather and his grandfather's fortune.

Mercenary fucking Coyote. If he thought she wasn't a vengeful mate, then he'd find out quickly how vengeful she could be. There was only one mate. Her soul was bound to his, even if his wasn't bound to hers. And if she was going to carry the scars of this mating to the very depths of her, then he'd carry a few on the outside, courtesy of her.

Scouring the dark web for any hint of a rumor that a Coyote was stepping up to a fortune—or a grandfather—she could feel the wild, enraged instincts clawing inside her for action. Demanding she go searching.

Only a fool searched with no idea what they were searching for. She wasn't a fool. That icy logical core that had slowly grown over the hours assured her of this. She might be burning in rage, but that cold, hard center kept her anchored where once Dog had.

A dry sob shook her. She'd cried for hours, screaming with the crazed pain that had destroyed her. She'd had her mother crying; Ashley, her sister Emma and Graeme's mate, Cat, had sobbed with her. Their touches hadn't bothered her. Her parents' embraces merely made her numb.

As she scrolled through yet another Breed-sighting site, her head lifted, instinct racing through her as she sensed the Breed heading down the hall. He moved with purpose, with regret. And he was coming for her.

Standing up, she closed the case on the tablet, smoothed her hands over the black skirt she wore and made certain the black sleeveless blouse was neatly tucked in. The four-and-a-half-inch heels weren't needed for confidence. Others expected her to dress a certain way, and she knew it might be best to give them what they expected.

The knock came at the door as she reached it. Opening it, she stared up at the Breed watching her with pain-filled eyes, his expression heavy with knowledge.

"Sweet Cassie," he sighed, the Scots burr a gentle sound. "I'll kill him for ya, I swear it."

"I'm sure that's not why you're here." He felt sorry for her, and as fondly felt as that pity was, it was so misplaced.

"Rule needs to see ya," he said. "I'm sorry, lass."

"Don't feel sorry for me, Styx." She stepped out and closed the door behind her. "Feel sorry for that Coyote. He's going to need your pity far more."

She didn't wait to follow him as she would have otherwise. Breed instinct had once demanded she do just that. That instinct no longer existed.

She stepped into the elevator, checked the watch she wore on her wrist and calculated the time to enter the next dark website she'd found earlier. She should have plenty of time. She doubted what she suspected was coming would take long.

It would kill the last of her soul, but it wouldn't take long.

"Cass, ya need to talk, I'm here," Styx said gently as the elevator stopped and they stepped out. "Ya know I'll always be here for ya."

"I know." She strode ahead of him for Rule's office, her head high, steeling herself for what was coming. "There's nothing to discuss, though."

Stepping into Rule's office, aware of her parents behind her, she faced Rule, Jonas, Brannigan and the three leaders of the Breed community, Callan, Wolfe and Del Rey.

"I'm sorry, Cassie," Rule sighed as she stopped in front of his desk, a grimace contorting his face as he shook his head heavily. "I'm so fucking sorry, sweetheart."

She'd known him since she was a little girl. She'd teased him over his name, played practical jokes on him as a teenager, stood in awe of him as she matured. Now all she could do was stand before him and wait.

"Get it over with," she demanded. "Just get it the hell over with."

She pressed her lips tightly together as he lifted two paper forms from his desk and handed them to her.

She accepted them slowly, stared down at each and felt herself shattering. The agony racing through her wasn't as sharp as it had been the day before, but she felt it shredding her soul.

No. No. She could hear the whisper of the spirit lingering behind her, a mother's disbelief and pain. And all Cassie could do was stare at the end of her world as she knew it.

Petition for Separation and Notice of Disavowal. Disillusionment, the reason stated. Permanent separation and disavowal. No contact. Talk about reaping what you sow.

"How ironic," she said softly, forcing herself not to tremble, but she couldn't stop the tear that fell from one eye before she could blink it back. "I'm the reason this petition even exists." She lifted her eyes to Coy Delgado and felt her breathing hitch at the compassion in his black eyes. "I'm so sorry, Del Rey." Her voice was strangled, the pain carving furrows into the already jagged pieces of her soul. "I didn't know . . ."

She didn't know how bad it hurt. How bad the agony could resonate inside the very spirit.

"No, Cassie." He shook his head, the rough sound of his voice filled with denial. "None of this is your fault, especially that." He nodded to the petitions. "I brought it on myself in my treatment of my mate, but you did nothing to deserve it."

But he'd been given a chance to win his mate back: His mate had agreed to one year's separation. Her mate had filed for permanent separation. She had been disavowed. There was no hope of seeing him again.

Like hell!

She dropped the paper onto Rule's desk. There wasn't even an objection she could file. She was denied any information they might have on his whereabouts. They couldn't even let her know if he was alive.

"Where is he?" she asked anyway.

She stared at Rule, wanting to beg and unable to. Instead, the creature Dog's desertion had spawned rose inside her like some demon filled with demented rage.

"We don't know." Rule shook his head, but he was lying.

She could feel that lie. He was staring into her eyes and he was lying to her.

She held his blue gaze, staring into it, searching for the answer, demanding he give it to her. That was her mate, and he would tell her . . .

"Goddamn, Cassie." His eyes rounded in shock as he came out of his chair, a snarl pulling at his lips as fury flashed across his expression as he prepared to launch himself across the desk. Her father pushed her behind him.

"What the hell?" Her father cursed, facing Rule now. "What the fuck, Rule?"

She didn't wait for his reaction. They weren't going to tell her anything. None of them would.

Turning on her heel, she stalked for the door.

"Cassie." It was Jonas who stopped her.

There was no demand, no order, just a gentle sound that tore at her heart and had the creature clawing inside her pausing.

She tried to make herself keep going, but this was Jonas.

"What?" Tilting her head, she waited.

"Did you really think that would work with an alpha of Rule's strength, honey?" he asked her gently.

"He knows," she snapped, hearing the odd sound of her voice, a melodic, haunting tone she'd have to consider later. "If he can lie to me, then he deserves whatever I can throw at him." She turned back to all of them, her head lifted, glaring back at them. "I do not accept that Separation nor do I acknowledge his Disavowal," she informed them, stabbing her finger in the direction of the incriminating paper still lying on the dark wood desk. "I will find my mate, with or without your help."

She was aware of her father watching her with narrowed eyes, his gaze thoughtful, intent.

"I can't tell you where he's at, and you knew that before you asked," Rule growled, trying to reassert the hold he would have had over her before she lost the anchor in her little world.

Her mate.

"I would have told you." There was only that agonizing pain, a feral rage beating at her brain, and the betrayal. "I wouldn't pull this bullshit on you, Rule, not after all these years. I would tell you."

Respect begot respect. If he could disrespect her and lie to her, then she could call him on it. He might be stronger physically, but she wasn't weaker, no matter what they wanted to believe.

"What are you going to do?" It was her father who asked the question, still thoughtful, watching her, gauging what he could sense inside her.

He was her father, and she loved him, but he wasn't her alpha any longer. He was her father.

"I'm going to kill him," she stated, aware of the surprise rippling through the room. "I'm going to find him, I'll find out why he did this, and if I don't like his excuses, then I'll kill him."

Jonas rubbed at the back of his neck; Del Rey's head turned, his gaze going to Callan and Wolfe in surprised reaction. Callan could only shake his head as Wolfe watched her carefully.

Her father nodded slowly. "Want some help?"

"Dash, no," her mother gasped. "She can't."

"She'll do it with or without our help," he stated, his gaze still locked with his daughter's, sensing the emerging strength, the depth of instinct she finally allowed free. "Let me watch your back, Cassie."

He could feel her searching for any hint of deception and let his lips quirk knowingly. "Have I ever lied to you? Deceived you?"

"No." Those blue eyes were blazing, like iridescent gems glowing with the pain trapped inside her. But what had each man in that room entranced was the way the blue was beginning to spread through the whites of her eyes. "Do you know where he is?"

He shook his head. "But I might know someone who does."

"Dash . . ." Elizabeth whispered his name, her hand tightening on his arm. "No . . ."

"It's time, Elizabeth," he whispered, dropping a quick kiss to her parted lips before following his daughter as she opened the door and left the room.

Dog had warned him months ago that his daughter was far more than he ever guessed, and Dash hadn't believed him even though he'd sensed something trying to break free inside her for years. What he was sensing now, though, he couldn't believe.

There had never been an alpha female not in title only. The mate of an alpha, though not physically or instinctively stronger than the males, commanded in her alpha's stead. It was a hierarchy thing, a part of nature. But he'd never heard of anything like what he sensed radiating from his daughter. She wasn't just alpha, she was what Jonas called Primal. A breed whose genetics went beyond human or animal. A creature spawned by determined strength, rage and called free in only the most extreme circumstance. But once called free, forever a part of the Breed that carried it.

"Weapon up," he told her as they moved down the hall. "I'll meet you in the lobby."

She swung around, her gaze piercing.

Dash grabbed her arm, snarled in her face, and grabbed

her attention. He was still her father, and if this was the path she was going to walk, then she'd better learn fast how to stay on it.

"You're strong, little girl," he acknowledged caustically. "But you have a hell of a lot to learn and your mate's not here to begin your education. Consider me a stand-in tutor. And you better believe I know a hell of a lot more about this game than you do. Accept it, and by God start learning now."

She didn't drop her gaze in submission but gave a quick nod in return, and he sensed the enraged creature inside her stepping back enough that his own instincts weren't bristling with the unconscious challenge.

"Now, you weapon up. I'll meet you in the lobby in half an hour," he informed her again. "And be ready, Cassie. You challenge the Breed we're going to meet, and he'll rip you apart. And there won't be a chance in hell I can stop it."

He might be making a mistake. It was entirely possible he was making a mistake, but if there was one Breed who could tell them where Dog had gone, then it was this one.

"Half an hour," she agreed, the change to her voice still a shock to him. It was smoother, a melodic sound that resonated with power and such a depth of pain, his heart broke all over again for her.

As he strode away from her, the memory of her screams as he rushed to the drive leading from the garage still filled him with horror. He'd never heard a scream like it. His instincts had never reacted to anything the way they'd reacted to those screams.

They'd echoed around her, resonated, and, he swore, pulled the animal he was to the surface with such instinctive demand he'd been shocked by it. The scream of an alpha demanding aid. Demanding they stop whatever agony was torturing her.

Pushing his fingers through his hair, he was aware of his wife catching up with him, moving silently by his side until they reached their room. She was scared for their daughter, uncertain of the decision they'd made when Dash had warned her of what he'd sensed in Cassie six years before. As that knowledge had strengthened over the years, they'd promised themselves they'd support her, no matter where it took her.

Her life, the dangers she'd faced, the choices she'd had to make, had been pushing her closer, and though he hadn't expected this, he'd promised himself he'd be there for her, no matter the direction that strength took her in.

The knowledge that the "fairy" who had guided Cassie was Dog's deceased mother might have surprised him, but he didn't doubt her. Cassie had always known things she shouldn't have known, made choices Dash knew were shaping her future, and there had been times, rare times, when he'd sensed something in Cassie that now made sense.

"This could be dangerous, Dash," Elizabeth whispered as he changed into his mission clothes and strapped on his weapons. "She could be hurt. You could be hurt."

Yeah, it was possible.

Sitting down on the side of the bed, he drew her to him, staring up at her with more love than he'd felt the day before, and the day before that. Over the years, he'd learned not to think that he couldn't love her more, because it grew daily, and his heart's capacity for it grew with it.

"It's her destiny," he told her softly. "Just as you were mine. She brought me to you, however she knew to do it. This is what she's been racing toward, Elizabeth, and I don't trust anyone else to watch her back as well as I trust myself. I don't know what she's facing, but I won't let her face it alone."

Tears filled her eyes, but they weren't tears of pain.

"Are you ever going to tell her the truth? That you're her father?" she asked.

"I don't have to tell her." He shook his head. "Cassie knows. She's always known."

REEVER ESTATE
UNDERGROUND LABS OF GRAEME PARKER

Well now, wasn't this interesting.

Graeme stood in the middle of his lab and stared at the young woman, his head tilted to the side.

The Primal had come forth the moment he caught her scent. Claws emerging, the markings spreading over his body, his gaze becoming sharper, clearing, picking up things a normal Breed had no hope of sensing.

And if he was watching her in interest, she was taking in nearly as much as he was. The blue of her eyes hadn't completely taken over the whites yet, and he doubted there would be markings, but one wouldn't know for some time yet.

"How fascinating," he murmured as his mate, Cat, and his brother, Cullen, as well as Cullen's mate, Chelsea, watched suspiciously from behind him. "Of course, so would your mate be. You'd never accept a mate weaker than yourself. How did I miss that?"

A frown snapped between those perfectly arched black brows and he could feel what was still trapped, fighting for freedom. This Primal was strong. What the body lacked in physical strength, the creature beneath her skin would make up for in other ways. Ways he might even find shocking.

"I wonder if it was the mating," he questioned, speaking more to himself than to those standing in the cavern with him. "A hybrid thing, do you think?"

It was the first hybrid mating, he consoled himself. It could be something that emerged in hybrids. If so, the Breed community could well be screwed. There was also a chance it was merely an anomaly.

"Did you sense it?" He turned to her father as curiosity got the best of him. "Has it always been there?"

Dash's sharp nod was all he needed.

"Hmm." Retracting the claws was easy enough; the stripes remained.

Primal to Primal, she would respect nothing else.

"Are you Primal as well?" He turned his attention back to Dash and caught the Wolf Breed's quick shake of his head.

"Not hereditary, then." He sighed, smelling the strength of Dash's paternal mark on her. "We'll have to discuss this in depth, you know."

"They're not here to talk, Mr. Hyde," his brother's mate reminded him. "I warned you of that."

Yes, that was true; she had reminded him of that.

"I need blood, saliva." He let his gaze meet the young halfling's. "Give me what I want; I give you what you want."

Her eyes narrowed, the blue filled with latent power. He wanted to rub his hands together in glee. He'd been getting bored, he admitted. This would definitely liven things up.

"Graeme," his mate's voice held a warning.

"Cat," he answered her, though his gaze never shifted from that neon blue. "It's easy enough. She knows there's no danger in giving it." She merely stared back at him as he tilted his head and watched her.

"Can you speak?" he asked, amused.

"Quite well. Give me what I need. I'll take the samples myself," she stated.

That voice. Graeme could feel a chill moving up his spine at the haunting, hypnotic tone. It was beautiful. Crystal clear, pulling at the senses, at that inner part of a living being that made one need to give whatever the voice demanded.

"Can you work the pressure syringe yourself? I can lay out what you need," he told her, thankful that he had no problem with it. Denying this young woman would not be easy when she let this part of her free.

"I can." She nodded.

Graeme looked to her father quickly, seeing the clench of the Breed's jaw.

That voice. God help Breeds and humans alike when the Primal inside her was fully mature. That voice would demand everyone sit up and listen.

Turning away, he laid out what she needed—the syringe, a sterile swab—and watched as she extracted her blood into the three vials he provided. Three swabs. He had quite a bit of work to do.

She did it quickly, efficiently, as he moved to his computer, typed in the proper address and watched information scroll by. He'd been alerted to certain events as Dash called, and had followed the information until they arrived.

When Cassie Sinclair stepped back from the tray she'd placed the samples on, he quickly wrote down the information and handed it to her.

"You shouldn't go alone," he told her.

"She's not," her father spoke up.

Yes, this one would watch her back, but who would watch his? His influence on the young Primal was strong enough, the bonds of father and child stronger than the girl knew. But they were just two against whatever force awaited them.

"Cullen, shall we join the party?" he asked, aware of the young woman stilling, preparing. "Just to watch the father's back." He smiled as she narrowed her eyes on him.

"Good idea," Cat agreed quietly. "Chelsea and I will join you."

He tilted his head and stared back at Cassie. "It's your party. Are you agreeable?"

Her slow nod was a bit wary, but her agreement was all he needed.

"When I gut him, keep back." It wasn't an idle threat.

Dash grimaced, a look of concern flickering over his expression.

"You're going to kill him fast?" Graeme frowned, shedding his lab coat as Cullen handed him his weapon. "My dear, we need to discuss the idea of true pain. You'll rue the day if you show him mercy. Shall we discuss the merits of torture instead . . ."

The frightening part was the fact that she seemed all too willing to listen.

There was nothing but pure, white-hot, demented fury. The kind of fury that took hold at the sight of another's hands on his mate, restraining her, holding her back. The crazed rage as he was forced to remain still, silent at the sound of the animalistic screams and the knowledge that his mate was running desperately for him.

He didn't look back, but he didn't have to. From the second he'd seen her vaulting over the second bodyguard's car and landing in a perfect defensive crouch, he'd been attuned to her as never before. Even in those fragile moments, six years before, after she'd awakened in the hospital, her furious scream echoing around her, it hadn't been this strong.

He'd simply stared at the man who had brought his grandfather's offer to him and watched him slowly pale as Dog fought to hide the physical proof of that rage.

He hadn't gone this nuclear since he was a child watching the news report of the unidentified body found in a back alley, a hole through his heart. What had happened then had destroyed the small cabin and everything in it, as well as Dog's memories of how it had been accomplished.

When he'd awakened, he'd found himself inside the coyote mother's burrow, curled against her warmth along with her pups, as she gently cleaned his bloodied hands.

He'd been ten, wracked by such grief, such anger, that he'd lain in that burrow for days. Soldiers had found the cabin, set fire to it. They'd searched for him, along with several Coyote Breeds. As they neared the burrow, the animal that sheltered him stuck her head out of the opening, snarling at the Breeds. They'd retreated, sensing no more than her and her pups, and eventually gave up their search.

Dog could feel that rage tearing at him now, but he wasn't ten any longer. And he didn't let that creature control him. He controlled the beast, until he decided it was time to set it free.

The drive from the Bureau of Breed Affairs to the private airport was longer than he expected, several hours, he'd realized, when the human had given Mongrel the directions. Mutt caught up with them long before that, the Dragoon following close behind them.

"She shot Mutt," Mongrel informed him, his gaze wary as it met Dog's in the rearview mirror.

"I saw." He turned his gaze back to the human.

If the other Coyote was unable to drive, Mutt would have informed him of that as well.

"Your grandfather won't like blood in the plane." The weak-assed bastard cleared his throat and spoke hesitantly. "He's a very fastidious person."

Fastidious, was he? Didn't like blood?

"Shame," he grunted, his voice low.

The human held his gaze another moment before it flickered away. He'd obviously expected Dog to say something more. There was nothing more to say.

His grandfather was expecting a reunion of some type,

it seemed. His conditions had been exacting. Break from his mate, meet this ball-less bastard and fly to him. No doubt it was a trap, but it wouldn't matter. Whoever the Major was, he was going to die. His fastidious self was going to bleed like a gutted pig. Dog was going to make certain of it.

The little bastard sent to give him the message cleared his throat again. "She's pretty," he offered hesitantly and at Dog's glower almost pissed himself.

Now he knew what Graeme meant when he said everyone lost their bladders when faced with Breed rage.

The little man cleared his throat again. "Your grandfather has authorized me to answer any questions . . ."

"Shit, man, would you shut the fuck up," Mongrel snapped from the driver's seat, the growl in his voice demanding as his wary gaze checked the rearview mirror again. "He'll take your fucking throat. Pissy-assed pantywaist moron. Can't humans sense anything?"

The human in question tried to press deeper into the corner of the seat facing Dog's, paling as Dog smiled with icy disdain.

"How long is this flight going to take, if you're so authorized?" Mongrel snapped, obviously nervous about whatever he sensed coming off Dog.

"Th . . . the flight?" the human squeaked. "Five hours. It's just five hours."

Long enough. Far enough away from his mate. But an inch was far enough away from her.

He breathed in deeply, the scent of her still clinging to the shirt he wore. She'd worn it after he'd taken her the first time the night before. Wrapped it around her as she lay back against his chest and let him just hold her.

They hadn't spoken, though he'd sensed her fears, her worry. And when he'd known she wasn't willing to stay silent any longer, he'd taken her again. Drawn it out. Immersed himself in her pleasure, her pleas, her body straining against his as she orgasmed to his fingers, to his tongue, then again as he'd found his release and locked inside her.

That was ecstasy. That was the most pleasure to be found in any life. Feeling his mate coming undone at his touch, her soul touching his, filling his as he held her, feeling her becoming a part of his spirit.

He'd go mad eventually without her, and he knew it. Filing that petition had actually made him weak with the agony it had caused. Knowing he'd severed that tie, no matter how little it counted to the mating, would drive the beast inside him to insanity.

But it would protect her.

A Separation ensured that any crime he might commit against Breed Law, she wouldn't suffer for it. That was all that mattered, that his mate didn't suffer more than she would already. The Disavowal would keep Jonas or Rule from allowing her to know where he was, or to come to him once he was captured. And he would be. He was weak without her, he realized. His will to fight against Breed Law would be nonexistent.

His halfling.

He could still feel her wild fury beating inside his soul. He'd thought it would dull as the drive lengthened, but he could still feel it. Her tears, her screams. If the agony lancing through him didn't abate, then he wouldn't be able to contain it long enough to reach his prey.

He could have let it go.

That was what he told himself when the Breeds he'd found in Cassie's former suite had told him about their search for the Major and this man. The emissary, they called him. Their search of the emissary's computer files had revealed the information on Dog and Cassie, his surveillance of them sent to the Major.

Find the Major, the Wolf Breeds in Cassie's suite told him, contact them and they'd move in and take custody of him.

Yeah, he'd agreed to it. He'd contacted this puny-assed human and made all the right moves, and when he'd been told to walk away from his mate if he wanted his legacy, Dog had walked away.

Because of the danger to his mate.

Because the information the Wolf Breeds had downloaded and shown him had detailed the risk of the hell they could be drawn into if he didn't take care of the threat.

And in taking care of it, he'd be subject to Breed Law.

He'd lose his mate, no matter the choice he made.

Through the long, tedious limo ride, the even longer flight, he remained silent. He let the memories of Cassie wash over him, sustain him.

The scent of her, spice and a hint of sugar. Her kiss breathed against his lips . . . her rage.

Her rage beat inside his soul, mixing with his own, until he was certain madness lay in the next second.

Enduring it would kill him long before Breed Law managed to do so.

• CHAPTER 19 •

The mansion was brightly lit, well guarded, and inside it was her mate. Cassie narrowed her eyes on it, her gaze tracking, searching.

A pristine lawn stretched before her, with few areas for concealment. Landscape lighting was positioned to dispel the heaviest of the shadows, but at three in the morning, the human guards patrolling the estate wouldn't be at their best. That is, unless the motion sensors were set off or the electronic security staff were diligent.

Three two-man teams patrolled the outside of the house, along with the dogs that paced at their sides. The dogs didn't worry her too much. They were well trained, alert, but she'd already touched their senses, soothed them, assured them only friends were invading their territory that night.

Now she just had to find her mate..

He was in the house; she knew that for certain. She could feel him waiting. Was he waiting for her? Did he sense the enraged, betrayed fury getting ready to descend on him?

"Don't use your eyes," Graeme hissed, the mangled feline sound reaching her from where she crouched atop the wall surrounding the estate, hidden by the heavy branches of a locust tree. "Use your senses. Your mate is the reason that creature that strains inside you exists. Mate to mate. You'll find him if you let it have its way."

Mate to mate.

She was going to skin her mate out and take his hide home. She'd hang it on her wall and die of grief.

A hard slap at the back of her head nearly knocked her from her perch. The scrape of sharp claws against her scalp accompanied the less-than-gentle tap. Before she could twist and defend herself, she found herself with a face full of Primal Bengal. Stripes, sharp canines and all.

"Close your eyes," he hissed, now crouched at her side. "He's a part of you. Find him."

She closed her eyes, sensing the value of whatever he had to teach her, needing it. The closer they'd gotten to the estate of Aaron C. Ryder, the more the rage had built inside her.

It connected them.

The wild near insanity of that fury was all that bound them. She'd given herself to him, heart, soul. But in the long hours after he'd driven away, she'd realized he hadn't given himself.

He had touched her soul, filled it, just as he'd filled her body, and she hadn't even realized that he hadn't let her into his own.

As she let her senses reach out, her eyes slowly opened again, her senses alerted to the spirit she'd become so used to as a child. The shimmering form of Dog's mother, faint, so faint, wavering against the darkness, stood on the lawn just beyond the tree hiding them from view.

Turning, the spirit pointed to a first-floor window, the one in the exact center. An office of some sort, or a library, she guessed, barely able to glimpse shelves of books through a crack in the shielding curtains.

She could feel Graeme tensing, rumbling growls barely heard, as he must have sensed the spirit.

"First floor, center window," she told Graeme. "He's there, but he's not alone."

Mutt and Mongrel were with him, but they weren't the only ones.

"There's something out there," Graeme muttered, the low growl beneath his voice filled with impending danger. "Something not natural."

And Breeds were?

"She's with me," was all Cassie said, feeling his start of surprise as the spirit turned back and waved her forward imperatively.

Before the Bengal Primal could stop her, she dropped from the wall, crouched, then raced across the lawn in the exact line the spirit indicated. Following the faint presence, she slid into the shadows at the far side of the house and crouched within the decorative brush growing alongside it.

There, she waited, watching, aware of Graeme, her father, Cullen, Cat and Claire as they moved more slowly into position alongside her.

"Back door," Graeme breathed into the night. "I'll be with you; the others have the guards. Give the signal when you're ready."

When the spirit she followed was ready.

She met the gaze of the distraught mother as she waited, knowing it sensed what she was fighting to hold back. Fear filled a mother's expression as compassion lurked in her gaze.

The guards passed, moved along their perimeter, the dogs looking, sniffing the air; they were wary but continued silently as she glared at them and urged them on.

As they passed the corner of the house, the second team was nearing; the spirit moved quickly.

Staying low, Cassie followed swiftly, aware of Graeme behind her as her father and the others moved to disable the guards.

They slipped into the house, the unlocked door opening and closing silently behind them.

They entered what was obviously a break room for the guards, thankfully deserted. The spirit didn't pause as she led them through the darkened rooms before stopping outside a set of open double doors.

The sound of voices had her flattening to the wall, trusting the shadows to shield her as Graeme seemed to disappear into another set of shadows.

To protect you . . . the wavering image whispered as she slowly disappeared. *All to protect you . . .*

♦   ♦   ♦

His grandfather.

Yeah, it was definitely his grandfather. Dog stared dispassionately at the old man, seeing his father in the old man's features, but not in the scent of corruption and desperation.

He remembered his father's scent. Gun oil and ammunition; below it, honor, strength. Grief.

He'd grieved for his mate until the day he'd died.

Aaron lowered himself stiffly to the leather sofa facing Dog, tired gray eyes lifting to where Dog stood silently in the middle of the room.

He shared blood with this man. He could smell the blood bond, and he cursed it.

Mutt stood next to the entrance with one of Aaron's security guards. A former navy SEAL. A hard-eyed soldier who watched curiously. Dog couldn't sense hatred or prejudice coming from him, but he sensed a determination to do his job and protect his employer.

Behind him, Mongrel stood with the other security guard. That one reeked of hatred and discontent. Humans. They never listened to all those Breed documentaries they watched that preached the acuity of a Breed's senses to pick up such emotions.

"I was surprised to learn you filed for Separation as well as a Disavowal from the woman you'd chosen as your mate," Aaron commented, watching him closely. "I expected you to object to disavowing her."

"Why did you expect that?" Let the bastard dig this hole a little deeper. If he was lucky, very lucky, then he might say something that would exonerate Dog when he cut his throat.

Aaron lowered his graying head and stared at the drink he held. Regret spilled from him. It didn't overpower the scent of core evil, but it was regret.

"Your father," he said before he tossed back the drink, then lifted his gaze to Dog once again. "He was a good son. A loyal son. Until your mother. Even after her death he refused to come home no matter my attempts to convince him."

"Yeah, he could be a little stubborn," Dog drawled coolly. "He might have blamed you for her death, though, feared for his son's safety. Little things like that can make a man stubborn, I hear."

It could make a man hate. His father had hated this man and Dog knew it. Not that he remembered his father saying it, but he'd known it, even as a child.

"Yes, it can." That regret once again. The bastard. "Before he went into those labs to train the Breeds there, Carson, your father, was a hardened soldier. He knew the value of the program, understood the work they were doing there. All that changed with her, though." He watched Dog for long moments, as though he expected him to say something. "She didn't even have a name. He called her Angel, though."

His mother was an angel, his father had told him more than once.

Dog could feel his skin prickling with the fury he held back, his head filled with so much rage it threatened the control he had a stranglehold on.

"Chet, get me another drink," Aaron ordered the guard at the back of the room.

Dog let a smile curl his lips at the resentment that tore through the soldier, the feeling that he was better than some servant to take such orders.

"Chet doesn't think much of playing bartender," Dog warned Aaron, watching the surprise that filled his lined expression. "Thinks he's too good for it."

Aaron shook his head. "Chet's a good boy. His father was on Carson's team. SEALs. They don't come any better."

"Hmm," Dog muttered before giving the man a mocking smile. "Keep thinking that. Now, my time's rather limited. Would you like to tell me why you suddenly want to claim your Breed grandson when the order to find me and turn me over to the Council was the order that went out when I was a child?"

Aaron accepted the drink from the soldier, though Dog detected a sudden wariness that hadn't been there before.

"Age brings a different perspective." Aaron breathed out roughly. "Both my children are gone. The legacy I'd leave behind at my death is gone." There was the faintest hint of a plea in those eyes as Dog stared back at him. "Carson haunts me." He swallowed tightly. "Choices I made then haunt me."

Dog wanted to laugh. What held the enraged bark of laughter back he wasn't certain.

"And you think threatening me with Cassie's safety, with revealing my bloodline to the Genetics Council without the benefit of your fortune to protect me, is the way to handle that? What makes you think I need your fortune to protect me?"

"It's not the fortune." Aaron watched him now with a calculating gleam in his eyes. "It's information you want, isn't it, Cain?"

"Dog," he corrected him smoothly.

A frown snapped between Aaron's gray brows. "Cain . . ."

"Cainis. I believe the translation is 'dog,'" Dog corrected him. "My name is Dog."

"You'll take the name Cain," the old man gritted out. "It's a family name given to the oldest son in each generation stretching back over a hundred years. Your father was Carson Cain, my name is Aaron Cain."

Yeah, yeah, good old family legacies, right? That hadn't done his parents a lot of good. "And my name is Dog," Dog finished for him.

"As I was saying," Aaron continued with a disagreeable snap. "It's information you want. Information I have and would be more than willing to provide you in exchange for your agreement to not only disavow your mate, but also the Breeds as a whole. You'll take your place here, as my heir, and take over the various businesses. If you conduct yourself as I wish, in one year, I'll turn over the information I have on the Genetics Council. Extensive information."

That bark of laughter escaped; Dog couldn't help it. "And why should I trust you have information that the Breeds haven't acquired?"

Aaron turned to Chet and nodded.

Oh, Chet wasn't a happy little soldier if the scent of malicious anger coming from him was any indication. But he was a good little soldier evidently. He collected a large envelope from a side table and stepped to Dog, extending it silently.

Keeping his eye on Aaron, Dog opened the file and extracted the pages within. There were three. Names were redacted, but there was no doubt it was a printout from a larger file detailing the identities of three of the Council members who sat on the Genetics Council.

He went over the information carefully, in case the pages somehow disappeared in the bloodshed coming. It was quite interesting, surprising really. If he'd been in the mood to be surprised.

Tucking the pages back into the envelope, he secured the

flap and handed them back to the soldier. Old Chet wasn't expecting that. He took the envelope hesitantly, looking back at his boss as though asking for guidance.

"It's yours." Aaron watched him warily. "All of it will be yours in a year . . ." He trailed off as Dog shook his head.

"If your identity is turned over to them, you'll never be safe," Aaron threatened him.

"Oh, good old Chet will take care of that either way," Dog drawled, the look he gave the soldier assuring him he knew exactly what he'd do. "Spies rarely keep such things to themselves. And he's a good little Council bitch, aren't you, Chet?"

The soldier straightened, his hand settling on the weapon he wore as Dog chuckled knowingly. "That can be discussed later." He turned back to Aaron. "That's not the information I want."

He could sense a vibration in the air, silent but steady, danger moving steadily closer as Chet made up his mind to kill. Not yet. He wanted to survive the bloodshed, Dog sensed. But it would come soon.

"What more could you want?" Confusion flickered across Aaron's expression.

"I want to know what makes a man put out the order to kill his own son." Dog wanted proof. "What made you think that hunting him down like an animal and threatening his woman, murdering her, then going after his child, would work for you?"

"There was no order to kill." Aaron labored to his feet, grief, anger, hatred, flooding him. "Carson was to be returned. He was supposed to come home." He stalked across the room and slapped the drink to the bar before gripping the edge with both hands and shuddering. "He left them no choice. The Council gave the order if they couldn't take him alive, to kill him." He turned back to Dog, his face heavy with the weight of that loss. "He chose to die."

Incomprehensible. Aaron C. Ryder couldn't imagine

how his son could choose to die rather than turning his son over and accepting that his father had been behind his mate's murder.

"But you gave the order to kill Angel," he guessed. "Didn't you?"

The old man sighed heavily. "I gave the order. God forgive me."

"He's the only one that might," Dog admitted, aware of Chet moving to protect his boss, the soldier next to the door tensing.

"You can't do anything, Cain." Aaron shook his head heavily. "I'm a United States senator. All you can do is request your Breed Law be enacted. Killing me is the same as suicide. Your own people will hunt you down."

"They won't have to." Dog shrugged. "You don't understand, Senator. I might have disavowed my mate to protect her from you and your fucking twelve, but that's nothing more than paper. If it takes my life to ensure her safety, then I'll give it. Gladly."

He didn't bother to pull the knife he had hidden. He wouldn't need it when the time came. The two soldiers were tense, hands on their weapons, hard gazes tracking his every move.

"If he dies, she'll die anyway." The soldier who spoke from the door did so without anger, without warning. It was a statement, nothing more. "That order's already out. The sniper who deactivated that window and took a bead on her was just a warning."

"You?" Dog asked without looking at him.

"Not me," he denied. "I don't kill women. Not for any amount of money. And I don't know who it was. But he'll kill her."

"You'd have to get past the ghosts that protect her first." Dog snorted, aware of the few times even he had sensed something otherworldly following her. "How do you think she's survived this long?"

Evidently, the good senator had heard the rumors of Cassie's visions.

"Now, do you want to die for this bastard?" He slid a look to the soldier he'd actually regret killing. "You can walk out. No harm, no foul."

"You can't kill him, Dog," the soldier said with a sigh. "I can't let you do that."

It wasn't out of loyalty. The odd note in the soldier's voice mixed with his regret.

Dog shrugged. "Doesn't matter. I'm going to kill him." He gave the senator a hard, cold smile. "For my mother. For ten years of grief my father suffered, for your betrayal. The danger you represent to my mate. I'm going to send you to hell, you son of a bitch."

He was poised to jump for Chet first, trusting Mutt and Mongrel to ensure the other two represented no threat. Before he could reach for the bastard, a knife flew past his nose and buried itself in the soldier's chest, piercing his heart.

He knew that knife. Right past his nose it flew; a breath closer and he'd have lost precious flesh.

"Are you crazy?" He whirled around just enough to catch the full impact of his mate's fist as it slammed into his jaw, and all the wild rage in her snarl as she swept his feet out from under him.

His ass hit the floor, and as shock reverberated through his brain, she straddled his chest, another knife lying against his throat as he stared into the most mesmerizing sight of his life. Neon blue eyes, the color bleeding fully into the whites, witchy, otherworldly. There was a snarl on her lips and all those wild black curls flowed around him as she bent her head, glaring at him with furious outrage. And in that second, he felt her as he never had before. Her creature slammed into his senses as his tore aside the shields he'd had in place to protect the last of his soul.

Son of a bitch. His halfling had come for him. Her intent

was to taste his blood perhaps, but still, she'd come for him and she wasn't just demanding her due of him, she was taking it. She was his equal and she was letting him know it. She'd never walk behind him, she'd never fully submit anywhere but in their bed, and as she claimed that last part of him he couldn't help but grin.

"Goddamn, halfling, you're so fucking beautiful, you steal my breath. Son of a bitch if you don't . . ."

CHAPTER 20

Cassie sat across the room watching the scene playing out before her as she flipped the knife absently, glaring at Dog, Rule, Jonas, Rhyzan and her father as they more or less interrogated the senator.

Cat, Chelsea, Cullen and Graeme had rounded up the security personnel. They were currently locked in the closet behind her as the two women talked quietly, leaning against the wall, discussing dresses of all things.

Graeme stepped back into the room after briefing the enforcers Jonas had flown in with him. Twelve Breeds were now tasked with securing the estate until they left.

She spared a glance for the insane Bengal. The stripes were gone, as were the claws. The whites of his eyes were normal now, the tilt less feline.

Bastard. He'd contacted Jonas somehow and she knew it. As though they needed him. She hadn't needed him to come riding in with the cavalry. She was handling her mate just fine without any help.

Dirty damned Coyote.

She spared him another look, receiving another of those

cocky grins he was famous for as he blew her a kiss. She bared her teeth at him before turning away.

Let him enjoy the escape for the moment; her time would come. A time when he didn't have help.

A soft male chuckle had her shooting Graeme a hateful look as he plopped into the chair beside the low stool she sat on.

He was crazy.

Really. Teetering on insanity.

The only thing holding this Breed on the right side of rational thought was the mate who watched him with pure adoration.

Their bond was secure. They'd given to each other. This hard, savage creature had opened his soul and let his mate inside.

Unlike hers.

She flipped the knife, burying it in the wood floor with a hard *whack* as fury shot through her once again.

He could say he'd done what he did to protect her until hell froze over. It didn't change facts. The fact that any Breed alive could sense the soul-deep mark he'd placed on her, but he carried no similar mark.

"You're an interesting little thing," Graeme remarked quietly, quite seriously, as she stared at the depth the blade had sunk into the hard wood.

"How's that?" Resentment rose inside her in a wave.

He shouldn't have contacted Jonas.

"I really didn't think a female Primal was possible," he told her. "I can't wait to get back to my lab and figure out if the Primal instinct awakening was due to your Cross-Breed genetics or if it was carried by one or the other and simply mutated."

She glared at him from the corner of her eyes.

"You have a lot to learn," he sighed. "When the creature isn't so close to the surface, it will become easier. Your mate will help. He's actually learned a rather unique way of handling his own without the savagery taking over. I still struggle with that myself at times. Not that the beast is any less effective. Just different." Pure arrogance filled his expression. "You'll learn that as your mate guides you . . ."

"I have no mate," she gritted out. "I was disavowed, remember?"

He chuckled at that. "A piece of paper." He waved it away. "Sent to ensure you weren't endangered by his actions. I rather doubt Rule even noted it in the database."

"Doesn't matter." She lifted her shoulders negligently. "You can't miss it, Bengal. I carry his mark, but he doesn't carry mine."

Grief threatened to swamp her.

"Ah, Cassie." He sighed, shaking his head. "You're wrong. That Breed carries your mark to his very spirit. The moment you put that Coyote on his ass with your knife to his throat, even I felt that bond between you snap in place. If he'd kept you out before, in that second, he opened his soul and let you flow inside him. When you're fully rational again, you'll realize it."

"I am fully rational." She gritted her teeth, pushing the words through them.

He chuckled again. "Come here."

Cassie growled as she gave in and rose to her feet, following the Bengal as he led her to the ornate mirror positioned over a sideboard.

"Look, little Primal," he urged softly. "Look at your eyes."

She looked up and froze. The whites were gone, her blue irises almost glowing, filling her eyes and sparking with fury within her face. Her hair framed her face, unbound, curls rioting over her shoulders and down her back, giving her an otherworldly, witchy look.

"Dog told me once his mate was a siren. That her voice could make grown Breeds weep, that her eyes could mesmerize, and from the moment he'd set his sights on her, she ensured he didn't slip into that black void his soul was becoming. Primals ride the edge of madness, or at least, it seems the males do." His head tipped to the side as he regarded her through the glass almost quizzically. "Perhaps you're simply an anomaly."

She leaned closer, staring at her eyes. "How do you make it go away?"

He sighed heavily. "The Primal never goes away, but it rests. You awaken it; it doesn't awaken itself. When you know the danger of losing your mate is over, then it will sleep. It won't awaken again until you call it forth. And it gets easier to awaken it without that phenomenon. Though you'll learn how much sharper your senses are when it's fully awake within you."

Pulling back, she lowered her head and moved over to the low stool she'd claimed. She jerked the knife from the floor and tucked it in the sheath at her thigh once again.

Graeme settled back into the chair next to her and relaxed with a heavy sigh.

"Will you give me more blood when I need it?" he suddenly asked. "I have quite a few tests to run. I'll need more."

She rolled her eyes. "Why the hell not?" Resting her elbow on her knee, she propped her chin in her hand and breathed out heavily. "When are they going to just fly him over Jonas's volcano and be done with it?"

Graeme suddenly leaned forward, looking at her with almost excited interest.

"So, that rumor's true? Do you know where it's at?" he asked almost gleefully.

"Restrain yourself, darling," Cat laughed, pushing his shoulders back and perching on his lap. "You'll frighten Cassie off if you're not careful."

The powerful Breed almost pouted, but his arms went around his mate, his chin resting on her shoulder. "Want to slip away?" he suggested, blowing in his mate's ear. "I'll make it worth your while."

"You will anyway. You're so easy, Graeme . . ."

Cassie tuned them out, unwilling, unable, to listen to their banter. She was still too raw, too ragged inside.

Rising to her feet, she decided she'd had enough herself. It was time for her to return to the Bureau. She'd had enough of this house, the stench of hatred and corruption.

How the hell Dog's father had survived here as a child and young man she couldn't fathom.

"Cassie." Jonas stopped her as she reached the doorway.

"I'm leaving, Jonas," she snapped, aware of Cullen, Graeme and their mates shadowing her.

Throwing her hand up in farewell, she passed through the doors and strode through the house, heading for the foyer. There were no fewer than three heli-jets parked on the lawn now. She could be back at the Bureau in a matter of hours and send it back when they dropped her off. Jonas would no doubt be here for a while. And she was tired of sitting, waiting.

She had things to do.

◆   ◆   ◆

"You got this?" Dog snapped out the question to Jonas as Cassie left the room, heading, he knew, for one of the heli-jets outside.

"Go," Jonas agreed. "I'll call another transport from DC. It can be here in less than an hour."

"Dog." Dash stopped him before he could get away. "What happened in that garage . . ." He grimaced, his expression tightening at the memory of it. "Whatever's tearing her apart . . ."

"I know what happened to her," Dog assured the other Breed, the lashing guilt he felt over it impossible to let go of for the moment. "She'll be fine, Dash. I swear it."

There was no other comfort he could give the father who hurt for his child, who hurt with her, struggled to protect her.

"I'll hold you to that." The Wolf Breed nodded abruptly. "Make sure she is."

◆   ◆   ◆

The sun was coming up when Cassie stepped back into the apartment at the Bureau. She shed the lightweight black jacket she wore in the living room, paused at the door to the bedroom and kicked her boots off. The snug tank came off next, dropped carelessly just inside the bedroom door; the pants were shed just inside the bathroom.

She wasn't wearing panties.

Dog leaned against the door frame and watched as she adjusted the temperature, then stepped beneath the shower, her head lowering to allow the steamy spray to saturate her hair.

She hadn't spoken on the flight back, despite several attempts by the others to engage her in conversation. She'd withdrawn so deep inside herself that Dog had felt the beast rising inside him again, desperate because he couldn't sense her.

It had been Graeme's quick response, a cautioning shake of his head and the warning to wait, that had allowed him to find the control to ease back. That crazed Bengal carried a beast inside him unlike any Dog had ever sensed. If anyone understood the enraged fury consuming Cassie, then it would be him.

The sheer wild agony he'd felt echoing in his soul until that second he found himself flat on his back had eased. It wasn't comforting, though, because the sense of aloneness he felt was worse. She'd pulled so far away from him that he could barely sense the emotions she was struggling to contain.

He'd been ten when the creature rose inside him. Ten when it had torn free. It had taken three days for it to retreat, to allow reason, sanity, to return to the boy he'd been. He'd be damned if he'd give Cassie three days. No way in hell would he let her drift in that black void alone.

Stripping and dropping his dirty clothes in the basket he'd always seen her use before, he activated the additional showerhead and stepped in with her. The little growl of warning and impending violence that sounded from her throat had him grinning.

"Savage little halfling," he teased her, soaping his hair as she glared up at him before turning her back.

Her eyes were still that amazing neon, burning like flaming gems within her pale face. Once the Primal, as Graeme called it, retreated, exhaustion would claim her. And by God he intended to have this settled before her system completely shut down on him.

"Pissed at me, are you, baby?" Filling his palm with her scented shampoo, he buried his hands in her hair before she could avoid him, tightening them and holding her in place as a snarl escaped her lips.

Savage little beast she was.

He was filled with regret at the reason, but almost overwhelmed by pride as well. That enraged little creature had done what grown Breeds couldn't. She'd put him on his ass, her blade at his throat, and he'd seen the threat in those raging blue eyes.

"Yeah, you're pissed," he sighed, working the shampoo through the lush curls that rippled down her back to her hips. "Not that I blame you. You have every right."

What he'd done to her threatened the very core of the mating, and he knew it. He had not just allowed but also ordered another Breed to lay his hands on her, to restrain her as he drove away. He'd legally disavowed their mating, separated himself from her at a time she felt she should have stood at his side.

What he'd done was unforgivable, and he knew it. But she would forgive him; he couldn't allow her not to. She was his heart, his soul.

She was stiff, unresponsive, as he caressed her scalp

with firm motions, working the shampoo through the curls. She refused to relax against him, to still the anger coursing through her.

"You were outside that room, you know what happened, you know why it happened," he told her quietly. "You can be pissed, Cassie, you can be hurt, you can rage from now to hell and back, but it won't change a damned thing, baby."

He continued to work the lather through her hair, rubbing the strands between his fingers, bunching them, massaging her scalp.

"If it would take away the pain I caused you in that garage, I'd let you slice my throat a thousand times over," he told her then and felt the almost imperceptible shudder that raced through her. "For as long as I live, I'll know what I did to you, I'll live it in my nightmares, because I felt every second of it shredding my own soul."

She tried to jerk away from him, rage echoing in the low, furious growl that filled the shower. His fingers held her firm, gripping her hair with one hand, the opposite arm wrapping around her hips to jerk her back against him.

"There wasn't a second, not an ounce of your pain that I didn't fucking feel," he snarled. "Let go of your anger long enough to sense the truth of that."

She stood as stiff as before, the water coursing over them, brilliant white suds rinsing around them, silky soft, but not as soft as the long strands of hair caressing his body.

He could feel that rage still whipping through her, destroying both of them. Resting his forehead atop her head, he breathed out heavily, fighting against the devastation he remembered sweeping over him.

"Mutt didn't want to stop you," he whispered, feeling the flinch that raced through her body.

His eyes closed, remembering the sight of the other Breed's hands on her bare arms, hearing her screams of pain and feral fury.

"I couldn't risk you, halfling," he whispered. "Ryder had

his own son murdered, the woman his son pleaded for him to accept so she'd be safe, so their child would be safe. He hunted them down like animals and the only thing that saved me was his uncertainty at the time that I existed." He could never understand the evil that blackened men's souls. "I hid for three days in a burrow with a coyote mother and her pups, huddled against those tiny creatures for warmth, and I swore I'd never allow anyone else to suffer at his hands . . ."

"You betrayed me." Ragged, torn with pain, but still the most beautiful voice he'd ever heard in his life. "You let him touch me. Disavowed me. You left me."

She tried to jerk away from him again, nearly managing it before he caught her hair again and spun her around.

He should have kept her back to him. The creature that had risen inside her was once again dormant. But the sight of that creature spilling into her eyes was better than this. Gem bright, overflowing with tears and filled with pain.

"Look at me, Cassie," he whispered, framing her face with his hands, knowing he couldn't hide from her now; all she had to do was look. "Do you hurt alone? Did you suffer alone? Would I have ever done any of those things for any reason other than to save you?"

Fury erupted in her eyes. A woman's fury. A mate's rage.

"I'm your mate," she cried, her finger stabbing at his chest as the scent of her reached him then, sweet, pure, on fire. "It's my place to face whatever you face. You can't save me from your actions, you moron," she all but screamed. "You took all of me and left me with nothing."

"Look at me!" he yelled, gripping a handful of sodden hair and forcing her head back. "Look at me, Cassie. Do you believe you don't have all of me? For even a second?"

She owned him.

"I will skin your ass out, hang your hide on my wall, and I swear to you, I'll find such a bad-ass Breed to mate that you'll cringe every second in hell if you pull this shit on me again." She was shaking, but with anger rather than that feral, primal rage that had filled her before.

"One mate," he snarled, unable to believe she'd make such a threat. No, as he stared down at her, he seriously feared that was more than a promise. "Get rid of me, half-ling, and there is no other."

A snarl curled her lips, a feminine growl of power vibrating in her throat. "Fucking bet me."

By God, she meant it. She'd actually try.

She wouldn't succeed, but she'd try. The very thought of it was terrifying.

And he was a sick bastard, because his cock was harder than hell, fully engorged and throbbing with something so far beyond lust that he had no name for it.

"Fucking test me." He jerked her to him, lifting her from her feet until her face was level with his. Her knees gripped his hips, the lush, heated folds of her pussy teasing the head of his dick. "Even consider attempting another mate for any reason, I'll show you exactly how I'll deal with it."

She bared her teeth at him, eyes narrowing. "I dare you."

· CHAPTER 2I ·

She dared him.

Dog couldn't help but chuckle as he tightened his fingers in her hair and dragged her head back. He took the kiss he wanted. The glands beneath his tongue were swollen, throbbing, the mating hormone so potent now it was like a rush, an incredible high as it hit his system.

Turning, he pushed her back against the wall, one hand going to her rear, filling his hand with one side of the rounded flesh and lifting her where he needed her.

Dare him?

He prayed to God she didn't expect nice and easy. The sound of those words slipping past her lips was like throwing gasoline on fire. The flames whipped through his senses, seared his brain cells and released a torrent of lust.

Slanting his lips over hers and pumping his tongue between her lips, he forced her to take the taste of him. When he pulled back and her tongue followed, he took hers, trapping it between his lips and drawing on it, licking at it. The spicy sweetness sending the flames in a rush of white-hot intensity tore the last of the restraint from him.

There was no holding back with her now. There was no closing even a small portion of his soul to her now. The mating bond was like a live wire connecting them, merging them together. Heart to heart. Soul to soul.

Tearing his lips from hers, his kisses rained down her neck as he groaned, feeling hers against his neck. Her teeth raked against the line of his throat, stealing his breath. Her tongue licked over it before her lips closed on his flesh and drew on it, marking him. But he was always marking hers. His teeth nipping enough to abrade the skin, before licking over the wound, just over the heavy vein that ran there.

Her arms wrapped around his shoulders, and her hips rocked, caressing the head of his cock with the slick, hot folds of her pussy. The heated moisture spilling from her coated the engorged cap of his erection, warmed it, sensitized it. As the broad head pressed against the entrance, a hard ejaculation of the hormone-filled pre-cum pulsed inside her.

Bending his head farther he captured the hard bud of a nipple, sucking it into the heat of his mouth, tonguing it as a groan tore from his chest. The taste of her, the feel of her . . . It wasn't even logical what she did to him, what she made him feel. Just the scent of her close to him was enough to soothe his soul, a soul he'd been certain he didn't possess before he saw her in the lens of his gunsights.

Pulling back from her breast, his fingers tightening on her ass, he held her in place and another pulse of pre-cum spilled inside her as she nipped at his shoulder. The heat of her pussy covered the head of his cock, the entrance clenching on it, sucking at his flesh.

Tensing, he thrust inside her, feeling the ultratight, slick heat of her pussy clamping down on his dick, tightening, caressing every inch, forging inside her. Her teeth bit down on his shoulder, a strangled cry tearing from her throat as he felt those sharp little teeth break the tough skin and the searing spill of that hormone infusing it.

His cock throbbed, flexing with another jetting pulse of the hormone inside her, sensitizing her, ensuring her pleasure.

"Fuck," he snarled as her tongue lapped at the wound, a smothered cry echoing around him. "Like a hot little vise . . ."

He didn't pause, sending his cock burrowing inside her deeper, pushing inside her until he was lodged balls deep and her cries were like a symphony in his ears. The snug flesh rippled, sucked at his cock.

He couldn't hold back. He couldn't hold on.

Holding her to the wall and bracing his body, he began thrusting, retreating, then filling her, each thrust inside her increasing the hunger, the need, until he swore he could feel parts of his spirit become infused by her, pulling her into his soul.

Animalistic groans spilled from his throat as he moved faster, harder, stroking inside her as the sensations turned to flames licking over him, setting everything inside him aflame when he felt her tighten further, felt her orgasm rip through her and trigger his own release.

He swore it was never ending.

The most intense release he'd experienced since the last time he knotted her tight little pussy. The swelling of his cock inside the clamped muscles had him growling at her shoulder, his teeth locked in it yet again. Filling her, destroying him, as his seed pumped from his dick in exquisite ecstasy.

"Ah God, Cassie . . . Halfling . . . I fucking love you. My life . . ." He threw his head back, teeth clenched as a snarl of pure, lashing rapture overwhelmed his senses.

He was surrounded in a pleasure that went so deep, filling every corner of his soul and healing the wounds life had placed there. A pleasure filled with hope, with savage determination to hold on to her, and a ferocity of such emotion it swamped him.

Not simply his emotion, hers. They mixed, wrapping around each other, filling each other, binding them together in a way he'd never believed possible.

Always.

A part of each other.

◆   ◆   ◆

Hours later Cassie came slowly to awareness. The room was dark, the bed warm, her mate lay at her back, surrounding her.

And they weren't alone.

She opened her eyes slowly and stared at the misty form of the couple. Carson and Angel. Parents who had been unable to pass to a place where there was no worry, no fear, because their fierce devotion to their son refused to allow them to leave his side.

So much so that his mother had searched out his mate, found her in danger, and left her mate to watch over their son while she watched over Cassie.

Her head tilted in understanding, knowing Cassie's thoughts as she always had, as her mate looked on in approval.

Seeing you grow, your strength, your heart, has been a joy, Cassie, she whispered across the bond they'd established years ago. *I could not have chosen a better mate for my child, nor wished for one truer. He was born, just as you were, not created. My mate raised him with love, taught him rather than trained him, and the heart he possesses is one more fierce than any but you could know. And know, we'll always be close if there's a need.*

Cassie stared back at the spirit, only then realizing that a part of her had feared Angel wouldn't be there to warn her when danger came too close.

We can both be near, together now, Carson assured her. *Tell our son of our love for him.* That emotion resonated so deep and pure from the male spirit that Cassie felt tears fill her eyes. *He's the best part of both of us. And he has fulfilled every dream his parents ever had for him.*

She would.

"Thank you," she whispered, a breath of sound. "For everything."

For her safety as a child, for the guidance, but most of all, for her mate.

No thanks needed, Cassie, Angel assured her. *Build your lives now, see your way through the trials together and love each other with everything you are. The future won't be easy. There are battles yet to come for not just you and Dog, but for all Breeds. Stay true. Follow your instincts and your heart. And always love . . .*

They faded away slowly, going wherever the spirits went until they sensed they were needed.

"Thank you, Cassie." Strangled, filled with awe, Dog's voice had her rolling quickly to face him, to stare into his eyes and the well of emotions that filled them.

Love, wonder, joy and the sadness that came from the realization of what was lost when the world stole his parents.

"Thank you, little halfling," he whispered, his eyes damp as his palm cupped her cheek. "For your heart, for my parents."

"You saw them?" Surprise filled her. No one had ever seen them before.

"I saw them. I heard them. Finally. I dreamed of them together as a boy, and now you've given me that dream." His lips touched hers. "Every dream I've held, Cassie, you've brought to life."

His lips brushed against hers, a gentle, heated caress that reaffirmed his words. The kiss was a benediction, a promise, a vow.

It was everything they were meant to be.

She was what she was, what she was meant to be, in her mate's heart, in his arms.

Finally, no longer a cross breed, but a mate.

Dog's mate.

✦ EPİLOGUE ✦

Ah, threads, Graeme thought as he read the message sent to his tablet. More samples would arrive within the hour, another Coyote Breed Mating, more questions. He loved the questions. Along with his mate, it was all that kept him sane.

It seemed for a while the Breed scientists were focusing on the Coyote Breeds, believing the anomalies of the Mating Heat within that species held the answers they were looking for, and that two former Russian scientists had found a key with the vaccinations they'd invented over two decades before. The vaccinations were interesting, as were the Coyote anomalies. The Wolf Breeds, though—now they were *interesting*. Their inability to conceive even within Mating Heat was becoming rather a problem for the females.

At least, it had been. The scientists were searching in the wrong direction, but to be certain, he needed a Wolf Breed mating, now didn't he? Wolf and human. Preferably an Alpha male. And wasn't it just fortuitous that he knew just such a couple, he thought with innate satisfaction. A Mating long overdue.

Not that this one would be easy. A more stubborn female he'd only met once. His own mate was of course more stubborn, but he liked to think he had the best in all things, now didn't he? But this female, she would give his own mate a run for the stubborn money.

The sound of the door opening at the top of the circular metal stairs had him pausing. The scent of anger, hurt, stubborn will, and determined pride mixed with that of emerging Mating Heat. Rather like the scent drifting from the connecting cavern. He had to cover a smile. He wondered if this young woman had the slightest suspicion of the determined Wolf that would die before he ever truly released her.

Ensuring his expression was suitably filled with sadness and regret, he watched as Khileen Langer moved down the stairs. Long, sunlit red hair was pulled back into a neat little braid, exposing her worried expression and the delicate lines of her face. Dressed in jeans, boots and a tank top he'd dared his own mate to wear, she moved down the stairs, the roiling emotions she felt touching his very narrow vein of compassion.

"I'm here," she announced quietly as she took the last step. "I need to hurry, though, I have an appointment in town with Cassie Sinclair. For some reason she's decided I should be in her wedding party." And she was genuinely confused over that, it seemed.

Lifting the syringe he had laid close by several hours before, he watched as she turned her shoulder to him. Her profile was downcast, something too thoughtful, too somber reflecting in it.

Pushing the pressure syringe to her shoulder he injected the hormonal treatment to still the effects of Mating Heat, then stepped back.

"That's the last injection, Khi," he told her quietly. "I'm sorry, but your system can't handle much more."

He was a very effective liar, sadly.

Poor Khi. The time for running was now at an end.

✦   ✦   ✦

Khileen Langer stared at the Bengal Breed, certain she couldn't have heard him correctly. It wasn't possible. He had to be wrong.

Graeme Parker was like Dr. Jekyll, Mr. Hyde and the Einstein of Breed genetics and mating bullshit all rolled into one. He knew his shit backward and forward. It wasn't possible that he wouldn't have an answer to this.

"I'm sorry, Khi." He stared back at her, somber, compassion reflecting his expression. "There's simply no way to go any further with the serum. The Mating Heat is simply adjusting to it too quickly. If I keep messing with your system in this way then it could kill you."

"Could kill me." She latched onto the words desperately. "You're not certain, though."

A grimace tightened his face and he shook his head at the objection.

"Kill you, paralyze you, it could make the Heat worse, it could cause severe internal bleeding or all of the above," he growled out, flashing her an irritated look. "I've run all the probables and those probables say that another increase in the strength of the injections to be highly ill advised. You're going to have to face this now. There's no delaying it any longer."

She could feel herself shaking. Fear, desperation, grief. Emotions she'd been holding on to for the past two years were beginning to race through her, threatening to escape all hope of control. She was shaking her head, staring at Graeme pleadingly, certain he had to be wrong.

"Graeme, please . . . ," she whispered.

"Khi, this has gone too far and for too long," he said with quiet firmness. "You and Lobo need to figure this out . . ."

"No. No." Her hand sliced through the air as rage slipped the tether she'd kept on it.

As long as there was hope, she'd been able to keep the

anger at bay. As long as there was a chance she'd been able to take each day with some semblance of control.

"Khi, the waiting is killing you and it's killing Lobo. You have to settle this with your mate," he told her, not for the first time.

"No." She shook her head again. "Tiberius will be back . . ."

"With his mate," he broke in on her words, staring down at her gently, regretfully. "Tiberius has mated, Khi. He's returning to the estate with his mate to take his place as Lobo's second-in-command. Your mother's death has been confirmed. Tiberius is mated. Lobo won't hold back any longer."

She stepped away, feeling as though she'd taken a blow. Breath catching, she barely restrained a cry of disbelief, certain she couldn't have heard the Breed correctly. She couldn't have; it wasn't possible.

"Despite your claims of hatred for him, Lobo seems to have found himself unable to tell you this. And I'll warn you now—you're pushing him too far. He's your mate. An Alpha Wolf who has restrained himself to give you time to adjust to what you know is the truth. It's time to begin adjusting to it." Graeme's tone hardened, his eyes taking on that freaky, scary look she always pretended didn't bother her.

"Then I'll leave . . ."

A bark of laughter met the claim. "And do what, girl? Once the Mating Heat begins burning inside you do you think you can hide it? And it will burn, Khi. You've delayed it to the point that once it kicks in every Breed for a mile or farther will sense it. If you don't allow the mating before this happens, then you'll drive Lobo crazy with it. You don't want that." The warning was another she'd heard before.

She knew what he believed would happen, how the Heat would snap alive inside her once the hormone he was injecting her with lost all effectiveness.

"I don't want him," she snapped, the anger pushing past her control. "For God's sake, Graeme, he was my step-father."

He grunted at that. "You know that marriage was one of convenience only . . ."

"He was still married to her." She was almost shaking with fury now. "It doesn't matter if she's alive, if she's dead or somewhere fucking in between."

Jessica Langer Reever. She'd ensured the death of her first husband, attempted to kill her Breed husband, as well as her only child. She was pure evil. She had no heart. She had no soul.

"Doesn't matter, Khi," he sighed heavily, shaking his head as he began shutting down the various machines he'd used to run her blood samples that evening. "Married or not, whether his wife was dead or alive, that's your mate. You know it; he knows it. And the time to face it has come."

She couldn't face it. She couldn't allow it to happen. The woman he'd married wasn't just any woman. It was her mother. And it didn't matter what Graeme believed—she knew, *knew* that Lobo had had sex with that conniving bitch. She'd known it since the week after her sixteenth birthday when she'd walked into her mother's bedroom and caught them.

She swallowed tightly, hatred and disgust welling inside her at the memory. Naked, their bodies sheened with sweat, Lobo's powerful muscles flexing, his hips driving between Jessica Langer's thighs as he buried himself inside her. The memory of it enraged her, burned inside her like acid and ate at her in ways she couldn't explain.

She was fighting to breathe, to keep from screaming at the injustice of the position she found herself in. She couldn't accept it; she couldn't bear it. Besides, it wasn't Lobo she loved but Tiberius. Tiberius, who had mated. Who was re-turning to the estate with the woman he loved. And that was all her fault. If he hadn't left, if he had loved her, then she wouldn't have to face mating a Breed she hated.

"Khi, you need to talk to Lobo," Graeme advised her then. "Don't keep pushing him. Don't keep challenging him."

"There has to be a way to stop this." There had to be.

But he was only shaking his head. "I've done everything I can do, ran every test I can think of. There's no way to stop it."

"So I should just accept it?" She sneered, feeling a shudder race through her body. "I should run upstairs and spread my legs for that bastard and let him steal my goddamned choice from me?"

He actually had the nerve to roll his eyes at her.

"That temper of yours is gonna get you in trouble, girl," he grunted. "And lying to yourself isn't going to help you either. Grow up. You're not sixteen any longer and Tiberius never was a good stand-in for Lobo. Admit why you want to hate him and deal with why you don't."

Her lips thinned.

He thought he knew so much. Him and Lobo both. They thought they knew so much more about her than she knew herself.

"Go to hell," she snarled, turning on her heel and stomping to the curved staircase that led from the underground caverns where Graeme kept his mad scientist lab to the house above it.

She'd be damned if she'd give in to any of them so easily, especially that bastard Wolf, Lobo. He sickened her. Enraged her. He'd married a woman to ensure he could establish his pack and ignored everything else. He'd ignored her bruises, he'd ignored her disappearances, and he'd ignored every pleading look she'd given him to make it stop. He'd ignored it for his pack. And she'd ignore him and his damned Heat now. And she'd find a way to make him pay for it.

✦   ✦   ✦

Lobo stepped from the connecting cavern as the door lead-ing into the main house slammed above them with enough force to echo into the underground rooms.

Sliding his hands into the pockets of his slacks he looked up, stared at the door and sighed heavily. God help him. If he could change any of this he would, for her. If he could have ensured a mating between her and Tiberius, it would have destroyed him, but he would have done so. For her.

"Oh, stop feeling so damned sorry for her," Graeme growled, disgust filling his voice. "If you and Tiberius would stop allowing that girl to bury her head in the sand and hide from the truth, then you'd all be far happier."

Would they? Lobo wondered, still staring at the stairs, the scent of his mate in his nostrils, her need increasing his, reminding him why he stayed as far away from her as pos-sible.

"She's so very young," he sighed.

And he felt so very old sometimes.

"Ten years?" Graeme snorted. "Keep burying your own head in the sand, Lobo, and someone's gonna knock you in the ass. You may even cause Khi more pain than she's al-ready known. That might piss me off."

And of course pissing off Graeme just worried the hell out of him, Lobo thought mockingly.

"You lied to her," he pointed out to the Bengal. "Mul-tiple times."

Graeme shrugged. "Tiberius may well mate before he returns, and as for the hormonal serum, there are some anomalies showing up in her that I want to study before she receives more. I believe it could be detrimental for the in-jections to continue."

"What sort of anomalies?" Lobo tensed, staring back at Graeme suspiciously.

The Bengal frowned almost as though confused. "I'm

still studying the anomalies," he murmured, his expression turning strangely thoughtful. "I do know the hormonal serum is reacting oddly on the Mating Heat hormones in her system, though she's likely not realized it yet."

And what exactly did that mean?

"Reacting oddly in what way? Is she okay?" For a Breed who had never known fear, what he felt was strangely similar to the descriptions he'd heard.

"Oh, it won't affect her health." Graeme waved the thought away. "The projections I've been running aren't conclusive yet. I'll let you know as soon as they are."

Mad fucking scientist, Lobo thought in disgust. Some days, Graeme seemed to have the answers to any Breed genetic or physiological problem that could arise. Then, on odd days, he could be amazingly reticent.

"Graeme, what's going on?" Lobo could feel a suspicion that went beyond the surface now. Something the Bengal wasn't saying, but should be.

"As I said, I'm not yet certain," Graeme reminded him. "I will be certain to let you know, though."

Lobo felt his jaw tense, frustration rising inside him. As though he needed more frustration.

"How long does she have?" he asked then, glancing up the stairs once again. "Before the Heat kicks in?"

Graeme paused, the green of his eyes darkening over the gold as his lashes narrowed.

"Twenty-four to seventy-two hours," he said, his expression becoming a bit brooding. "No more than seventy-two, definitely." He finally nodded.

Seventy-two hours. Not nearly long enough to find a way to make her understand when she refused to discuss more than the time of day with him. Not nearly long enough . . .

• B R E E D   T E R M S •

Armored F-16 Dragoon: Vehicle based on the Armored Sergeants Dragoon but weaponized and more advanced.

Armored Sergeants Dragoon: Vehicle with the same design as the Dragoon Elite but built primarily for off-road use.

Breed Appropriations Committee: Group responsible for regulating expenditures of money collected from various persons and governments whose political and/or military arm were found to be involved with or funded, knowingly or unknowingly, Breed research and creation.

Breed Criminal Cabinet: Breed and human members who act as a grand jury of sorts to decide if Breed Law has been broken and if a matter should be referred to the Breed Tribunal. The Breed Criminal Cabinet is part of the Breed Defense Initiative.

Breed Defense Initiative: Measure created by Cassandra Sinclair, Kane Tyler, Malachai Morgan and Braden Arness for the defense of Breeds or humans accused of breaking Breed Law.

Breed Law: Mandates of laws signed by President Marion as well as all state-elected representatives and members of

Congress that govern the treatment, punishment, acts of prejudice, hatred or other species-related crimes against Breeds, their communities, mates or children. Because of the number of elected and military officials as well as government-backed scientists who were involved in the creation and cruelties inflicted on the Breeds, the laws were created and approved to remain intact for eternity, unless otherwise abolished, amended or designated no longer needed by the Breeds themselves.

Breed Ruling Cabinet: Organization that governs and enforces the mandates of Breed Law within the Breed society. Comprised of an equal number of each Breed designation of the Breed species as well as humans.

Breeds: Humans genetically enhanced and/or altered either before or during conception with any DNA designated as non-human.

Breed Tribunal: Group that oversees laws governing Breed society. Rules on crimes against Breeds or the Breed communities by Breeds, their mates or any human affiliate who signs the agreement of Breed mandates that rules the Breed communities. Comprised of the members of the Feline Breed Tribunal, Wolf Breed Tribunal and Coyote Breed Tribunal, as well as the elected Breed commander and the director of the Federal Bureau of Breed Affairs.

Bureau of Breed Affairs Oversight Committee: Panel of several elected senators, Breeds and foreign ambassadors tasked with overseeing the running of the Bureau, the actions of its director and the official missions Breeds participate in for allied countries.

Condition Alpha: Protection and highest level of security to ensure the lives of the members of the Breed ruling families.

Their location and protection during danger are kept under the highest level of security.

Council Breeds: Breeds whose loyalties remain to the scientists and those backing them.

Council Soldiers: Both Breed and human soldiers who follow orders given in the apprehension or death of those in the Breed society.

Coya: Mate to the Coy Leader.

Coy Leader: Head of all Coyote Breeds and/or packs. Base location is Cidadel, overlooking Haven, Advent, Colorado.

Desert Dragoon: Powerhouse vehicle built mostly for desert use. Rumbles dangerously at low speeds.

Dragoon Elite: Vehicle that sits low to the ground, built for speed and agility on congested highways and city streets. Equipped with minimal onboard weapons and two seats, with a trunk and back seat area that's empty to allow for storage, bullet-resistant windows with a protective film covering that confuses telescopes or other devices used to observe occupants, and explosive-and IED-resistant undercarriage and frame fully armored.

Federal Bureau of Breed Affairs: Oversees the Breed communities, any protests or accusations against them and all government payments to the Breeds as a whole. Director of the Bureau chairs any committees concerning the Breeds as a whole.

Feline, Wolf and Coyote Breed Tribunals: Judicial bodies comprised of three pride or pack alphas and six generally elected members of the community to oversee any general crimes against the community or the members of the community. Overseen by the Pride or Pack leaders.

Female Alpha: Naturally born female Breed with the same inherent sense of command and inner strength that male alphas are born with. Such a female can become a Primal. Any female Primal is an alpha female, but an alpha female is not necessarily a Primal.

Genetic Flaming: Sudden flaming or awakening of once-hidden Breed genetics after a long period or even a lifetime of recessive Breed genetics. Usually occurs between ages twenty and twenty-three after the genetics have lain dormant or recessed. Symptoms include body temperature over 107 degrees, convulsions, hallucinations, flaring animal instincts such as enraged growls or snarls and attempts to bite or scratch.

Genetics Council: Group of twelve who oversee the funding, research and creation of the Breeds.

Ghost Team: Team of Breeds tasked with protecting the ruling families when an inordinate amount of danger threatens. Separately the Breeds in Ghost Team are highly effective. Together they are the most deadly team of Breeds known.

Hybrid Breed: Breed born naturally of a Breed-human mating.

Law of Self-Warrant: Law that decrees that any Breed may, one time only, accept the punishment and/or death for any criminal act that the Breed believes would cause his or her mate, child, parent or other associated relative undue harm.

Mating Heat: Chemical, biological and pheromonal reaction between a Breed and his or her mate that causes extreme arousal, the inability to allow touch from the opposite sex except from the mate and in extreme cases, extreme discomfort during the height of the Heat, from any touch beyond the mate's. It is believed that this occurs only once for a Breed.

Nephilim: Most popular definition is the offspring of human females and male fallen angels. The title has been given to a group of hidden Breeds who so closely resemble their animal cousins that they appear as two-legged animals. Often used by human parents to frighten their children into good behavior.

Patrol Water Cruiser: Watercraft used in large lakes or near shore in ocean/sea patrol.

Petition to Disavow: Physical divorce of sorts that ensures a mate isn't affected by any crime his or her mate makes after the mating. No contact is allowed after a disavowal.

Petition for Reconsideration: Petition requested by a prospective Breed mate to have a first mating reconsidered, should a mate show two prospective Breed mates. Forces the mate in question to spend a predetermined amount of time (nonsexual) with the filer of the petition to disprove the viability of the first mate.

Petition for Separation: Petition requested by a Breed to separate from his or her prospective mate for a predetermined amount of time, though no longer than eighteen months.

Prima: Mate to the Prime Leader.

Primal: Preternatural creature whose awakened senses and/ or strength can sometimes defy even fatal wounds. Most Breeds know only their human and animal personalities. In the Primal, a third designation becomes known. The Primal's sole reason for existence is to protect the Breed, to ensure the safety of its mate and/or children. There are currently only four known Primals.

Prime Leader: Head of all feline Breeds and/or prides. Base location is Pride Sanctuary, Buffalo Gap, Virginia.

Psychotic Emergent Feral Fever: Most violent and least controllable of the feral fevers.

Pure-Blood Societies/Purists: Group that believes Breeds should be exterminated to ensure their mutated genetics aren't allowed to mix with those of humans. They believe in a pure-blood society.

Rogue Breeds: Breeds with no official ties to the Breed society, either known or unknown.

Supreme Societies/Supremacists: Group that believes Breeds are animals, despite their human origin, and they should be returned to the labs for scientific experiments and used only to benefit humankind.

Unknown: Navajo. A group of secretive, unnamed warriors in war paint who rescue, transport or aid Breeds, humans and hybrids in escaping the Council and their soldiers. They have aided the disappearances of dozens of Breed children. Rumor suggests Leo Vanderale financially backs this group.

CASSIE AT SEVEN

Dash Sinclair. That's the name you want, Cassie. Choose Dash.

Seven-year-old Cassie Colder stared at the name that the pale, translucent finger pointed to. Her heart raced, fear was an ugly taste in her mouth and desperation had the tears she couldn't shed threatening to well in her eyes. But when the fairy pointed to the name, all she could do was hope.

Dash Sinclair sounded like such a nice daddy's name. She bet Dash Sinclair didn't hit his little girl or scream at her. She bet he loved her and he took care of her like a daddy was supposed to do.

No, Dash Sinclair would never hit his little girl or scream at her, the fairy that always followed her whispered in her ear. *He will love his little girl. But he has to find her first.*

Cassie looked up from the paper cautiously, her gaze going around the schoolroom just to make certain no one else could see or hear her fairy.

Raise your hand, Cassie, before someone else chooses

his name, her fairy demanded gently. *He's the one we've searched for. The only one that can help your momma . . .*

Her hand shot up.

That mention of her momma had her heart racing, had the fear returning. Someone had to help her momma. She was determined to save Cassie. And the bad men who kept chasing them would kill her momma if someone didn't help them.

"Cassie, do you have a name?" Ms. Davies asked, her voice nice but not as gentle and filled with warmth as the fairy's.

"I have a name, Ms. Davies." She nodded quickly. "Dash Sinclair. Can I write to him?"

Ms. Davies lifted the list in her hand, her dark eyes going over it before a small smile tugged at her lips.

"I liked his name myself, Cassie. You can have Dash Sinclair, then," the teacher agreed.

Hope grew stronger within her.

It was a wonderful daddy name and if she was really lucky, then he didn't have any other little girls and he would like her enough that he would come help her momma.

Very good, Cassie. Her fairy bent next to her, her pretty face gentle and approving, her blue eyes filled with warmth. *Now, remember the rules. You can't tell him your momma's secrets. Not yet.*

Cassie gave a little nod, hoping no one else saw her. She knew the rules but she didn't like them. She was so scared the fairy was wrong and she and her momma would be caught before help came, before someone could make all the bad men go away.

And her momma was getting so tired and worried. She didn't laugh like she used to, and though she always smiled whenever Cassie looked at her, that look of fear was still in her momma's eyes.

Cassie, you must stop worrying, her fairy cautioned her softly, a stroke of warmth drifting over her cheek where the fairy's fingers moved over it. *I promise I'll watch over you and your momma. Now, be good, obey the rules and do as I told you and one day, your momma will laugh again. I promise you.*

And her fairy had never broken her promises to Cassie.

Since that first night when her own daddy had tried to give her to the bad man and the bad man had killed him, her fairy had been there.

Dash Sinclair is a wonderful daddy's name, Cassie. Just remember that. And he will save your momma. Just as soon as your letters save him . . .

IRAQ, TWO WEEKS LATER

He was dying.

That knowledge drifted through the darkness Dash Sinclair found himself within as he became aware of the fact that he was . . . aware.

He'd have been amused if the part of himself that had awakened had the ability to be amused. Sadly, the only ability it seemed to have was keeping him alive when all he wanted to do was give up and drift away.

He was thirty years old, no doubt lying in yet another hospital, buried beneath more drugs, the clock ticking off the seconds, the hours since he'd known there was no avoiding the missile he'd heard whining its way to the chopper he and his men were in.

The eleven men he'd commanded for the past years had been laughing, teasing one another, sharing their plans of how they'd spend their leave once they landed.

How they'd leave the harsh desert behind for six weeks and return to the States. They'd return to family, girlfriends or simply friends. They'd be welcomed, hugged and pulled back into the lives they'd left behind to fight a war halfway around the world.

They wouldn't return to an empty tent and they wouldn't

search for missions to take until the unit came together once again.

Now they wouldn't be returning home either.

The blurred, distant knowledge that the soldiers he'd commanded were dead weighed on him. That knowledge didn't affect the beast that pulled him from that place where he could just drift away, though. Snarling and clawing, the animal dragged him back, held him with each fierce heart-beat and refused to let go. That secret, hidden part of who and what he was snapped at the darkness, threatened to wreak havoc, to break free and reveal itself if Dash didn't pull himself from oblivion.

And all he wanted to do was let go . . .

Every day of his life had been survival. No friends, no family, no one to call his own. Claiming someone meant making explanations. It meant trusting someone with his secrets. Secrets that could reveal who he was, what he was.

It was a risk he couldn't take.

He was alone. And so tired of merely existing rather than living. And why was he living when the men he'd commanded, men with friends, families, wives and lovers, were dead?

"Well, Dash, it would seem you have a fan . . ." The voice of his commanding officer, Colonel Thomas, pene-trated the darkness and the hidden primal rage. His words caused Dash to jerk alert despite the pain that assailed him as he did so.

He had no fans.

No friends or family.

And he had lost his unit.

He was damned tired of hiding and fighting, and he couldn't let himself just sleep. And now the animal he had always fought to deny was awake as it had never been be-fore and forcing him to listen, to pay attention.

"A nice little girl named Cassie sent you a letter. Let me

read this to you real fast. I'll answer her until you're well enough to do it yourself. But I have a feeling this little girl would get right pissed if you didn't eventually answer . . ." His commander cleared his throat. "Listen close now. You don't want to miss a word of this." And he began to read.

"I liked your name best when the teacher gave us the list. Dash Sinclair. It has a very nice sound to it, I think. Momma said it's a very brave, very handsome name, and she bets you like it lots. I thought it sounded like a daddy's name. I bet you have lots of little girls. And I bet they are very proud of your name. I don't have a daddy, but if I had one, then I would like a name like that for my daddy."

He had created his own name. Long ago. Far away. Created a name he had prayed would hide his past. Then he had fought to change himself as well. But he didn't have lots of little girls and he wasn't a daddy. The words his commander read seeped into his brain as a sense of urgency began to fill him.

"My momma, her name is Elizabeth. And she has black hair kind of like me. And pretty blue eyes. But my eyes are kind of blue too. I have a really pretty momma, Dash. She makes me cookies, and even tells me it's okay to talk to the fairy that lives in my room with me. My momma is really nice.

"My momma says you are a very brave man. That you are fighting to keep us safe. I wish you were here with us, Dash, cause sometimes my momma gets very tired."

Even though he was in pain, barely conscious, a sense of alarm surged through him. He could hear her fear in that simple sentence, read by the colonel, who didn't seem to recognize it. It was a plea for protection. And he knew in that moment he'd have to fight to live.

He had to live.

He had to save Cassie and her momma.

Dash saw Cassie, small and delicate, whimpering in

fear. But in bright, vivid colors, he saw her mother, desperate, frightened, poised in front of her daughter like a protective she-wolf, snarling in fury.

Why did he see that? Why did the image taunt him?

It was little Cassie who wrote to him, but with each line about her mother, each description, each phrase concerning the momma who looked after her, Dash's worry and need grew.

His sense of possessiveness, his hunger, his inborn knowledge that somehow, some way, Elizabeth and Cassie belonged to him, began to strengthen inside him.

Yes. The name Dash was a good name for a daddy. For Cassie's daddy. But it was also a good name for a mate. Elizabeth's mate.

The primal instinct of the animal he'd always denied refused to rest now. His senses became sharper and he became stronger as he fought against the pain and weakness to heal himself.

Twisting shadows of violence and the dark bloody stains of death began to emerge and coalesce around Cassie and her momma as the letters came to him. The child and her momma were his, and they were in danger.

He had to live.

He had a reason to live now.

"My momma says you must be a very kind man. Kind men don't hit little girls. Do they?" As his commander read that line, it echoed in his head, over and over again, allowing more of the fury, the strength and abilities he'd always allowed to sleep, to awaken.

"Damn, Dash." Colonel Thomas sighed. "That didn't sound good at all, did it? Some men just aren't worth the air they breathe, now are they?"

So innocently phrased, yet with a wealth of meaning. He strained within the dark agony that filled him, fought through the layers of pain to find consciousness, to heal. To live.

His mate. His child. They needed him.

And his commander was right, some men simply deserved to die.

As he fought to heal, grew stronger and swam from the bleak, black pit he'd sunk into, he waited for more letters. For that fragile thread of awareness that had the animal snarling, clawing to be free.

"My momma says there might not really be fairies but it's okay if I think there are. 'Cause nothing don't exist if you don't believe in it. And if you believe in it, then it's real as sunshine. I believe in you, Dash . . ." Thomas paused before asking him, "You going to let her down now, son?"

But the question went unanswered.

Dash could hear a cry when his commander finished the letter. It was inside his head, a woman's tears and muffled sobs. But it was the child's words the colonel read to him as he fought his way back.

A battle he often feared he would lose.

"My momma says leprechauns should be real. That gold at the end of the rainbow sounds really nice. I promise, Dash. I know a real fairy. I told Momma and she smiled and said I could ask her in for cookies and milk if I liked. I had to tell her that fairies don't eat cookies and milk. They really like candy bars . . ."

The kid's letters became a lifeline through long, bitter months of recuperation. It gave him something to hold on to.

He had no one. He was a man alone in the world and he had thought this was the way he wanted it, until Cassie's letters. Until a little girl introduced herself and her mother to a man literally dying of the loneliness that filled his world.

The letters were often peppered with amusing, cute little displays of affection toward a mother who apparently loved her daughter very much. And the daughter showered him with a sprinkling of the love her mother gave.

"Sometimes my momma is sad," Colonel Thomas read.

"She sits alone in our room and stares out the window and I peek through my eyes and I think I see tears. I think she needs a daddy too, don't you?"

The soldiers who accompanied the colonel ribbed Dash over that one. But Thomas shushed them quickly and continued to read.

Dash was conscious now, and growing steadily stronger by the day as he fought to heal and to get to Cassie and her momma. He fought like the animal he was, because of the woman's tears and a little girl's fears.

I wanted to send you a sparkling present for Christmas, she wrote just after Thanksgiving. *But Momma said we just didn't have the money this year. Maybe for your birthday, she said, if you will tell me when it is. So, I emailed Santa instead. I told him exactly what he was to get you but I bet your other little girls already thought of it too. I wanted a bicycle, but Momma said Santa might not make it this year. I told her he would. This year, Santa would know I'm big enough for a bike. I'm seven years old. Seven years old is a good bike age, I think.*

He was reading the letters himself, devouring each word.

With each letter, she wrapped around his heart, with her youthful wit and humor and her belief in everything good in the world. He wanted her to have that damned bike. He wanted her to know Santa looked after good little girls who saved worthless hides like his. He wanted her to know he was coming for her.

"Send her the bike," he demanded the next day when the colonel came to check his progress. "And this." He pushed the list into the colonel's hand. "For Christmas."

Christmas was for kids. He'd always heard the men in his unit sigh whenever the holiday came around and they received the cards and presents and grinned like kids themselves. Dash had begun making himself scarce years ago during that time of the year. It always made his men uncomfortable, almost guilty, because cards and presents never came in his name.

He knew even adults longed for something, someone, to remember them on that day, no matter how small the present or how simple the card.

That Christmas, Dash received a card with a note inside, and his own present. The note read, *Major Sinclair, Cassie still believes in Santa and I'd like to keep that alive in her for as long as the world allows. She wrote Santa and asked him to send you the enclosed present. Please consider this gift from Cassie and Santa.*

For the first time in his long, weary life, Dash received a present and felt his heart swell in his chest. The sturdy silver chain and St. Michael medallion opened emotions inside him that he had no idea how to process.

Elizabeth and Cassie had sent him someone to watch over him, he thought. The patron saint of the U.S. Army, for a mangy damned soldier who had never known the warmth of a Christmas gift.

Two weeks later, Cassie herself wrote back.

I got my bike, Dash. Momma was really surprised. On Christmas Day I was sure Santa didn't trust me yet. My bike wasn't under the tree. Then the doorbell rang and when Momma answered the door there was my shining red bike. It had my name on it. It was just for me alone and it was brand new. And it had a helmet. And I have gloves. And I have elbow pads. And I have knee pads. And there was even a present for my momma from Santa. Can you believe it, Dash? It was the best Christmas ever. Santa even remembered my momma.

He nodded as he read the letter.

"Thank you for sending the presents," he told the colonel, glancing over at where the other man sat, his expression quiet as Dash worked the weights strapped to his leg.

The long robe would keep the mother warm until his

arms could do the job. Cassie had said her momma was often cold . . .

"There's a problem there, isn't there, Dash?" The colonel nodded to the letter Dash carefully folded and tucked into the small bag next to his side.

"No problem, Colonel," he lied. "Just a little girl . . ."

◆   ◆   ◆

For over six months the letters came every other week like clockwork. Dash had begun to mark his progress with each one. His level of strength, the full mending of broken bones, internal injuries and torn muscle. With each letter, he pushed himself harder.

Then he learned there was something that could push him to strengthen himself faster and allowed the parts of him he'd never let free to surge through his body.

Cassie's letters stopped.

The first week, he excused it.

She and her mother moved a lot.

Too much.

A few days here. A month there, maybe a week at the next location. They stayed on the move, steadily working their way west.

She'd write again as soon as her mother paused long enough for Cassie to post her letter, Dash assured himself.

The next letter would arrive any day.

At three weeks late, he contacted a private investigator through the colonel to find the little girl and her mother. He turned over the previous addresses, all the information he had on the mother and child, and began to prepare himself to leave.

He could feel the imperative need building inside him, the instinct that the danger Cassie and her momma faced had increased.

Finally, three weeks later, the investigator's report came in.

Colonel Thomas, I regret to inform you that little Cassidy Colder and her mother, Elizabeth, died in a fire that overtook their apartment building several weeks ago. The bodies were unrecoverable, but there is no doubt that they, along with several others, were caught in the blaze. There was some trouble associated with the child and mother, rumors I've heard of a contract on their lives. Please let me know if you would like me to obtain more information . . .

According to the report that accompanied the letter, neighbors had heard the screams, had seen the apartment building explode, had watched the flames overtake it in a matter of minutes.

The explosion had originated in Elizabeth Colder's apartment while she and her daughter had been inside. What few remains could be found hadn't been identified yet, but according to official reports, there was little doubt it was the little girl and her mother. The remains had disappeared, possibly misplaced, according to the coroner, though the investigator believed they'd been stolen instead.

Dash felt his world crumble. The little girl who had saved him, who had given him his will to live, was gone.

For days he sat silent, staring broodingly at the ceiling, the weight of the medallion Elizabeth had sent him heavy on his chest.

For so long he had been alone. He had awakened each day knowing he had no one. Had gone to sleep each night feeling the loss. Yet while he lay near death, God had brought him angels. Only to take them away once again. It was a terrible blow to the soul he thought had withered away years ago.

He knew only blood and death. Had never known innocence until Cassie and her momma, Elizabeth.

Elizabeth.

His Elizabeth.

In thirty years of living, Dash had never claimed any one person as essential in his life. He had grown up knowing his survival depended on having no one, knowing he was different, knowing how imperative it was that he hide those differences. He had made his own way in life, had literally raised himself as best he could until he was old enough to join the Army.

He had made the service his home. The men he fought with, though not close to him, had given him a base to interact, to sharpen his intellect, to learn how to lead.

For twelve years, he had done just that. Led. He moved up the ranks, joining the Special Forces and proving his capabilities there. He had thought he hadn't needed anything more.

Dash realized now how wrong he had been.

Elizabeth's and Cassie's deaths tore a wound in his soul he couldn't explain. He had never touched the woman, had never held the daughter. She wasn't his mate and her daughter wasn't his child, yet his heart screamed something different.

His soul howled at the loss and some instinct, some inborn knowledge, refused to allow him to deny the bond that existed between him, mother and child.

"Dash, you have to snap out of this." Colonel Thomas sat beside his hospital bed a week after the report had come in, his green eyes somber, intent. "These things happen, son. You can't explain them or make sense of them. At least you have a part of her to remember."

Dash stilled the howl that wanted to rise to his lips. He had nothing. A pile of fragile letters wasn't enough.

Not nearly enough.

His fingers curled into the sheet as he stared up at the dull white ceiling silently. They thought he had sunk into depression. Lost his will to fight. Nothing could be further from the truth.

He had one last battle to fight before he could give in to the soul-deep need to rest.

Vengeance.

It kept the blood pumping in his veins, kept his heart beating in his chest.

He gave his commander a long, brooding look. "I want to know what happened. They were running from something. Someone. I want to know who."

He should have already known. He'd just been so certain he would get to them in time.

Colonel Thomas sighed wearily, his gaze compassionate. "What does it matter, Dash? They're gone."

Dash felt fury engulf him. It mattered. It mattered because he intended to exact his own form of justice. "I want to know. Contact the investigator. I want the information before my release."

He had his plans in place. The investigator could provide the background he needed, and then Dash would finish the job.

"So you can do what?" Colonel Thomas leaned back against his chair, watching him with a frown. "You'll be assigned a new unit . . ."

Like hell he would be. He was finished fighting other men's wars.

"I was given the option to return stateside on deactivation." It was all he could do to keep from snarling. "I won't be returning to duty, sir. I've had enough."

Surprise glittered in Thomas's eyes and Dash knew why.

He'd been in the service since he was eighteen. He hadn't once taken a deactivation. Twelve years he had given to first the Army and then to the Special Forces units. He was one of the best, a natural leader and a savage fighter.

But he'd had enough. The unit he had fought with was gone.

The little girl and the mother who had seen him through the need for death were gone.

He needed justice.

He needed a way to balance the scales, and he needed to find the part of himself he had hidden for most of his life so he could exact payment for their deaths.

His commander sighed again before nodding. "I'll call him tonight. You'll have what you need."

He rose to his feet, staring down at Dash for long, silent moments.

"Vigilantism is a crime. You know that, don't you, Dash?" he asked him cautiously.

Dash smiled. A slow baring of his teeth that he knew the commander would recognize. Dash was one of the best for a reason. He knew what he was doing. And he knew how to do it right.

"They have to catch you first," he said softly.

While Dash waited on the information, he worked on completing his recovery. He was rarely still. He exercised his body and his mind constantly, making certain each was in peak condition. When word came through that the information was being sent to the stateside location Dash had chosen, he packed his duffel bag and prepared to leave.

"Major Sinclair, you have a letter." The private met him as he stepped from the tent to head for the airfield. "Colonel Thomas said you were to get it asap."

Taking the letter, he saluted the soldier absently as he stared at it, predatory anticipation rising inside him.

He knew the handwriting, not the name, Paige Walker, but the carefully written words were all Cassie.

He opened the letter quickly and scanned it, a rare, enraged growl rumbling in his chest before he could stop it.

I know you must have lots of other little girls to love. Momma says you must be married with children and don't need us. But we need you, Dash. Please help me and my momma before the bad guys get us. I used to be Cassidy Colder, but Momma says now my name is Paige Walker. Paige Walker's okay, I guess. And here. This is Bo Bo's kerchief. So you know it's me. Momma says you will think the splosion got us. It hurt Momma, but we're okay. Please help us, Dash.

It had been hastily scrawled and the words sent terror chasing down his spine.

Inside the envelope was the locket he had sent her for her eighth birthday, a picture of herself and her mother inside. The mother looked haunted. Big blue eyes stared in startled awareness at the camera while the girl smiled charmingly.

The small red kerchief it was wrapped in had been around a little teddy bear's neck that he had asked Colonel Thomas to order for her. Bo Bo, she had named it. He could smell her on it. Baby powder and innocence. But there was another scent, Elizabeth's, and it sent his hormones howling. Pure female seductiveness. Dark, sweet, like a summer rainfall.

His eyes narrowed on the picture in the locket, rage shaking his body at the thought of anyone daring to hurt either of them.

They were his. And no one dared touch anything or anyone belonging to Dash Sinclair. A rumble of pure menace echoed in his chest, a growl of foreboding, a promise of retribution.

The hunt was on.

He would go after the enemy later, though.

First . . .

First, he had to find the family he had claimed in the darkness of pain. The mate who needed warmth, the child who needed protection. He would find them first. If along the way, a few of the enemy died, too bad. It would be a few less to kill later.

He was a Wolf Breed.

Dash Sinclair had known what he was even before the news of the Breeds exploded around the world.

Thankfully, in him, the genetics had recessed and were only identifiable on the genetic level, rather than the physical. It was the reason he had been marked for death at a young age. But it was also the reason he had survived after his escape from the labs.

He had joined the Army as soon as he was old enough, had fought and killed and done his best to hide right under the noses of several of the men who had funded his creation. He knew who they were. He had seen them at the labs when he was just a child, remembered their faces clearly.

Dash never forgot the face of an enemy.

Over the years he had become confident, strong, and aware of his strengths in a way that kept him from making mistakes. He never told anyone what he was. Never took the chance of confiding in friends. Hell, he had never made friends. He was surly on the best of days, and downright dangerous any other time. Most people knew to steer well clear of him.

The enemy wouldn't know that. The enemy wouldn't know who he was or what he was before he struck, before he killed.

As soon as his mate and his child were safe, they would learn, though. And it was a lesson they would learn hard.

Not today. Not today.

Elizabeth Colder chanted the words with silent determination as she ran through the dirty, run-down halls of the apartment building, fighting to get to the basement and the only avenue of escape left to her.

If she was lucky—God, let her be lucky—the men ransacking her apartment hadn't seen her in the hall. They wouldn't know she was aware of their presence and escaping. They wouldn't catch her before she could get away.

In her arms, held tight to her, the too-small, terrified body of her eight-year-old daughter clung to her with arms and legs, her shudders noticeable even as Elizabeth raced down the stairwell.

She fought to breathe, to go faster, to get away.

As she hit the bottom step she heard the door above them crash open and knew they were out of time.

Out of time.

"There she goes!" Furious, filled with the excitement of the chase, one of the men called out an alert just as Elizabeth rounded the corner and found a burst of added speed as she saw the opened door of the laundry room.

She prayed it was empty. She didn't want another innocent life destroyed because of the hell she and her baby, Cassie, were forced to live. She couldn't bear knowing the cost someone else would have to pay in her fight to escape.

Reaching the door, she slammed it closed as she entered the laundry room and hurriedly pushed the bolt in place before shoving the chair next to the door beneath the knob and jumping for the washers.

"Up, Cassie. Out the window." She lifted her daughter to the washers and pushed her to the open window as she climbed onto the appliance behind her.

Urging Cassie through the window, she was right behind her when the sound of the door crashing inward sent rage and terror tearing through her. Clawing her way through the small opening, she felt a shard of broken glass cut across her waist a second before the sound of a weapon discharging.

Fire burned across her leg as Elizabeth pulled herself free of the window.

Jumping to her feet, she ignored the pain.

It was bad, bad enough that tears burned her eyes and she was forced to lean more on her left side, but not enough to halt her flight.

Thank God Cassie was already in the car, the driver's-side door open, just as she'd taught the little girl to do. She was lucky the car hadn't been stolen yet, not that it was worth stealing.

She jerked the keys from her back pocket and within seconds the motor was running and she was pulling from the alley and shooting across the main road into the next alley. She'd already planned an escape route, already had another car in place, just in case this happened.

In the past two years she'd learned the tricks to surviving, to escaping. Too many near misses—far too many, actually—had forced her to learn. She felt like a mouse and the enemy was a cat watching her in anticipation.

"You're bleeding, Momma," Cassie whispered, her voice trembling, shaking just as hard as her thin body.

Yes, she was, too much. Dammit, she didn't have time to stop either. Not yet.

"Just a little cut, baby. Nothing to worry about," Elizabeth promised, glancing in the rearview mirror, then at the little girl. "Buckle your seat belt."

She checked the mirror again.

The other car wasn't much better than the one she was in and the tires were just as worn. That wasn't going to help, she knew, as she saw the snow falling in the air and remembered the weather report.

A coming blizzard.

God help her. She wasn't going to go far in a blizzard and she knew it.

It wasn't the first time Elizabeth had prayed in the past two years, and she prayed she and Cassie would live to pray another day. She had a feeling this was the end of the line if a miracle didn't come soon, though.

Unfortunately, she'd learned that miracles were few and far between in real life.

"I'm sorry, Momma," Cassie whispered, staring straight ahead, her expression dazed, her face white. "I'm so sorry . . ."

Cassie said that too often, as though she could stop any of this.

"Cassie, this is not your fault," Elizabeth snapped, not for the first time. "None of this is your fault."

And there was no convincing her daughter, not that Elizabeth could blame her. She alone had witnessed her father's murder, had seen the man who had killed him. She believed it was her fault because the man who killed him told her to watch and she'd obeyed him.

Elizabeth wanted to scream, to rage at whatever forces

had converged on the very night Dane had insisted on having Cassie with him. Why had he allowed his daughter there, knowing his life was in danger?

Rather than saying anything more, Cassie huddled into the seat, shivering as much from fear as the cold. There hadn't even been time to get her coat. All her daughter wore was the sweater, jeans and sneakers she'd worn down to the basement. In a blizzard she'd be more than defenseless against the cold. Both of them would be.

As soon as she switched cars Elizabeth knew she'd have to find some place, some way to hide them for just a few days. Just long enough to contact the only person who might have the power to help them.

It would be a risky move, she knew. She didn't even know the man who had made the offer of help should she ever need it. She didn't know him and she sure as hell didn't trust him, but she knew she wouldn't escape the next time they found her. The next time, they'd kill her and then there'd be no one to save her baby.

But she was out of options.

And she didn't see a miracle anywhere in sight . . .

◆   ◆   ◆

Dash stood still, drawing in the scents of the small ransacked room, and felt rage wash over him. He'd been so close. So damned close to catching up with Elizabeth and her child, only to have those chasing her manage to get ahead of him.

Over the past six weeks he had investigated Elizabeth and Cassidy Colder until he knew even the most minute detail concerning them.

He'd made contacts while in the Forces. Contacts that owed him, and he pulled in each favor he could draw on once he reached the States to learn everything he could to ensure their survival.

Cassidy Colder was a little girl living on borrowed time.

A child with a price on her head and a mother fighting to save her. The lengths to which Elizabeth Colder had gone to save her little girl made his gut tighten in fear each time he thought of the information he'd collected. Such a small woman should be protected, cuddled, just as the child should be, not running in fear for that child's life.

Yet that was exactly what was happening.

Staring around the small living room of the apartment from where he stood in the doorway, he drew the scents that lingered there inside his nostrils and let the information filter through his senses.

He could smell the little girl's terror, her tears, just as he sensed her mother's rage. He snarled silently at the scents, allowing them to fuel his rage. The men chasing them would pay.

Eventually.

He picked up a child-sized jacket, brought it to his nose and drew in deep.

Innocence and the smell of baby powder clung to it. But the fact that it was here and not wrapped around Cassidy's small body sent chills snaking down his spine.

It was damned cold out there. A little one would freeze quickly in weather like this. Not that the jacket would do her much good, ripped in half as it was.

He picked up a woman's sweater next and did the same.

Ahh, there was a smell a man would die happy to know. Female, fresh and clean, a hint of baby powder but filled with the delicate scent of womanhood.

His.

Dash stared around the room again. He wasn't far behind them and it was obvious they were still several steps ahead of the men chasing them.

He smiled slowly.

He'd find the woman and child first. It was too cold, too brutal out there to go hunting for the enemy with no assurance that what was most important was safe first. And

Elizabeth and Cassie were most important. Their safety was paramount; even above the hunger to feel the enemy's fear as death came for them was the need for the woman's warmth and the child's safety.

In the middle of the room a little girl's doll was ripped apart, stuffing littering the room. Clothes were shredded, books ripped in half. He knew the smell of the enemy now and he drew it in, memorizing it, making certain he never forgot it.

Cassidy and her mother must have come in after the destruction of their temporary home.

A small basket of clothes sat by the door, left forgotten but undamaged. Laundry. Doing the laundry had saved their lives.

He dropped the garments. They wouldn't be needed after he found them anyway. He had everything they would require packed in an SUV. He had made certain that once he found Elizabeth and Cassie, they would want for nothing. He took care of what he considered his, and everything inside him screamed out in possession of Elizabeth and her child.

He stepped into the apartment and moved silently through the room, aware of the hidden bugs placed within it. He had smelled them immediately upon stepping through the doorway.

His lips twisted into a cold smile. He was dealing with amateurs. There would be little challenge in taking them out when their time came.

The scent of Elizabeth's fury and fear went no farther than the door, so he knew she hadn't taken time to investigate the destruction.

She was smart.

He'd been chasing her for weeks and only in the past days had he gotten close enough that he knew the end was in sight.

She wouldn't be easy for the others to catch up to. After

he found her, they would never have a hope of capturing her.

But first, he had to find her.

He backed away from the doorway, closing the door silently before turning and drawing in the scents along the hall. Moving past the basket of clothes, he headed for the far end of the hall.

Moving carefully along the dirty passageways, he followed the scent of the woman and child down the stairs and then to the basement and into the communal laundry room.

There, a small window had been pried open. Stepping to the line of washers, he reached up and removed a tattered piece of flannel from the broken window above the machines and brought it to his nose.

Once again, Elizabeth's scent filled his senses. She had cut herself escaping. Blood marred the soft, worn fabric. But she had been smart. Smart enough to know the enemy was watching the front entrance. Over the past two years since she'd been on the run with her daughter, Elizabeth had grown in strength and instinct. She was smart and intuitive. She was learning to hone the abilities she needed to stay on the run and proving herself to be adept at evading the enemy. He'd seen proof of the fact that she'd learned to use her wits where she lacked physical strength.

As Dash stood there staring at the fabric, his fingers running over the dark stains that marred it, he felt another presence begin to disturb the air that flowed in through the opened door.

Animal senses snapped into place, increasing his ability to draw in and separate each individual smell with lightning-fast instinct. Strength filled his muscles, hardened them. Calculating, predatory, confident, he let the animal out to play.

And the animal demanded blood.

Dash paused, his head turning slowly to the partially opened door as a new scent began to mix with that of fabric

softener, detergent and stale water. A scent that had his lips
curling in a silent snarl of predatory fury.

The scent of the enemy was insidious. The stink of corruption and furious intent. It wafted through the cool basement air, dug into his senses, filling him with the need for
blood. The prey was moving closer, unaware of the predator
waiting for him.

The enemy was on the prowl, stalking him now, fool-
ishly moving from cover to investigate a stranger's interest.

Dash was looking forward to the confrontation.

He stilled the warning growl that rose instinctively in
his chest. The smell of cold steel moved closer, the tread of
cautious steps. There was only one. He was confident, but
filled with arrogance, bloodlust, and weakness. It was that
weakness, that overconfidence that would destroy him.

Dash smiled. He'd so rarely felt the well-honed strength
that flooded him now, the mercilessness or icy logic that
now infused him. He'd fought to be human, forgetting for
far too long that he wasn't human. And men such as the one
he faced now deserved no more mercy than a quick death.

The man moving toward him was no more than a flunky.

No true threat.

A hired gun and little more. Disposable. It was a good
thing because he wouldn't leave the building alive.

Silently, Dash waited.

He didn't have to wait long. The door swung open
slowly, revealing the lean, tense form of the fool who believed himself to be a true killer.

He was a man full grown. A gamma trying to play alpha
with an animal he had no idea existed. Dash allowed his
lips to curl into an anticipatory smile, knowing the other
man wouldn't see it for the lethal threat it was.

"Can I help you?" he asked softly, the graveled sound of
a growl at the back of his throat ignored by the other man.

"Getting nosy, stranger?" the enemy grunted as he carefully closed the door and aimed his weapon at Dash's chest. "Put your hands up where I can see them and don't move funny or you're dead."

Dash lifted his arms, hands behind his neck, the fingers of one hand curling around the hilt of the large knife concealed in its sheath between his shoulder blades.

The blade was eighteen inches long, the hilt eight. Secured in a leather sheath attached to a shoulder harness and deadly when Dash wielded it. It surpassed deadly when training merged with instincts and strength that went well beyond human.

Oh yeah. Now he could play.

"Just checking some things out." Dash narrowed his eyes, aware of the gun barrel's angle, straight to the heart.

A silencer had been attached to the barrel. The other man was a cautious bastard; Dash gave him credit for that. But only for that. Otherwise, he was less than smart. He should have realized the threat Dash was and killed him instantly. If possible.

That was what he would have done.

Instead, the little slug wanted to play. Dash liked to play. And he knew for a certainty that his opponent would fall. It was the way of the beast. He could sense the weakness facing him. Overconfidence glittered in the enemy's eyes as the need for pain scented the air around him.

"Who are you?" Beady brown eyes narrowed. Thick, oily, sun-streaked brown hair fell forward, framing a less-than-intelligent forehead.

"Not your concern." Dash shrugged as he allowed his lips to curl with insulting mockery. He refused to give respect to a creature so lacking in morality that he would hunt a child. "Who are you?"

Dash watched the other man closely, the shift of the lanky body beneath the ill-fitting, though expensive, coat he wore, the confident way he held his weapon. The other man was used to killing and he was used to doing it the lazy way. He wouldn't expect to face a man of Dash's capabilities.

It was almost too easy. Dash sighed. It was a shame; he would have enjoyed a fight.

"You're too nosy, dude." The surfer boy accent grated on Dash's nerves. The casual disrespect of the attitude was reason enough to kill him. "Way too nosy."

"Not nosy enough, perhaps." Dash watched the other man's gaze carefully as he allowed his smug smile to deepen. "She got away from you again, didn't she?" he said, taunting the younger man. "Elizabeth's smarter than you are, *dude*. Back off now while I'm willing to be merciful."

The challenge was made. Dash made certain the insulting derision in his voice was clearly understood. There was no fight here, no conflict. The enemy's blood would be shed, period.

Angry color filled the other man's cheeks, his gaze glittering with the need for violence as he stepped closer.

He would want to be closer, to be certain the bullet killed rather than maimed. To watch the pain and fear he hoped to see spilling into Dash's eyes as the blood spilled from his chest.

He let the man fantasize for a moment.

"She'll be a tasty treat to the rest of us when we give that little girl to the boss," the surfer boy sneered. "You like her too, big boy? Too bad. You're dead."

The other man thought he was close enough. His finger was tightening on the trigger.

The knife slid from the leather sheath with a whisper as Dash swung his arm, wrist twisting at the last second, dragging the blade across the tender flesh of the enemy's neck. The other man's eyes widened in surprise even as his jugular split beneath the blade.

Blood formed along the narrow slice. A heartbeat later, thick rivulets began pouring from the wound.

"No, dude. *You're* dead." Dash allowed the animalistic rumble free, glorying in the smell of blood, the bite of triumph and predatory strength that filled him.

The animal flexed inside him. Powerful muscle shifted, filled with strength, and the leash on who and what he was slipped another notch.

Dash slid to the side with smooth precision as the reflexive clench of muscle tightened the man's finger on the trigger. The bullet whizzed harmlessly past him.

Blood pumped in a wide, vivid arc, splattering across the sleeve of Dash's custom-made leather jacket and draining the life from the cruel gaze of a man who would kill a woman and her child.

The body fell heavily, sightless eyes staring back in macabre astonishment as the crimson wash of blood spilling over the cement floor widened beneath his head.

There was no remorse in Dash's heart for the death. Some animals were just plain rabid in the soul, and this one was one of them. There could be no regret for putting the world out of the misery they brought.

Casually, he dragged the blade over the dead man's denim leg, cleaning it quickly before checking the body for any usable information.

There was a phone number on the back of a wrinkled blank business card. No name. Dash tucked the card into his inner jacket pocket. Money. He tossed it by the body. A message to his boss. Keys.

A picture of the little girl and her mother. This too, Dash tucked into his jacket's inner pocket.

Seconds later, confident that the man carried nothing that could be traced back to Elizabeth, Dash rose to his feet, replaced the knife in the sheath, and used a discarded towel on one of the machines to clean the sleeve of his jacket. He threw it over the face of the dead man before striding to the door.

He jimmied the lock before closing it behind him, mak-

ing certain it couldn't be opened easily. The apartment
building echoed with the laughter of families, of children.
He didn't want to chance a child walking in on the bloody
scene or an innocent bystander taking the blame for the
death. Not that he thought there would be many who would
feel the loss of the man he had killed.

Dash stalked back to the front entry, then into the frig-
idly cold winter evening. As though he had nothing better
to do, he ambled around the building, heading for the alley
in the back, hoping to pick up more information there.

Elizabeth and Cassie had gone out the window that led
into this alley. He doubted he would find much but he had to
check to be certain. Being cautious had gotten him this far;
he wasn't going to slack now.

He didn't see the navy blue sedan she was driving,
thankfully. At least they were in the warmth in the vehicle
rather than the biting cold of the frigid winter air. He knelt
in front of the open window of the basement, surveying the
displaced snow beneath it. The footsteps were barely vis-
ible now as they led to a set of tire tracks a few feet over.

No, they weren't too far ahead of him if the tracks in the
snow were any indication. And if he wasn't mistaken, the
bastards chasing them, minus the one he had just killed,
were still watching the building.

His hackles had risen the moment he stepped from the
front door and felt malevolent eyes following him.

Dash looked around carefully as he rose to his full
height and began checking out the tire marks along the
wide alley. From the looks of it they had left in a hurry.
Checking the tracks he was certain matched the sedan, he
guessed Elizabeth had headed into the heart of town. She
wouldn't stop there, though.

He sighed heavily as he stared into the twilight sky.
Snow peppered his cheeks and forehead and the smell of
the air indicated a blizzard was well on its way.

They wouldn't be able to run for much longer tonight.

He should find them soon. Keeping his steps casual, he moved back to the front of the building and his own vehicle. The four-by-four SUV would be traded in farther down the road for the military Humvee waiting at a local reserve depot. It would make short work of the lousy road conditions and keep him moving when no other vehicle would dare try.

To catch the woman he had claimed before he ever saw her face, Dash knew he would need that advantage. It was also a vehicle the enemy was unfamiliar with. That edge would be important in the coming days.

He watched the rearview mirror carefully as he drove out of the parking lot and pulled his cell phone from the holder at his hip. Nine-one-one was a quick call. Brief and to the point. A dead body, nothing more.

All the while, he kept the white Taurus parked across from the apartment building in his peripheral vision. Yep, definite interest from the single occupant inside but no attempt to follow.

They were certain the kid and her mother would return. They had no idea that the woman was smarter than a whole unit of dumbasses. He shook his head and made the turn that would lead him in the direction instinct assured him Elizabeth had taken. His hunt was nearly at an end.

Then he could begin playing in earnest.

. . . *when we give that little girl to the boss* . . . The dead man's words slid through his mind again.

Every piece of information he had said that the price on Elizabeth's and her child's heads was for death, not capture. Yet the gloating words, the truth that rang in the other man's voice, was unavoidable.

There was more going on here than the report he'd been given.

Far more.